THE END OF DEMOCRACY

THE FAILURE OF THE EGO SELF AND THE SEARCH FOR UNITIVE CONSCIOUSNESS

A NOVEL BY DON CARROLL

ISBN: 0982926529
ISBN-13: 978-0-9829265-2-9

THIS IS A WORK OF FICTION

DEDICATION

For Will and Nora

ACKNOWLEDGEMENTS

I am indebted to Susan Whiteman, Gilda Syverson, Suzanne Leitner, and Reita Pendry for their kindness and skill in reviewing the original manuscript and giving me countless suggestions that greatly contribute to the value and enjoyment of this novel. I am again deeply indebted to my assistant Buffy Holt for her skill, creativity and diligence in the often arduous process of bringing a novel to publication. Buffy is an imaginative writer herself and her passion for and commitment to the writing life makes working with her a joy.

Dear Reader,

Sometimes a pause makes all the difference. There may have been times a fortuitous pause saved you from a turn in your life that would have taken you down the wrong road for years. I certainly have experienced those times when I did not stop to see a clearer picture of what was before me and proceeded willy-nilly.

So, dear reader, I beseech you, with as much forthrightness and honesty as I can, to pause before reading this book and to consider my suggestion; indeed, my heartfelt advice, that you should avoid reading this novel even if you would do so with the most considered care.

Yes, dear reader, it is my honest belief that reading this book is tantamount to continuing forward willy-nilly. Frankly, there is nothing to be gained by your reading this book and potentially much to be suffered. If you are a stout-hearted American you will find that the suggestions in this book could erode the very foundations of your belief in the ideal of American democracy. If, like so many of us, you are a person who has come to view the American system of government with great cynicism, then by reading this book you are only likely to be adding fuel to the fire of that corrosive perspective.

I know I face obstacles in your considering my advice. First, it is likely you read the first book in this series, *Hacking Toward Consciousness*, and there you were asked to consider discarding that book, yet you must have endured and read it in order to get here. So you come having discarded my initial advice and I know the chances of convincing you now so belatedly are dim, but please pause and reconsider. Or, perhaps you have not read the prior book, and you are coming to this one without having the chance to have seen how the characters here have been shaped in crucial ways. Either way, my plea is the same. To those of you in the first group, I say—enough is enough, heed my second warning. And to you in the second group—those who have not read the first novel—not only do you face having the foundations of belief about American democracy shattered, you will be experiencing that without having followed the growth of the book's characters to understand what has prepared them for the disillusionment you will face alone.

However, since you now hold this book in your hands or have it on your screen, if you find that you are unable or unwilling to follow my advice, then I beg you not to let anyone read this book except those whom you believe have managed to read the first novel to a conclusion and come away with their faith not totally shaken and in some paradoxical way strengthened. I admitted to all in my letter to the readers of the first book that it is possible that a few true spiritual seekers might navigate through that book and pay no greater price than the benefit of reading a riveting and suspenseful story. However, except for those few who received a negligible entertainment value, without coming at the dear price of their souls, most should have simply discarded the first book and avoided risking suffering and loss altogether.

What I am trying to say is that only those who are true spiritual seekers with an enormous capacity for mystery and wonder can, I believe, have both their religious beliefs and their political beliefs shattered without grave harm. It is one thing to have your religious beliefs run roughshod over as the first book might have done for many of you. It is quite another to have your secular beliefs about government destroyed. For we are a nation of secular fanatics more than religiously committed people. Our views about government are in fact for many our most important religion. So this second book should only be read by those true spiritual seekers who are sufficiently grounded in the mystery of life that, notwithstanding having seen precious Christian religious ideas undermined in the first book, are also willing to step into the possibility of a similar blow to their ideas about the American government.

Why expose yourself to such uncertainty? Many who are cast adrift from all moorings about their life never make it to the other shore. Heed my warning: it is not too late! Discard this book now. I would suggest that in doing so you make sure that it does not fall into the hands of the naive or uninitiated.

Let me stress to you the authenticity of my warning by telling those of you who do not know that I am a character in this book. This warning is coming from the ultimate insider. Do not proceed thoughtlessly, for once an ideal is shattered there is no way, without continuing your spiritual journey to an even deeper place, to realize the beauty and possibilities contained in the broken, fragmented pieces.

Very sincerely yours,

Father Charles F. "Cloudy" Hay

CHAPTER 1

Charles Redmon was not sure what to do. This was not a good state of affairs for a CIA section chief. He always felt his skills were sharp and analytically precise when he was deciding what to do about one of the bad guys. When it came to handling another officer, or in this case a former officer, Redmon got confused.

For the tenth time Redmon opened the thick personnel file of William Dawson. The file was thick not because Dawson had been disciplined or incurred problems as an officer. Rather it was thick from the accumulation of regular service awards in his personnel record over twenty years before he retired. In fact, if there was anything remarkable about Dawson's record, it was that there was nothing remarkable about it.

Dawson's background made him perfect CIA material. He came out of the solidly conservative Midwestern Corn Belt and had been recruited into the CIA directly from college during the height of the Cold War. Dawson had been assigned to Afghanistan back before the Russian invasion and then at various trouble spots around the globe. Over the years he had received a number of special commendations. The last five or six years before he retired, he had spent at headquarters in Langley,

Virginia running other officers and working on specific anti-terrorism projects.

Dawson had been married and then divorced. This did not signal a problem these days, since it was the norm that most officers ended up divorced. He used alcohol; however, there was no suggestion that he used it excessively and no evidence of illegal drug use or abuse of prescription drugs. His financial condition was modest though adequate. There were apparently no major financial dilemmas on the horizon for him.

Redmon scratched his head. He would be delighted if most of the new officers looked as good on paper as Dawson did. Still he was unsure what to do. Part of the reason for his uncertainty was that he could not understand why in the world the 1776 project had been authorized in the first place. It seemed to him a little bit like the investigation of flying saucers that had gotten the agency such ridicule years ago. He looked again at the project's color coding. Whatever this inquiry was about, it was coming from way up the line, maybe the top. And ever since James Jesus Angleton drove the organization nuts trying to ferret out double agents, the safest way for him to handle the investigation was to play it strictly by the book.

One such approach would be to simply call Dawson in and tell him that he had gotten caught up in an agency investigation. In fact, Dawson had all the top secret security clearances needed and the agency could offer him a job as a consultant on this project. Most of the really dirty work was done by consultants for the agency these days anyway. This had developed as the default pattern of how to deal with anything the agency wanted to keep just beyond the view of a congressional oversight committee.

The other approach would be to continue to keep Dawson under surveillance and see if he led them anywhere. There was not a huge risk in this approach, though Redmon knew there was a long history of spectacular failures by the agency being able to spy on former officers. Somehow if a former officer felt the Company was after him, the ex-officer could mobilize a level of paranoia that had in the past created bizarre, unwanted results for the Company and the publicity nightmare of tell-all memoirs.

Redmon sat back from his desk. He pushed his spectacles up on his balding head and swiveled his chair so he could look out the window into the interior courtyard. This view was one thing about the new headquarters building he really liked, that and the tulips out front in the early spring. If the truth be known, he was looking forward to retiring in another year himself. The life of a CIA officer was bipolar. You were either caught up in a wave of manic excitement, or there was simply the depressingly dreary grind of day-to-day monotonous information gathering.

He turned back to his desk and looked one last time at Dawson's file. He noticed for the first time that Dawson would be having a birthday in just a few days. He closed the file. As so often happened to him, his uncertainty prescribed that he would follow the most cautious approach. He put Dawson on 24-hour surveillance and ordered his cell phone and e-mail tapped. Maybe something would turn up. If not, there was always the option to call him in later and ask him to be a consultant on the project. You always had more control over someone who thought he was working for you.

CHAPTER 2

William Dawson was back in his cramped Alexandria, Virginia apartment. Coffee was brewing. He was up again early, as he had been every day since he had returned from Turin, Italy where he went to the International Enneagram Conference: *Exploring the Outer Edge of the Enneagram: Ancient Sources, Future Revelations*, in order to try to find out what happened to his long-ago first love, Melissa. Sleep was eluding him.

The best time of day for him to try to get some clarity about what was happening in his life was early in the morning, with a cup of good strong coffee. He poured his cup two-thirds full of coffee and added another third of warm milk, then stirred in half a teaspoon of agave sweetener. He opened his kitchen window to get some fresh air. Even early in the morning the air was warm and sticky with a sourness that he reckoned came from the miasma of power just across the Potomac.

Dawson closed the window and cranked his air-conditioning down to a lower temperature. The coffee was both bitter and sweet in his mouth, just the way he liked it. He began to replay events in his mind. He had met Melissa in Kabul, Afghanistan years earlier before the Russian invasion. She was there as a Peace Corps volunteer. Dawson was there as a CIA officer.

Dawson had never met anyone as remarkable as Melissa. He had fallen deeply in love with her. She had the ability to control her energy field, and she had for a brief time let Dawson inside. She also had remarkable clarity of mind and purpose. Six months after he had met Melissa, his rotation in Afghanistan was over and the Company transferred him. He kept in touch with her for a while but eventually communication stopped. Learning how to be a good spy seemed to be the most important task, to save the world from communist threats.

The bottom line was that Dawson had been too distracted by his Cold War mission to worry about having a personal life. Eventually he got married to an attractive woman. This seemed like the right thing to do at the time, the next step in some sort of life logic. Perhaps they were right for each other, because she was also afraid of any real intimacy, and having a husband who was always gone suited her for a number of years. Then suddenly it didn't and she left.

Working for the Company meant that his natural reluctance to commit was completely rationalized by the higher value of serving his country. He hardly remembered now what his wife looked like.

Dawson was deeply moved upon reading the letter Melissa's mother, Mrs. Dowling, sent to him. He'd only been retired from the Company for a few months when he began to sink into depression and isolation. Mrs. Dowling had given Dawson a letter from Melissa that was to be delivered to him if anything ever happened to her. When he read that letter Dawson realized that years ago he failed to listen to his heart and go after the woman he loved. The hole in his heart had only grown larger over the years.

At the Enneagram conference in Italy, he met Blaine Astrid. She was much younger than he was and an odd sort of woman. Yet something about her seemed invitingly familiar. Dawson had spent most of the week of the conference with Blaine, either going to the conference sessions or exploring first Rome and then Turin. At the end of that week, the hole in his heart was not quite so large.

The last day of the conference Dawson found out—with Blaine's help—that Melissa might still be alive. It appeared that Melissa was at the conference, but did not contact Dawson when she discovered that he was being watched both by the CIA and a shadowy group that was also keeping her under surveillance.

Dawson had come to the second great relationship crossroads in his life. He had the opportunity to invite Blaine into his life or he could devote himself to the task of chasing after Melissa, his first elusive love. As happened with Melissa years before, he froze at the most crucial time. When Blaine saw that he was stuck, she made her own plans to find a new life for herself by going to work for a computer software company in Berlin.

Dawson knew it was also hard for Blaine to trust. Probably much harder than it was for him. She had left the door of their relationship open; although with her across the globe in Berlin, that didn't leave much opportunity for someone as out of touch with his own heart as Dawson.

Now he was back home and the excitement of the conference and being with Blaine was over. There were absolutely no leads to go on about how to find Melissa. The mystery of her disappearance was murkier than ever. Dawson got up and poured another cup of coffee, added the milk, now lukewarm, and a little bit more of the agave sweetener. He loved the bitter sweet taste of his favorite coffee first thing in the morning. He wished his life could taste like his first sip of coffee. For now there was no sweet taste in his life, only bitterness. A bitterness from having failed in some fundamental way to come to terms with his own life, and the awareness of that failure seemingly coming too late.

Eventually the caffeine buzz focused his attention. His training with the Company clicked back in. Go back to the beginning. Assess all the details. See the big picture and notice as much what is missing as what is present. He took out a legal pad and began writing.

Sometime prior to his meeting Melissa in Afghanistan, she had an extraordinary spiritual experience there. Like Native American visionary Black Elk on a vision quest, hers was a Moses-on-the-mountaintop experience. Experiences such as Melissa's are usually not sought, but come by some divine surprise, as was the experience of Bill Wilson, the co-founder of Alcoholic's Anonymous, in Townes Hospital when he had almost completely given up on life. Melissa's experience had qualities of all these mythic experiences and occurred at St. Issa's pond, a place where legend had it that Jesus visited in his travels, not far out of Kabul. Because of his visit, the pond was known by the name given to him in his eastern travels, St. Issa.

Like all truly transformative spiritual experiences, Melissa's experience was very physical. As a result of her experience Melissa learned how to control her energy field. When she got back to the United States she continued her spiritual journey. She received guidance from a spiritual director who used the Enneagram in providing spiritual direction. The Enneagram is an ancient system going back perhaps to Christ, and at least as far back as the early Desert Mothers and Fathers who lived in the second and third century after Christ. Even then an understanding of its principles was used as a spiritual tool in guiding initiates into spiritual transformation.

The Enneagram seems to have been used by many mystical traditions, including Christian, Sufi and Jewish mystics working with the Kabbalah, whose tree of life pre-figures the Enneagram symbol. However, use of the Enneagram in spiritual transformation remained largely an esoteric oral tradition until the 1970s.

Dawson wrote on his legal pad: *first thread—emergence of the Enneagram into public knowledge after centuries of use in esoteric traditions as a tool of spiritual transformation.*

The next thread was about himself—*what has been happening to me for the last twenty years?* Dawson knew from his Company training, that everyone suffers from their own limited perspective. To solve a problem that seems insolvable, one first must get a larger perspective. He had not developed a lot of knowledge about the Enneagram, but after attending the Enneagram conference in Turin, Italy he had at least begun to have some limited insight into his own personality. The

Enneagram had given him a way to begin to understand his innate perspective and its inherent shortcomings.

Dawson was an Enneagram type six. From what he had learned about the six he understood why the Company liked to recruit sixes as officers. Sixes experience the world as deeply unsafe. They react to this feeling of insecurity by looking for beliefs or institutions in which they can put their trust. Thus a six is often very loyal to a cause or an organization, such as the Company, ahead of everything else. It is hard for sixes to trust another human being and develop a relationship of intimacy, because that other person could always betray them.

A six's natural level of paranoia was helpful to the Company. The six walks into a room and immediately senses where the sources of danger are. Sixes respond in two ways to their underlying fear of the world. Some sixes have a phobic response, meaning they withdraw because of their fear. Other sixes respond just the opposite; that is, they move directly toward the object of their fear so they will not have to actually experience the feeling of their fear, though the energy of their fear is what generates their response. These are counter phobic sixes, and the type of six the Company preferred.

From his experience at the Enneagram conference, Dawson realized that because sixes are always responding to fear, which they may simply experience as a generalized anxiety, their energy is out of touch with who they are and what they value. They are overly connected to those emotions that signal danger, and cut off from the emotions that define their values. This limitation on his perspective was hard for Dawson to understand, because he was very aware of his emotionally reactive fear patterns. However, sixes are out of touch with those emotions that give them a sense of centeredness and a feeling of being safe in the world.

So the thread of his limited perspective was at least partially clear to Dawson. He was unable to act upon connections important to his heart because of his fear of betrayal. Because of that he had not committed to Melissa when he fell deeply in love with her years ago. Later he never really formed an intimate relationship with his wife in their marriage. And he had been unable to follow after this strange young woman Blaine Astrid, whom he only recently met in Italy, and who had moved him deeply in some new way. His experience of life's meaning was restricted because he never had the strength of faith to act on what was important to his heart.

Dawson was a good officer because he was always trying to collect more information to understand a situation. His gnawing anxiety drove him to extraordinary efforts to find new facts. More facts were not important to matters of the heart.

Dawson was quite good at going along with what seemed appropriate and what was expected. That had gotten him one marriage and a lot of loneliness. He put down his legal pad. Finally he thought he was getting it. The danger of his six perspective, the way that he would sabotage his life, would be that he would not follow through sufficiently to find Melissa, and at the same time he would let Blaine slip out of his life. The six traits that served him so well in the Company were the weakest thread in his personal life.

Most of his life Dawson responded to challenges by taking action. The Company liked this part of his personality. For the first time in his life he thought maybe before he jumped into action that he would see if he could *change something basic in my internal way of being.* As he wrote this on his legal pad he was not sure what it meant. But, he felt the rightness of this conclusion. Perhaps hanging around all this Enneagram stuff was making a difference. If he was going to find Melissa somehow he would have to change internally first. The old Dawson would not be able to find her. How would he be able to change? He didn't have a clue, but he knew who might.

He went to his computer and clicked on his last message from Father O'Donnell, whom he had accompanied to the conference in Turin. Father O'Donnell had been planning to return to his hermitage in the Southwest after the conference. From the schedule he had sent to Dawson much earlier, it appeared Father O'Donnell might be another week or two at the monastery before he went into seclusion up in his nearby mountain hut.

Dawson pushed back from his desk. It was already late morning, and for the first time since he returned from Italy he felt, not exactly a sense of joy, but maybe a glimmer of hope.

CHAPTER 3

Blaine was worried, worried about Rat. It seemed impossible to her that she could be worried about anyone or anything. Never in her wildest imagination could she have conceived of the life she was now living.

Following the Enneagram conference in Turin, Blaine had gone to Berlin with Rat. He had helped her find a small apartment in central Berlin. It was within walking distance of the storage room where Rat lived and also an easy commute to the new job that Rat had gotten her at DAP AG, a German software development and consulting corporation, which provided software applications and support to businesses all over the world. DAP was headquartered in Wolfsburg, Germany, and Blaine was lucky to be able to start working for DAP in the Berlin office.

While her new apartment was small, by European standards it was spacious for one person, and for Blaine it was the most luxurious place she had ever lived. She had borrowed some money from Rat in order to furnish the apartment with inexpensive and well-designed furniture from IKEA. She liked the sparseness of the Scandinavian design as well as the warm quality of natural blond wood. Every time she came home she would put her arms around herself and squeeze in disbelief that this was really her home. It was a long way from hacking her way out of a mental institution.

She was beginning to learn a bit of German, although her colleagues were all willing to speak to her in English. Her main challenge at work was the teamwork approach which the software company used. She had never done anything except work by herself. Gradually, she was starting to enjoy the interaction with others that was a part of a group creative work process. It reminded her of how she collaborated with Rat and other hackers.

Blaine's social life was also something her former self would never have dreamed of. There was always some geeky guy at work coming up and asking her out for coffee. These guys were always so weird that Blaine had begun to feel more normal, more comfortable in her own skin, than she had ever felt in her life.

Still most of her time outside of work was spent with Rat. Their relationship remained in this no-man's land between friendship and romance. Rat knew how deeply Blaine had fallen for Will Dawson in Turin, and Rat had been the shoulder that she had literally cried on when Dawson had gone back to the United States to pursue his quest to find the mysterious Melissa. Rat would never admit it to himself, but Rat was as in love with Blaine as he had ever been with anything that didn't plug into a wall socket and the Internet. He had been in love with her from the time he first met her at the airport when she came down the exit corridor dressed all in black with a tattoo winding down her left arm and metal piercing her eyebrows, nose and tongue. The more Rat was with Blaine, the more he idealized this unusual woman who seemed just out of his reach.

Because all relationships for Blaine with men were uncomfortable, at least because they all had been that way up to now, she was able for the most part to let the unknown nature of her relationship with Rat just be. She was so grateful to Rat that her gratitude prevented negative emotions from the uncertainty of the relationship's meaning, stirring too strongly in her. At least that is what she told herself, for Blaine truly believed that she did not have the normal range of feeling emotions most people did. Instead, what she had as a result of what she had been through in her life were survival instincts honed to a fine edge. Her survival skills, she believed, had displaced normal feelings of kindness, compassion and perhaps even love. Whatever love was. At least that had been so until Professor Gallagher befriended her and until she had met Rat in Berlin and then Will Dawson in Italy.

Her friendship with Rat, plus something else with him she could not quite define, was an emotional anchor to her as she absorbed the newness and wonder of her move to Berlin, her new job, and being the object of attention by techie German men. After she left Turin for Berlin, Blaine gave up most of the metal that she used to pierce her body. She settled for a few rings in her ears and, for the most part, wearing clothing that covered up how extensively her body was tattooed. It was extraordinary for her to feel okay about herself without having to protect herself by making a statement through her appearance that she was different. Her previous fashion statement, taken at face value, revealed more accurately than anyone could have guessed her history of dark inner turmoil and outer struggle to survive.

In celebration of her new comfort with her appearance, Blaine had also stopped wearing all black. She could tell that whenever she was worried or anxious about something she would automatically slip back into a black outfit for the day. Most of the time she enjoyed wearing bright colored tops that fit her slender, lithe body in a way that said she was comfortable with herself. Despite her new life in Germany, feeling comfortable with her scarred body was still a bit of a stretch, a stretch she was making toward a new kind of freedom.

Now she realized, that for the past two days, she had only worn black. Today was Saturday and she did not have to go to work. Rat was too busy to make plans to go out with her during the day, though she would see him later in the evening. She spent most of the morning wandering around the Kreuzberg District where she lived. It was a bit touristy with people going to see Checkpoint Charlie, but there were many quaint neighborhoods and tranquil parks. She found herself walking through the network of trails and rocky areas in Vikoriapark. She sat down by a beautiful, deep waterfall.

For the first time she realized what was beneath her sense of worry—a concern for Rat's safety. She had a gut feeling that he was involved with guys in Ukraine who had developed the Conficter worm. It was one thing to hack into the data banks of others, to help correct the injustices of modern life. She, in fact, never had a second thought about creating a transcript for herself that showed she had gone to college and done well. Or, about changing her data in the mental hospital records and getting herself discharged with medical approval after she had run away from that evil institution. However, sending out worms, particularly something as lethal and stealthy as Conficter, was a whole different ball-game.

Conficter was the talk of all her hacking buddies back in late 2008 when it first appeared. The worm had exploited a specific defect in the Microsoft operating system at port 445. Ports were designed to transmit and receive particular kinds of data and the Microsoft operating system has more than 65,000. Windows opens port 445 to perform certain tasks like issuing instructions for file sharing or print sharing. In October 2008 Microsoft issued a security bulletin with a patch to repair a hole in port 445. The problem was that a "remote procedure call" could allow the port to be opened. The patch that Microsoft issued in October 2008 in theory closed the port to unauthorized entry. However, within a few weeks of the Microsoft warning, the Conficter worm began to spread into millions of un-patched computers.

The Conficter worm was astonishing. When it entered an un-patched computer through port 445 it immediately patched the hole it came through to keep out other worms. It also sought to prevent the computer from receiving security updates from security service providers. In addition it disabled the Windows system restore tool that allows users to reset an infected machine to a date prior to its infection. The most important unanswered questions about Conficter were how and when the creator would communicate with the massive group of infiltrated computers.

In computer jargon the infiltrated group of computers is called a botnet. The larger the botnet, the greater its potential menace. Botnets are used by criminal enterprises to distribute malware, steal private information or just generally engage in fraudulent schemes. Botnets can be bought or leased in underground criminal markets. Conficter is the largest known botnet. Conficter, Rat would say later, is the mother of all computer worms. It was the target of the greatest amount of computer expertise and effort to stop its spread and disable it.

So far all the efforts to unravel Conficter were unsuccessful. The creator of Conficter apparently waits patiently to put the extraordinary power of millions of networked computers to work for some malevolent purpose. Blaine was aware before she left the United States for Berlin that even among the sophisticated hackers in her online community, no one knew what the ultimate purpose of Conficter might be, or who the creator of Conficter was.

Blaine would have to talk with Rat about Conficter. Rat usually worked with at least two or three computers at a time in his storage room. The other day when she had been passing behind him she had seen information about Conficter on the screen of one of the monitors. If Rat really was involved in some way with Conficter he was going to be the target of every criminal prosecutor in the world assigned to prevent Internet fraud. Well, she mused, *no going to be, or maybe about it*. He probably already was the target. She knew that Rat was one of the most accomplished hackers in the world, and she also knew that in his heart he was a Robin Hood hacker. Conficter was not about helping the poor.

Blaine looked at her watch; it would be time to meet Rat in just two hours. She got up from the park bench and began to walk back to her apartment.

* * *

Blaine enjoyed getting ready to meet Rat for dinner. She had hardly ever used makeup in her life, but since she had gotten to Berlin, she had begun wearing light eye makeup to work. Tonight she found herself applying heavier, darker eye shadow. She realized it made her look more like the single German girls her age she saw when she went out at night.

There was a knock on her door.

"Hey, Rat," she said, "come on in."

"*Liebste, du siehst schön,*" said Rat, all the time wriggling his nose at her in his endearing rat-like manner. "Let's go, I am starving. There is nothing like a hard day saving the world from the arbitrary power of despotic computer networks to give a guy an appetite. I need cheese!"

They headed back over to Viktoriapark and to Golgatha, one of the most popular beer gardens in their part of the city. They got beers and hung out there for a while. It was too noisy to have the conversation with Rat that Blaine wanted to have, so after a while they left and wandered down one street and then another. Finally they found a quiet Turkish café. They went in and ordered kebobs and tabouli salad.

Blame screwed up her courage and started. "Rat, there's something that I have been meaning to talk to you about that really has me worried." She paused. "Is there something you aren't telling me?"

Rat was suddenly all attention. His nose was quivering. "Oh, Blaine, I am so sorry you have been worried," said Rat, "I have been keeping something from you, and I guess the truth is I just don't like talking to you about this guy Dawson. I know you really care about him, Blaine. So here's the deal. With the help of the Wiz, a hacking buddy of mine in the U. S., we have been watching Dawson. He must really be in some kind of trouble. The CIA is all over this guy—monitoring his phone calls, monitoring his location by where he goes with his cell phone, and reading his e-mails. There is also somebody else out there, who is much stealthier and a bit further removed who is checking his e-mails. The Wiz and I don't know who else is watching Dawson besides the CIA, but we know from past experience that whenever there is this level of surveillance, no-good is about to happen."

Rat paused, then he concluded, "I suggest we immediately communicate with Dawson through a non-monitored route and let him know what he is up against."

Blaine was stunned. She immediately forgot that she wanted to talk to Rat about Conficter. She knew in her gut that Rat was right. Will must be in some kind of deep trouble and he certainly needed their help.

"Rat, how in the world can we communicate with him from this distance in some fashion that is not being monitored?"

"Well, I have thought about that and my friend the Wiz can set something up. All we need to do is tell Dawson what is going on. After all, your friend is a spy boy isn't he? He should know what to do next."

"You're right, Rat," said Blaine. "All we need to do is just let him know how closely he is being watched."

"Okay," said Rat, wolfing down the rest of his kebab and thrusting back his shoulders as if to say he was ready for action, "let's head over to the storage room right now and we can set something up to alert Dawson that can happen first thing in the morning in the U.S."

CHAPTER 4

Gordon Slade found Joy.   Joy was at Boston's Logan airport to meet him at Terminal E when his Air Alitalia flight arrived from Rome.

Even now, two days after Joy had met him at the airport, Slade was trying to steady himself back into his old rhythm as a private detective. He had been on an emotional roller coaster. When he received word while in Turin at the Enneagram conference from Joy's mother that Joy was missing he had been deeply shaken.

Slade was a man who was cynical about life. This outlook suited his profession. However, it was problematic in his relationships with women. Slade also suffered from being a ruggedly handsome man with an easy-going disposition that one of his friends had remarked literally charmed the pants off women.

It wasn't that Slade had a problem with relationships. He was a master at playful, charming relationships, but he was unwilling, or perhaps unable, to be emotionally vulnerable with a woman.

Most of his livelihood came from providing the evidence necessary for a betrayed spouse to get even in court. He saw on a daily basis the huge downside to becoming open and vulnerable in his personal life with a woman.

For months, Slade had been going out with Joy off and on. Joy worked as a librarian. She wore glasses that tended to slide down her nose because the lenses were thick to compensate for extreme nearsightedness.

Slade was not sure why he was attracted to Joy. She was probably a few inches over five feet tall. Usually at work she wore her red hair pulled back so tightly that stress lines appeared in her forehead above her temples. Her hair was then tied behind her head like a twist of rope. She appeared to have a good figure, possibly a little more buxom than normal for a woman of her small size. Slade did not have any accurate knowledge about this. She wore drab librarian clothes that camouflaged her body, and all of his charming attempts at romantic conquest had been rebuffed.

She also wore particularly clunky, ugly librarian shoes. Slade tended to judge people by the shoes they wore. At least until he got to know someone well, Slade was convinced that shoes said more about a person than anything else. Joy totally failed the shoe test. Despite it all, Slade was attracted to her and had continued occasionally for months to try to make her another successful conquest.

Shortly before he left on his trip to the Enneagram conference Joy suddenly appeared more interested in having a relationship with him. Somehow it seemed that his interest in the Enneagram had raised him substantially in her estimation.

THE END OF DEMOCRACY

The last time they had been out together before his trip to Italy, Joy had begun to share with Slade a little more of her rich interior emotional life, and Slade had found himself even more attracted to her. Slade had discovered that they were both alike in that they each were very emotionally self-protective. Joy was protective in her shy, introverted way. Slade protected himself with a persona that was outgoing, easy and charming, that immediately put other people at ease when they were with him and allowed the real Slade to remain undisclosed.

Now, two days after feeling a surge of unexpected emotion upon Joy meeting him at the airport, Slade stuffed his lanky body into the front seat of his Olds and turned the key. The engine fired up immediately. Slade smiled to himself. The car had seen a number of Boston winters and General Motors had stopped making this model back even before Detroit collapsed in 2008, but somehow just getting on the road in his Olds made him feel younger, like he was part of an older, more innocent era. He pulled out from the side street near his condo onto the thoroughfare and headed up to the North End where Joy lived with her mother.

Joy met Slade at the front door of the neat brownstone she had lived in all her life. The home her parents had moved into years before she was born. Upon seeing Joy, tension lines around Slade's eyes immediately relaxed, softening his face. Her normal stress lines had vanished at the airport when she recognized how upset this man had been when he thought she had disappeared. They had not re-appeared. For a long moment all Joy and Slade could do was simply look at each other with silly grins, overloaded with more emotion than either was used to processing. They were both relieved when Joy's mother came out of the kitchen and called them to come for a cup of coffee. As they walked to the kitchen, their physical motion eased their emotions.

Joy's mother turned to Slade. "Gordon, do you want yours black or would you like a little milk and sugar?"

"Black is fine," said Slade.

"I must apologize again for causing you so much alarm while you were on your trip to Italy. I was just beside myself when I could not get in touch with Joy." She turned and glared at her daughter still obviously caught in the middle of both her anger and her relief that her daughter's absence had only been because she had gone for a four-day silent meditation retreat without telling her, or anyone else.

"Mom, I thought we had finally gotten past this. I told you how sorry I was that I neglected to leave you a note, but after all, I am 34 and I don't have to keep you constantly informed of where I am. Anyway, if you need to fuss more at me about this, let's do it later. Right now, I am just so glad that Gordon came by to see us this morning."

Slade nodded at Joy and smiled, aware that Joy was aligning herself with him and not her mother.

"It sure is good to see you both," said Slade. "What a great day for us to get out of the city. Joy, are you still up for a drive out to the Berkshires?"

"Gordon, that would be wonderful. I feel like I have so much to talk to you about and I am a person who usually doesn't do much talking. That's strange, isn't it?" Joy lifted her head and looked directly at Slade. She never went on like this, talking about what was actually happening inside herself. She smiled at Slade and unspoken words seem to tumble out of her into him, and his unspoken words came back to her sealed with his smile.

"Mom and I have already been working on sandwiches for us. I made you a big turkey pastrami with sauerkraut and Russian dressing."

Slade was pleased that she remembered what his favorite sandwich was. He was the one who usually remembered quirky details about others. He smiled at how comforting it was to have another person think of something small that mattered to him.

"What about pickles? Should we take some?" asked Joy.

"If you have some of those garlic dills like we got at the deli before I left on my trip, that would be great," said Slade.

"Okay, and I got us a bottle of wine from someplace you will probably know about in Sicily. I don't drink the stuff you know. I thought you might like it and you would be able to tell me a good story about how the sun shines on the Sicilian hillsides where the grapes grow." Joy raised her eyebrows and gave a mocking expression of paying homage to one who knows all things.

Slade grinned again. He couldn't believe Joy was teasing him because he always had an opinion about anything being discussed. And, he could not have imagined before meeting Joy, how much fun it could be just to talk about what food you would be taking on a picnic.

"Oh, and I also have a fortune cookie for you," said Joy with a huge smile, and she handed Slade a small cookie wrapped neatly in clear cellophane.

"Should I open it now?" asked Slade. Joy nodded.

Slade opened the cellophane. He took out the small cookie and broke it in half. He pulled out a little strip of paper and popped half a cookie in his mouth. He unrolled the paper. It read: *"You will find in the Mystery the manna."*

Slade looked at Joy's smiling face. He was puzzled. "This doesn't sound like a Chinese fortune."

Joy took the other half of the cookie from his hand and put it in her mouth. "Mom, the steel trap mind of the professional detective is clicking in," she said teasingly. "It is from my new job. I haven't quit the librarian position, but I have a new part-time job creating fortune cookie sayings. They are not the old-fashioned fortune cookie sayings. A Jewish guy we know opened up a fortune cookie factory in Brooklyn. Except, like I was saying, it's not your traditional Chinese fortune cookie he is making. He makes fortune cookies for the spiritual journey. We make several varieties, including Sufi, Kabbalist, Tibetan Buddhist and Taoist. And I am one of his consultants on the fortunes that go in the cookies for the mystical Christian line and

the Enneagram journeyer cookies. What do you think of that?"
"I am amazed as always by you, Joy," said Slade. "Just when I think I'm getting to know you a bit, this whole new part opens up." It was all he could do to keep from pulling Joy close and kissing her deeply, except Joy's mother was standing just a few feet away in the hall completely ruining the opportunity.

"Time for you kids to be hitting the road," said Joy's mother.

Slade smiled sheepishly to himself. If the truth were known, and he was not exactly sure what the truth was in this particular instance, he might really be closer to the age of Joy's mother than to Joy's age. However, he was feeling more like a kid than he had felt in a long time.

Joy closed the lid of the picnic basket and Slade grabbed it by the handle and headed for the door. She stopped in the hallway to pull on an old BU sweatshirt and grab a Red Sox cap.

Slade opened the trunk of the Olds and put in the picnic basket. Joy got in the passenger seat and waved at her mother standing in the doorway of the row house. Slade turned the key. As always the Olds immediately sprang to life. Slade looked over at Joy. "You sure look like you're a long way over there."

"Well, I can fix that," said Joy. She reached down, unbuckled her seatbelt and slid across the wide, bench front seat of the Olds until she was right up next to Slade.

Slade realized that when he was with Joy he saw things differently. He was attached to his old car, and he had never actually been able to figure out in his mind why. Now he reckoned it was because it represented to him a more community oriented time in American history. Back before the rampant individualism of the bucket seat. He would keep fighting the rust that got so much encouragement from the salty-winter, Boston streets. Joy reminded him of a sense of community that was important to life.

They drove for a while without saying a word. Joy leaned the top of her head against his right shoulder. He could feel her energy as she snuggled up against him. There was nothing he needed to say or do. For a moment he let go of the iron grip he tried to keep on his life. In that moment he experienced something he had not felt in many years, something that tasted of salt and being young, in a sailboat, out on the sea.

CHAPTER 5

There was a knock on the door. *Who in the world could it be*, wondered Dawson. He had been up since early morning getting his gear organized for his trip out to the Southwest to try to meet again with Father O'Donnell.

Probably some of those young kids passing out tracts, he thought. Often he liked to spend time engaging them in discussion and challenging some of their ideas about their religion. He definitely didn't have time for that today. He'd have to send them off promptly.

When Dawson opened the door the young man standing before him was not holding tracts in his hands, but a large white box.

"Mr. Dawson?" inquired the young man. Dawson nodded tentatively.

"I have a delivery for you."

Dawson looked out in the parking lot and there was a white panel truck with a sign emblazoned on its side which said: "All Occasion Gourmet Organic Catering."

"Are you sure this is for me?"

"Aren't you Will Dawson?"

"Yep, that's me. Okay, thank you very much." And with that Dawson took the white box he was handed, closed the door and retreated into his kitchen.

Dawson immediately opened the box. He could not believe it. There was a beautiful chocolate cake, and in darker chocolate icing were the words Happy Birthday, Will.

Will had completely forgotten that today was his birthday. What was even more shocking was that he knew absolutely no one who would be interested in sending him a birthday cake. Well, almost no one. He couldn't hold back the thought that maybe the cake was from Melissa. But he didn't even know whether she was alive. Then just as quickly he thought, maybe the cake came from Blaine. However, when he left Blaine after their week of romance in Italy, she made it quite clear that the ball was in his court. He took the cake out of the box and looked for a note beneath the cake or taped to the box somewhere. Nothing.

Gosh, he thought, *this cake really does look good.* I might as well have some. He put some coffee beans in the grinder, flipped the switch and then emptied the grounds into his French press. As soon as the water came to a boil, he poured it into the French press. It was hard to beat chocolate cake and good coffee.

After the coffee brewed for a couple of minutes, he poured it into his favorite pottery cup, added warm milk and a little bit of agave sweetener. He sipped the brew. Perfect.

He put the cake in the middle of the table and got a long knife. He was just about to complete the first slice into the cake when he felt the end of the knife strike something metal. He dropped the knife and ducked back into the hallway. His internal alarm system was on high alert. Somebody had sent him a booby-trapped cake, and he was probably extremely fortunate that the thing had not already exploded. He went into the room that put the most walls between him and the kitchen and sat down against the far wall and waited.

After a few minutes, when nothing had happened he went back into the kitchen. This time he laid the knife to the side. He picked up a fork and very gently began to scrape back the icing from the cake. Soon he was making his way into the moist rich cake itself. He lifted a tiny morsel of cake with the fork. He smelled. There was no trace of the plastic smell of explosives he had been trained to detect. He stuck the fork with the tiny bite on it into his mouth. Dark chocolate and sugar and the way each accented the other. He moved the bite around in his mouth. Nothing else. He swallowed. He could not believe how good the cake tasted. It was exquisite. He continued to meticulously work his way down through the cake.

Just before he got to the bottom his fork grazed something metal. Very gently he pushed away the cake from the metal object. He laughed. The object in the middle of the cake was a small metal Altoids box.

Dawson did not consider himself a big fan of Altoids mints,

though occasionally he would treat himself to a box of the cinnamon variety. He pulled the small box from out of the center of the cake. A strange way to deliver a box of mints.

Very carefully he opened the Altoids box. Inside there were no mints, just a small scroll of paper which he carefully unwound. He read:

Dawson,

Blaine would have liked to have written you, but she is waiting for you to visit her first. In the meantime, she is worried about you and wanted me to let you know the danger you are in. Consider this a curiously strong warning. Your telephone, e-mail and location are being monitored by the CIA. In addition, some other group is reading your e-mail. The level of surveillance is sufficiently intense that Blaine is worried that the same thing that happened to Melissa, whatever that was, may happen to you. I will keep monitoring your surveillance. Do not carry your cell phone with you unless you want the watchers to know where you are. Do not try to call or e-mail us using your regular telephone or e-mail. If you wish to communicate, I have set up a chat room that you can access. Do not use your computer to access it. Go to the website for the large daily newspaper in your town. In the background on their home page you will see a barely visible icon representing the Brandenburg Gate. Click on the icon. This will take you to another website where you can login. Your login is Altoid. Your password is your name spelled backwards with ones and zeros alternating between the letters. If you need help in an emergency buy a prepaid phone and call this number: 030/785 24 53.

Rat

Wow, what a birthday present—a chance to escape with his life. Maybe he was being overly dramatic, however, his long years of service in the Company left no doubt in his mind, as Blaine and Rat had surmised, that with this level of surveillance, his life indeed might be in jeopardy. The rule of thumb in the Company had always been: the greater the level of surveillance, the higher the value of the target, and the higher the target value the more likely the target would be caught in some kind of crossfire. How had he become a high value target? The only possible reason was obvious. The Company must have him under surveillance because of his pursuit of Melissa. All trails seemed to lead back to Melissa's disappearance. Probably they were not really after him as much as they were hoping that he would lead them to Melissa.

In fact, that was the message that Rat had given him before he left Turin: Rat felt that Melissa would have contacted Dawson if he had not been watched so closely by the CIA and some other organization. He would have to be much more careful. He began to wonder if the letter that Melissa's mother had given him, supposedly from Melissa, had actually come from her. Or, was the letter written by someone else to make him the bait that could be followed to Melissa?

Dawson went to his computer. He had made his reservation to Las Vegas through his own computer in his own name. He pulled up his reservation online. From now on he would need to be more discreet in his travel plans. It would cost him a hundred and fifty dollars he didn't need to waste to cancel his reservation.

He went back to his bedroom and pulled out an old metal file, that had once been a safe deposit drawer, from under his bed. When he retired from the company, almost without thinking, he had kept a few of the old identities he had once been assigned. He pulled out a couple old Australian passports and credit cards to go with them. Then he went into the kitchen and got the knife he used to cut his birthday cake, returned to the bedroom and pulled up the sheet from the bottom of the bed. He wiped the knife clean and made a foot long slice in the end of his mattress. Slowly he wedged the metal file box into the mattress. He would have to find a better hiding place. However, this would have to do for the time being. He tucked the sheet back into the foot of the bed.

Dawson went to the top drawer of his dresser and got out a passport pouch attached to a body belt. He put the two Australian passports and credit cards in the pouch and zipped it shut. He put the belt around his waist so that the pouch rested easily in the small of his back. He pulled on a T-shirt and a pair of jeans. He got out his jogging shoes and put them on, before finally pulling on a college sweatshirt. He went to the kitchen and stuffed the Altoids box with the scroll inside into the pocket of his jeans. He found a zip drive and inserted it into the USB port of his Apple MacBook Pro sitting at the kitchen table. He downloaded everything from his computer into the zip drive. Dawson used the encryption software on his computer to do an encryption update so that everything on his computer was encrypted. Then he shut the Apple down.

He looked at the chocolate cake, paused a moment, and then cut a large slab off the side maximizing the amount of icing he got. He put the remainder in the refrigerator. He sat at the kitchen table and quickly finished off the serving of cake. He got up, put his keys in his pocket and went out the front door of his apartment, being sure the door locked behind. He walked down the interior staircase. Rather than going out the front door of the apartment building he headed down to the basement where the apartment storage units were and where garbage collected from the trash chutes provided for each apartment in the building. As he stood inside the rear exit door from the basement, the stifling odor of ripe garbage filled the air. Still he remained there for a good long minute searching the outside scene. When he was convinced there was no one watching this exit, he pulled the door open slightly and slipped outside.

By moving through the landscaped common spaces between apartment buildings, without crossing the apartment complex's parking lot, he gradually distanced himself from his own apartment building. A few hundred yards up from the entrance to the apartment complex was a bus stop. He waited there to catch a bus to the nearest Metro stop.

He took the Metro Blue Line to Foggy Bottom and walked over to Georgetown. It was late morning but few people were up and moving about. This was a late-night part of Washington. He found his way to a small Ukrainian bar and restaurant just a block off 35th street. It'd been a couple years since he was there. Still, he knew the place well. The owner, Sergei Karsiloff, was very helpful years back during the fall of the Soviet Union. So helpful in fact that he was able to bring on board a couple of Ukrainian informants whom Dawson suspected were still being handled by the CIA.

The place had a **Closed** sign on the front door, but the door was ajar. Dawson walked inside. He saw Sergei sweeping up the remains from the night before. He waved.

"Come in, my friend," said Sergei.

Dawson wandered over casually.

"I bet you closed this place up last night too," said Dawson, "and here you are the first one in this morning."

"I can't complain," said Sergei, "business seems to be good here no matter what the economy is like. I think that means that there's never a bear market in politics. How can I help you, my friend?"

Dawson reached out his right hand and grasped Sergei's large hand.

"Sergei, I need your help and, as always, this needs to be extremely discreet. I mean just between you and me. Even if the Company comes calling, it never happened. You with me?"

Sergei's smile disappeared and his face knotted into an intense expression. He nodded affirmatively to Dawson.

"I need to do a couple of identity trades with you. Passports, credit cards—the works," said Dawson. "Can you help me out?"

"I think so," said Sergei, "I need to know the quality of what you're trading me?"

THE END OF DEMOCRACY

"Company produced all the way."

Sergei paused. They both knew that this meant that the quality of the forgeries was excellent, and it also meant that wherever they were used, there was a high probability that the CIA would be alerted.

"I need high quality from you in return," said Dawson.

Sergei nodded. "I think I can get what you need. What nationality are you giving me?"

"Australian," said Dawson, "and I would like Australian or Canadian in return if you can do that?"

"Probably, and would Kiwi also be okay? I will need several days. Did you bring some passport photos?"

Dawson pulled out his wallet and reached in and extracted three old passport photographs of himself, taken by one of those passport photograph vending machines several years back. He handed the photos to Sergei. "I will be back in three days. Can you have them for me then?"

"Barring any unforeseen difficulties, yes."

Dawson reached under his T-shirt and pulled around the passport pouch from the small of his back. He unzipped the pouch and took out one Australian passport and a credit card with the same name as appeared on the passport and handed these to Sergei. "I will deliver the other one to you when I'm back in three days," said Dawson. "Thank you, my friend." Dawson gave Sergei a big bear-hug like he had often seen Eastern European agents give each other in the old days. He had marveled then at how it was such a perfect expression of intimacy and threat at the same time. Now Dawson meant the hug in exactly the same way he had seen it given years earlier. The two men broke from their embrace and Dawson, without further words, turned and headed toward the door.

Dawson walked back to the nearest Metro stop and got the Metro to the King Street station in Alexandria. From there he walked to the nearest public library. When he walked in, he was delighted to find that there was no wait to use one of the library's computers providing public access to the Internet.

He sat down at a computer next to the window and turned the monitor discreetly away from the rest of the room. He reached into his jeans pocket and pulled out the Altoids box. He opened the box and pulled out the scroll. He clicked on the computer icon for Internet access and typed in *The Washington Post*. The online edition of today's paper appeared. He clicked on the tab for homepage. He had glanced at this homepage often enough before, but for the first time he studied it seriously. Finally he saw a faint, fuzzy image in the upper right-hand corner. Maybe it was an image of the Brandenburg Gate, but it was way too fuzzy for that to be clear. It looked like what might simply be a smudge on a monitor screen. He clicked on the smudge.

As Rat had told him in his message, Dawson was directed to another website. He logged in using the login and password that Rat had given him. There was only one other participant with access to the chat room, and that was Rat. Dawson typed: "Thanks for the birthday cake. It was delicious, and the mints were curiously strong. I don't know what's going on either, but thanks for the heads up. I will keep below the radar and check in with you again before too long."

Dawson looked at his watch. It would be early evening in Germany, so there was no reason Rat might not be at his computer and able to reply immediately. Of course, from what Dawson knew of Rat there was no time of the day or night when Rat might not be available to reply. Dawson waited a few minutes longer. He didn't want to keep this circuit open too long. In truth, he could not think of anything that Rat could really tell him right now in reply. The important thing was for Rat, and therefore Blaine, to know that Rat's message had been received. Quickly he pulled down another tab and set up a new Hotmail account. He added this new address to the bottom of his chat message to Rat with a note letting Rat know that it was new and that Dawson would only access it from public computers. Then he logged out of the chat room, got up and left the library.

When Dawson got outside he realized he was starving. The only thing he had eaten all day was his surprise chocolate birthday cake.

CHAPTER 6

As Gordon Slade drove thoughtfully from the North End back to his condo near Fenway Park, he suddenly realized his life was changing. He had just left Joy at her home where she and her mother lived. The time hiking with Joy in the Berkshires and then sharing a picnic was as idyllic a day as he could remember ever having.

What struck Slade the most as he thought about the day was that he had not simply observed his life with Joy, but he had been fully present in it. Somehow a new willingness to show up in his own life had emerged. He felt this change must have occurred because of Joy, though he could not put his finger on exactly what she had done. Maybe it was not anything that she'd done at all. Maybe it was the trip to Turin and his forced participation in the Enneagram conference on behalf of his client, Peter Wagner.

It would not be accurate to say that his experience with Joy was like his enjoyment of fine Italian shoes, or like having a really great meal at his favorite Italian restaurant in the North End. But it would not be entirely inaccurate either. There was a sensual quality to being in the moment with Joy that rang true to other pleasures. There was something else also. Some quality of trust began to emerge when he was with Joy which allowed him to let his guard down.

Usually when he was out with a woman he enjoyed his control over the liaison, watching as she responded to his charm. There was none of this with Joy. When he was with her he no longer imagined how he might connive to get her in bed. He was simply content just to be with her. Even the periods of silence that they had together seemed rich and full. His usual need to be entertaining and full of charm and wit did not arise.

Yes, he admitted to himself, there was a new sense of freedom and tranquility that he was experiencing in his relationship with Joy. He also recognized an uneasiness. He was simply not used to being in a situation like this. It was strange that tranquility could be so unsettling. But, he mused, if you're not used to experiencing peacefulness in your life and then suddenly do, that is a jolt.

Slade pulled up to his condominium parking space in Back Bay. His reverie came to an abrupt end. There sitting on his doorstep was none other than his old friend Will Dawson. Slade hesitated just a moment before cutting off his headlights. Oh no, thought Slade, Dawson is not looking too good tonight.

Slade got out of his car, put out his hand and pulled Dawson up off the step. "Couldn't get enough of me in Turin," said Slade. Then, more seriously, "Come inside and we can talk."

Dawson did not need persuasion. The two men went way back. They had been in criminology classes together at BU. Dawson had been there as a part of his preparation and training for the

Company, and Slade as a young rookie cop on the Boston police force.

The two men had often gotten together over the intervening years at Slade's condo. Slade bought his condo about ten years earlier when he got a big fee. His client had been a man. This was not usually the case. Sure enough, the guy's wife had been cheating on him. Slade had just gotten a pair of binoculars that included a digital camera. Dawson had been the one who had tipped Slade off that such equipment was available. When the pictures had been blown up into large glossies, including the one he'd gotten with the binoculars from a perch in a tree looking into the paramour's bedroom window, his client paid him triple his normal fee.

Even when he did a great job for clients, which he almost always did, his clients were usually so upset upon receiving evidence of their spouse's betrayal that their anger came out at everyone, including Slade. Not so with this guy, whose generous fee was the down payment on the condo.

There was really nothing remarkable about the condo, but like everything in Boston, it was about location. And the location could not be beat. Slade could walk to a Red Sox game at Fenway and walk downtown in twenty minutes. Plus he had the prize of his own parking space for his Olds.

Slade quickly unlocked the front door to the condo. He and Dawson walked straight into the kitchen. Slade flipped on the lights, opened the fridge and pulled out two cold Samuel Adams beers. "I hate to say this Will, you look awful. What's up?"

"Man, am I glad to see you," said Dawson. "About the time I was halfway here coming up on the train, I got to thinking you might be out of town for a week or more and it would be a long time sitting on the curb."

Although the two friends would often go for months without seeing each other, one of the most valuable lessons Dawson had learned working for the Company was the importance of having someone to talk through a case with. Over the years, Dawson and Slade had each used the other as a sounding board to get new perspectives when they were stuck on a case.

"I'm not exactly sure where to start," said Dawson. "Since I got back from Italy I have found out that I am under 24-hour surveillance by the CIA. They are monitoring my phone, my e-mail and my whereabouts through my cell phone location. I know from experience that when this level of surveillance is put on a target something serious is in the works."

The tone of Dawson's voice made Slade immediately attentive. Slade noted the dark circles under Dawson's eyes at the same time as he focused intently on what he was saying.

"I am not sure what to do, but for safety's sake, I have decided to go underground. Maybe I just don't like being followed. I need somebody I trust to talk with about what is happening. And to talk me out of going on the run if I am making a foolish mistake."

There was a pause. Slade took a long pull on his Samuel Adams. Then Dawson continued to talk, almost in a monotone, filling

Slade in with every detail he thought relevant. When he had finished the two men sat in silence. After a moment, from down the condo's hallway Slade's restored Howard Miller wall clock chimed the hour.

"I think you are right, Dawson, about the need for a low profile" said Slade. "This has got to be about Melissa. At first I thought it was just about the efforts at the environmental organization she works for to stop the public's rekindled fervor in favor of nuclear power. That might get the FBI involved, not the Company. Something bigger than we know about must be going on."

"You are right," said Dawson, "I think there is a bigger picture; it's almost like I can see the hazy outlines of it or at least the bigness of the outlines, and I still can't bring the picture itself into focus. I've decided to go out to the Southwest to meet with Father O'Donnell and seek his guidance. I am going under an alias. Here is a new Hotmail address that I'll be checking from time to time. If it's okay with you, when I get back East, I would like to come back to Boston and talk about what my next move should be. I may be gone awhile."

"Try to make it on a night when we can go over to Fenway Park and watch the boys play. I know you may not be a big Red Sox fan living down there in Alexandria, however, if you are going to hang out up here it's best to get your team perspective aligned." Slade looked away from Dawson toward the window—a gesture that allowed Slade to sink a little deeper into what he was feeling in the moment. He was aware that his causal banter was masking the gravity of the situation, not only for Dawson, but also perhaps for himself. If the Company was tracking Dawson closely they might know that he was visiting Slade right now. His life was finally taking a turn for the better because of his relationship with Joy. He sure didn't want to get involved with problems like Will Dawson was having if he could help it. But he realized why Dawson had come to see him. Even if it meant opening a can of worms, they both put loyalty to close friends first, before everything else. I can't turn my back on a buddy in need, he thought.

"Seriously, Will, I am troubled by all this. You can come here anytime you need to talk or need a place to stay, you know that."

Slade almost never called Dawson by his first name. Dawson was touched by Slade's friendship. Dawson knew that Slade meant the offer of help that he had given him. And they both knew that at times, in doing their work, they each had to go around the law in order to see that ultimately the law was served.

Slade sensed that Dawson was on dicey ground, but maybe his was the right approach. He was simply not sure. Rather than trying to give Dawson advice, he figured it was better to just give him aid and comfort. Maybe it was the time he had spent with Joy. He got up from the table and as he arose so did Dawson. Slade went around the table and put his arm around his friend's shoulder. Nothing further was said.

CHAPTER 7

Will Dawson had a long, circuitous trip to the Southwest. After he got back from his trip to Boston, he immediately went to Georgetown and picked up a passport, driver's license, and credit card in the name of Godfrey Adams, an Australian.

Dawson re-entered his apartment complex in Alexandria the same way he had left, by coming in, not through the main entrance to the apartment building, but up from the basement storage and trash area. He was not surprised when he touched the doorknob to the front door of his apartment and without even turning the knob the door gently opened inward. The door's closing and locking mechanism had been completely disabled when his apartment had been broken into.

Dawson looked around his apartment. Obviously whoever had done the searching, and at least for now he assumed it was the Company, didn't care that he knew his apartment had been searched. His clothes had been taken from his bedroom dresser drawers and strewn all over the floor. In the kitchen, everything was gone from the cupboards and cabinet shelves and now lay scattered all over on the counter and floor. His beloved Apple MacBook Pro, which had been sitting on the breakfast table, was gone.

Despite all his intellectual understanding of how the Company did searches and how the bureaucratic machinery of the agency ground mercilessly forward in an impersonal way, he felt a sense of outrage and deep survival-based fear from having his home and life invaded.

Dawson went into his bedroom and sat on the end of his bed and gently rolled from one butt cheek to the other. *Damn*, he thought, as he felt the edge of something hard beneath him, *what a sloppy job*. He got up and pulled the sheet off the mattress. Someone had obviously looked under the mattress, but no one discovered the hiding place of the metal box he had stuck inside his mattress before he left town. Dawson pulled the metal drawer out from in the mattress. He opened its lid. Everything appeared to be there just as he had left it. He took the contents from the drawer and emptied it into a backpack, along with his zip drive with all the encrypted files on his computer and the Altoids box.

Finding that his metal file box had not been discovered buoyed his feelings. He knew it was hard to compete with the Company's ability to track someone down, but the key was to stay one step ahead of them. He could probably do this as long as Rat could keep him up-to-date on the Company's search activities. He knew he had no time to spare. He had to get out of there as soon as possible.

Quickly he packed a duffel bag with clothes. He would have liked to have taken almost everything, but he did not want to leave the impression that he had moved out for good; best to let them use their resources watching the place for the next weeks or months. He took what he needed to have clothes for varying weather conditions. He opened the fridge and cut another slice off of his chocolate birthday cake. He rescued a plate that was not broken, put the large chunk of chocolate cake on the plate and snacked on it as he completed his packing. Gosh, that cake was delicious. He hated to leave the rest.

Dawson went to his desk, got a piece of paper and wrote his landlord a quick note, asking for his lock to be repaired and giving notice that he would be terminating his month-to-month lease at the end of the next month. He included a check to cover his rental payments through the expiration of the lease. Then he took his backpack and duffel bag down to the basement and stashed them out of sight behind a trash bin.

He went back up to the front foyer of his apartment building. He was careful to avoid standing where he could be seen through the narrow glass windows that were on either side of the apartment building's front door. He hoped he would not have to wait long.

Fifteen minutes passed before he heard the door of a unit on the second floor open. In a moment a young woman walked down the steps to the first floor landing. She was wearing flip-flops and a man's shirt with a bathing suit underneath. *This is great good luck*, thought Dawson.

He smiled at the young woman and moved as if he were going up the stairs. "Oh, I forgot to drop this off by the rental office, would you mind doing this for me on your way to the pool?"

The young woman pulled an iPod earbud out of one ear. She had not heard exactly what Dawson had said, however, she had seen him occasionally in the hallway and knew he lived in the building. She looked down at the envelope he had in his hand that he was holding out to her. Written on the front of the envelope were the words Rental Office.

"Sure, I'll be glad to drop it through the slot in the rental office door," she said.

"Thanks so much for saving me another trip back out in this heat," said Dawson, "I appreciate your help. Have a great day."

The young woman nodded at him, put the earbud back in her ear and headed out the door.

Dawson continued up the stairs. After the door to the apartment building had closed firmly behind the young woman, he paused for a few seconds then turned and walked quickly back down the stairs to the basement. There he collected his backpack and duffel bag, and having surveyed the scene from the exit to be sure there was no one keeping surveillance on the rear of the building, he cautiously slipped out of the rear door and made his way between apartment buildings toward the nearest street away from the entry drive to the apartment complex.

When he got to the street, Dawson found his way to the same bus stop where he had begun his trip to Boston to see Gordon Slade. As he stood at the bus stop, he practiced what he had learned with the Company, and more of what Melissa taught him about how to control his energy field. He drew his energy field in tightly around himself. Most people passing by in their vehicles would have had to look twice to even realize that there was a man standing beside a telephone pole next to the bus stop.

Bus service in Alexandria was not great and it was about thirty minutes before a bus came by. Fortunately, the bus on this route went right down Duke Street, near the Amtrak station. Dawson got off the bus on Duke Street and walked the short distance to Callahan Drive and the Amtrak station. He bought a ticket on the next train, The Carolinian, leaving at 11:12 a.m. going south. The good thing about train travel was no identity watch-list matching was used. He wanted to get a little ways out of the Washington area before utilizing his new identity to catch a flight west. The Amtrak train should be in Richmond, Virginia at 1:02 p.m., and he would have plenty of time to visit a bank before closing time.

As he emerged from the train station on Staples Mill Road in Richmond, Dawson noticed that down the street at the corner was a bank. He had a fair amount of cash that had collected in his metal file drawer. He went into the bank and opened an account in the name of Godfrey Adams and rented a safe deposit box. He went into the closet like room provided for customers to put items into their safe deposit box and closed the door. He poured out the contents of his backpack on the desk. Among the items that had been in the metal file box was the silver locket Dawson had given Blaine, which she had returned to him when he had left her in Italy. He picked it up and opened it. On one side was a tiny icon image of Mary Magdalene and on the other side a small photo of the two of them taken in Rome. He stared at the photo of the couple inside. Without thinking he put it in the Altoids box along with the message from Rat and his zip drive. He felt a wave of emotion and remembered one of the things that Father O'Donnell had told him on their flight to Italy: men who are out

THE END OF DEMOCRACY

of touch with their heart-centered emotions often love movies with cheap sentimentality.

So what, thought Dawson, if the locket made him suddenly feel weepy. He stuffed the Altoids box into the pocket of his jeans. Then he placed all of his old company identities and the remaining contents of his backpack, which was mostly family memorabilia, in the safety deposit box. He returned the safety deposit box to the bank assistant and watched as she returned it to the vault, locked it back in its slot and handed him back his key.

He put the key in the pocket of his jeans and left the bank. Dawson then walked to a branch of the Henrico County public library located in the Dumbarton shopping center. There he logged on to one of the public access computers and, following the instructions previously given to him by Rat, returned to the chat room Rat had set up for their communication. There was no new posting from Rat. Dawson sent Rat a message quickly outlining what Dawson had been doing since Dawson received the birthday message from Rat in the Altoids box.

After looking at a local street map in the library, Dawson left the Dumbarton Square shopping center and walked up Staples Mill Road. He took a left on Wistar and walked along it until he got to West Broad Street. There he caught a bus that traveled along West Broad to the Short Pump Town Center where the only Apple store in Richmond was located. He bought the newest generation iPhone with the maximum storage capacity and a small, powerful MacBook.

While he was still on his new computer in the Apple store, Dawson logged on to an Internet travel service to look for the next cheap flight going to New Mexico. He found a last-minute flight for a discounted price. He would have to spend a little time in Denver making connections. He bought a ticket in the name of Godfrey Adams and paid for the flight with Godfrey's credit card. For the first time all day, he began to relax. He had three hours to get to the Richmond airport.

CHAPTER 8

Charles Redmon did not like being called on the carpet. Particularly the carpet of an Assistant Director of the CIA where the Seal of the CIA, so beautifully etched in granite on the ground floor, was emblazoned right in the center of the carpet. His boss knew just as well as Redmon did that it was easy to lose track of a former officer. The officer would pick up on the surveillance early and know exactly how it was being done. It was no surprise to Redmon that Will Dawson had vanished.

There was some consolation. Redmon held it in his hand. An envelope marked as accessible to only those with the highest security clearance. On the outside of the envelope was a running roster of every individual who had seen the document inside. The Company was famous for letting officers know only a limited part of the bigger picture of what they were working on. But sometimes it happened, like now when the trail for Will Dawson had suddenly gone cold, the higher-ups would bring a section chief like Redmon in on the big picture. Redmon knew that bringing him into the bigger picture was seen as a motivational strategy, although he was already doing everything that standard operating procedure allowed him to do in pursuing Dawson. Still, knowing what was really going on always made things more interesting.

Redmon walked back into his office and closed the door. He glanced at the signatures on the front of the envelope. Included were the signatures of the Secretary of Defense, the Director of the CIA and the President's personal secretary. The President himself never signed for high-security documents; however, if his personal secretary did, it meant that what was in the document was presented to the President.

Redmon dropped into his old leather desk chair. He had brought it over from the old building to the new CIA headquarters at Langley, when most everybody else at his level had gotten new furniture. The chair reminded him of the good old days when he had first started working at the CIA, when the mission of defeating communism was clear. Everything was blurry nowadays. He pulled the report from the envelope and read its title: 1776—The End of Democracy. *Geez*, he thought, *the blurriness is getting worse.*

He settled into his chair and began reading the report. Redmon did not consider himself an intellectual. Exactly the opposite. He saw himself as a down-to-earth practical man. He was a boy who had grown up reading *Popular Mechanics*. He was fascinated by how things work. Quantum mechanics was quite a leap from popular mechanics. Still, Redmon immediately became intrigued by the report.

The report gave background on science's current understanding of quantum mechanics. Prior to the advent of quantum theory, scientists had believed that there was an objective reality operating under the laws of nature independent of human observation. In the early part of the 20th century, scientists discovered that certain subatomic particles could only be observed in certain energy states and not in between these states. In ordinary experience we perceive a logical linear progression of events. We move from the kitchen down the hallway into the living room. By analogy the way certain subatomic particles behave is to first be in the kitchen and then in the living room, without ever having walked the hallway in between.

Werner Heisenberg discovered that when subatomic particles were observed you could not know everything about them at the same time. Particularly, you could not know both the speed and the location of the particle at the same time. The state of the subatomic particle is always in some way connected to how it is being measured or observed. The report read:

> Heisenberg's discoveries shocked the scientific world. It appeared that the most fundamental aspects of matter were indeterminate. Then along came Niels Bohr and his fellow scientists in Copenhagen. According to the theory they developed, subatomic particles don't exist in one state or another but in all possible states at once. Only when there is an attempt to measure or observe a packet of possible states does the energy package become a particle. Somehow the existence of an observer brings a particular state into being.

> The Heisenberg Principle was hard for many to accept although it did explain beautifully the behavior of subatomic particles. Albert Einstein was one of the physicists who questioned Heisenberg's theory. Einstein sought to prove the independent existence of reality—that the physical properties of a particle exist outside of any observation.

The question of whether or not there needed to be an observer in order to make sub-atomic matter real wasn't the only mystery posed by the ongoing exploration of quantum physics. Erwin Schroedinger, who later won a Nobel prize, was the first scientist to predict that quantum particles were somehow entangled in a way that did not depend upon their physical location. His experiments showed that the properties of quantum particles were not fixed. If two particles were paired together and one of the particles was observed in a certain way, it affected the state of the other particle. This effect was instantaneous—that is, faster than the speed of light, and occurring regardless of the distance between the separated particles. John Bell, a mathematician, proved this "non-locality" of quantum particles mathematically.

In 1982 an experiment of non-locality was performed by Alain Aspect and his team of researchers at the University of Paris. This experiment showed that if the spin of particle A in an entangled pair is changed, particle B's spin changes simultaneously no matter how far apart the two particles are. The extraordinary conclusion from these experiments was that the form of an object's existence depends upon the form of other objects with which it is entangled.

At the same time that this research was being done by physicists on quantum mechanics, biologists were raising questions about how biological growth occurred. Early stem cell research back in the 1970s showed that if identical stem cells were placed in different environments, the stem cell in one petri dish would grow muscle tissue; in another environment the identical cell would grow nerve tissue; and in another environment, organ tissue. While each stem cell contained all of the DNA for the whole organism, something outside of the organism was what triggered a certain portion of the DNA to manifest. We may carry all sorts of potential within our individual DNA as human beings, but it appears that it is something outside of us which determines what is called forth.

Quantum physics and quantum biology seem to be headed in the same direction—that neither organic or inorganic matter exists independently in a concrete location, but everything is given its existence and its physical properties based upon the field in which it exists. Quantum physics and quantum biology become much more comprehensible once we let go of the idea that there is an objective material reality outside of the field of consciousness. Of course, the idea that consciousness is more fundamental than matter has a long history in Eastern traditions. This concept is totally alien to the Western mind.

Inevitably, scientists began to explore the question of whether quantum entanglement occurs between people as well as subatomic particles. In one experiment pairs of people were asked to meditate together for a period of time to establish entanglement. Then they were separated over large distances and hooked up to EEG machines. One of the meditators was then given a specific visual signal by a red light. When this red light flashed in the first meditator's eyes his EEG pattern changed and at the same time the distant meditators' EEG pattern changed in exactly the same way several time zones away. There is no conventional explanation outside of field theory which can explain these results.

There is also a long history in the psychic literature of people who are closely connected experiencing significant events together though they are thousands of miles apart. There are many stories of a father or mother waking up just before the time that a son or daughter is accidentally killed on the other side of the globe. These experiences are not limited to humans. Often a favorite pet has been described as having gotten very upset just at the time that something happened to its owner miles away.

Redmon took a deep breath. He was beginning to get some idea of how what was being presented in this paper might connect to its title. He kept reading.

Roger Nelson, a psychologist at Princeton, undertook experiments to see if human consciousness could have an effect on inanimate objects. The inanimate object in this experiment was a computer programmed to generate random patterns. The control was the random pattern generated before an event for an hour and then after the event for an hour. The purpose of the experiment was to determine if a significant event on the minds of many people created a field of consciousness that influenced the random sequence generated by the computer. Three events were examined. One included twelve people who were in a nine-hour Holotropic Breath workshop. The second included an estimated one billion people who watched the Academy

Awards ceremony in March of 1995, and the third event was the announcement of the verdict in the O. J. Simpson trial on October 3, 1995, which was estimated to have an audience worldwide on TV and radio of a half billion people. In each case the impact of the collective event affected the random sequencing by the computer to an order of between 1000 to one and 700 to one. In subsequent studies the greatest variance from predictable randomness occurred during the events of 9/11. The conclusion is that intensely felt experiences among people appear to affect the field in which even inanimate objects exist.

The unified field theory is the most commonly understood explanation today among religious scholars of how prayer works. The famous double-blind experiments by Dr. Larry Dossey with cancer patients showed remarkable results for those who were prayed for, even without their knowledge and by people whom they did not know.

Redmon paused to think about his own prayer life. It had pretty much dried up. He had grown up in the church and prayed daily for a long period in his life. However, the last time he remembered seriously praying about anything was when his mother died over ten years ago.

He turned his attention back to the report.

Our understanding of democracy, particularly Jeffersonian democracy, is based upon a non-quantum understanding of reality. Jefferson had a Newtonian view that if the public freely had information through freedom of the press, then the votes of everyone would end up electing the candidate who was in the best interest of the collective good. It was a cause-and-effect understanding.

Quantum field theory suggests that the whole premise on which the idea of democracy is based is unfounded.

We are governed not by the logical informed decisions of voters. Rather we are governed by how the collective field of consciousness is influenced. The media then becomes the controller of democracy, because in the media-saturated West, it creates the collective field. What controls the media? For the most part the media is driven by what creates corporate profits. Corporate profits in the media are driven primarily by stories and pictures of violence and tragedy. A media-driven democracy, at least in a capitalist country, is going to be primarily a fear-driven culture.

Unless, that is, there is another way to control the collective field of consciousness. This project, code-named 1776, was set up a year ago at the request of the President when it became apparent that there are individuals out there who, through training or other processes, have developed their consciousness to such an extent as to be able to control the thoughts of others. In quantum theory language they can become entangled in the thought fields of others and then, by analogy to the early quantum experiments, change the vibration of those thought fields. It all boils down to this: those who can control consciousness can, in effect, control the world.

One of those individuals who may have this ability is a former Peace Corps worker named Melissa Dowling. She had been working for an environmental organization when it came to the attention of an officer working on 1776 that she sought to change the thinking of certain senior officials working for a nuclear power company. The way Melissa's abilities were discovered was interesting. The agency set up a series of listening stations for a particular pattern of higher level electromagnetic waves that humans give off. The vibrational electromagnetic spectrum is huge starting from the slowest brain waves at .5 Hz and going up to cosmic rays at 10 to the 28th power. The agency constructed a vibrational template for enlightened consciousness by taking readings off of well-known conscious individuals such as the Dalai Lama. The signature image of enlightenment was a combination of low amplitude alpha and theta brain waves as well as waves going up to ten to the fourteenth power, which is the vibrational zone of visible light.

A footnote in the report noted that this might be the possible explanation of auras and the golden halos portrayed over heads in medieval religious paintings.

Damn, thought Redmon, *maybe the Company can chase down people who are enlightened, but we don't know how to achieve that for ourselves. At least not around here.* The agency was always being criticized by Congress for not being sufficiently creative in obtaining good intelligence data. From this report the problems were obvious. The agency lived in a field of consciousness of the bureaucratic mindset, which inevitably discouraged creative thought and innovation.

The report concluded that it was imperative for the United States to be the first to find a way to control the unified field of human consciousness. If not, Russia or China, or even worse, some failed state or terrorist organization would, and then it would be too late for the rest of the world.

Redmon squirmed in his old leather chair. Suppose the United States did discover the way to control the unified field of human consciousness. Who in the government would control how that power was used? Whichever political party was in power when the knowledge was gained would then be assured of staying in power forever. A foreign country, or group outside the United States, might not have the power to control the U.S., but perhaps more pernicious would be someone or some group within the United States believing in a self-righteous way that they must control the world's field of consciousness. Redmon felt a wave of nausea go through his body. Maybe it was time for him to retire. Things really were getting blurry.

CHAPTER 9

Manuelito was hot and tired. He looked down at Ooljee and the dog's tongue was hanging long out of the side of his mouth. Manuelito realized that his dog's instinctive effort to keep cool was turned up to the max. He would have to find water for Ooljee soon.

They had been up walking since dawn. It was only three days since the accident. The Navajo policeman had said little to him about what happened. All he knew was that his father had been on one of his weeks-long drunks and was driving their old beat-up Ford pickup home. His mother had been seated on the passenger side.

Manuelito's father was not a bad man. His father came from a proud warrior family. Manuelito's grandfather had been a famous Navajo Code Talker. There was a picture of his grandfather in the Code Talkers Museum that Manuelito's father had taken Manuelito to see.

There were many periods of six months to a year, and in one case almost two years, when Manuelito's father was not drunk. However, whenever his father did drink, just one beer was the start of at least a week long bender. During the sober periods

Manuelito's father had been attentive to his son and they had often gone hunting together in the winter, or fishing in the spring when the melt in Colorado caused the streams to run full.

Times had always been hard. First, there were not many jobs at all, and second, it was hard for his father to keep one with his frequent lapses into alcoholic oblivion. Yet Manuelito's life was not that different from any of his friends on the rez.

Manuelito's parents in a burst of enthusiastic delight upon the birth of their new child, had named him after Chief Manuelito, the great Navajo chief of the 1800's who fought the white Americans and eventually made peace with them on behalf of his people.

Chief Manuelito's name means "little Manuel." The diminutive in his name was probably given to him to signal the affection with which he was held, because he was a large powerful man. Manuelito's parents kept the diminutive suffix, maybe because somehow they knew their son would grow up to be of wiry build, tall and thin, and that other kids would call him "the Man."

The old Ford pickup veered over the center line as it went around a curve and hit a tractor-trailer coming from a food delivery in Tuba City. Manuelito imagined that his mother and father were arguing as they usually did when his father was on a drinking spree. All that Manuelito knew about what happened was that produce had been scattered all over the road and his parents were gone. Gone back to where, his people, the *Diné*, go, into the underworld. His aunt and uncle, whom he could have lived with, would not let him see his parents' bodies, which were promptly buried without much ceremony as was the *Diné* custom.

Manuelito left his home, which seemed right since it would have been torn down anyway if his parents had died there. It was not a logical process, making this decision about where to go that would fix the trajectory of the rest of his life. Rather, for Manuelito, it was an instinctive response to growing up in the schizophrenic world of native and white cultures. Somehow Manuelito was drawn to the one place that allowed both worlds to exist in some harmony. He knew that the experience of harmony—which he felt so often out in the wild, but could not define—was important.

So at sixteen, Manuelito, now orphaned, made his way to Father O'Donnell's monastery. Three years before when he was thirteen, he had taken part in a male puberty ceremony organized by Father O'Donnell and several distinguished *Diné* Singers. This was Manuelito's sole experience where the two cultures seemed to be in harmony. Father O'Donnell understood, just as the Singers did, how everything was connected.

While the Navajo culture gave more attention to Kinaalda as an expression of the female puberty ceremony, Father O'Donnell, with several elder Singers, had been responsible for assuring that young boys had the opportunity to participate in a male puberty ceremony. The ceremony was a Beauty Way ceremony to assure that Manuelito would walk in beauty and harmony for the rest of his life. The male puberty ceremony is triggered by a young man's first nocturnal ejaculation, and the female puberty ceremony by the young woman's first menstruation.

After Manuelito had his first wet dream the four day ceremony commenced. Each day he ran toward the East singing and yelling to wake up the gods and let them know that he had become a man. Although he was slightly built, Manuelito had great endurance and he ran a long way each day. Some of his friends ran with him though none were able to keep up. The four day ceremony paralleled in many ways the puberty experiences of Changing Woman's twin sons, Monster Slayer and Born for Water. The ceremony included a sweat lodge where Manuelito had a vision about what his life would be about. It was because of that vision that he was now returning to the monastery.

In Manuelito's vision, he was taken by an eagle to the top of the four sacred mountains: Hesperus Peak, Blanca Peak, Mount Taylor and the San Francisco Peaks that mark the boundary of the people's nation. At each peak he was asked to look on both sides, the land of the *Diné* and the land of the white man. The message he received was that he was to walk between both lands.

The *Diné* custom was not to discuss one's vision. He was only permitted to talk about it with two of the elder Singers and Father O'Donnell. The Singers told Manuelito that when the time came for him to walk deeper on the road of his vision he should come see Father O'Donnell. He was told by them that he would know when the time for this visit to Father O'Donnell had arrived.

As he walked along the road with Ooljee, he was not sure that he had any great knowing that this was the time. There were simply few alternatives for him. He knew that at sixteen if he lived with his aunt and uncle and hung out with his older cousins it probably would not be long before he ended up like his father.

THE END OF DEMOCRACY

He loved his father and he hated him. He could not have said it, but somewhere down deep he knew his walk, the long miles to Father O'Donnell's, was to escape the hate part.

It was surprising both how little he wanted to take with him and how little there was to take. Manuelito had crammed everything meaningful he owned in his school backpack. Of course, the most important thing for him to bring walked beside him—Ooljee. When Ooljee was a puppy his father had won him in a poker game, and gave him to Manuelito after the bender ended. Ooljee grew up spending almost every waking moment with Manuelito.

Because Manuelito took Ooljee to school with him every day, one of his instructors had given Manuelito an assignment to write about the dog's people. Manuelito had a starting place. His father was given papers for the dog, which certified that the dog was a Plott hound.

At first Manuelito had not been very interested in writing a school paper about his dog's people, but the more he read whatever he could find about the Plott hound in the small, cramped reservation school library, the more interested he became.

The Plott hound was like the *Diné* in many respects. They were hunters, arguably the finest hunting dogs in the world. The Plott hound was known for its courage, speed, heart, nose, loyalty and, above all, its intelligence.

In 1750, two young German immigrant brothers, Johannes and Enoch Plott left Germany, at about the age Manuelito was, and headed to America in search of a new life. They were the sons of a Black Forest gamekeeper and they brought with them five of their best hunting dogs. The two brothers brought two buckskin-colored dogs and three brindle-colored dogs. These dogs were of Germanic stock rather than traditional English origins as were most American dog breeds. The five dogs became the foundation stock of the Plott hound in America.

On their voyage to the New World Enoch died, and upon arriving in Philadelphia, sixteen-year-old Johannes Plott and his five prized dogs headed south to North Carolina. Over the years the Plott breed continued to be nurtured by the descendants of Johannes Plott. The Plott hound became the breed of choice among mountain hunters of bear and bobcat in western North Carolina and east Tennessee. There were many stories of these courageous dogs saving their master from human and animal attacks.

Manuelito concluded his school paper with the assertion that his Plott hound had come from dogs sold in the late 1920s by North Carolinian Henry Vaughn Plott into the Southwest. He ended his paper with a quote from author Cormac McCarthy saying the Plott hound was "without fear."

Ooljee might be without fear, but he still needed water. Manuelito spotted a hogan about a half-mile from the road up ahead. He would go over there and see if he could find some water for Ooljee.

Just then an old pickup truck pulled up beside him and stopped. It was only about the third or fourth vehicle that had gone by in either direction all day. He was not surprised that the pickup truck was stopping to offer him a lift even though he had not had his thumb out. Hitchhiking was never a problem on the reservation, though many people preferred not to pick up a hitchhiker with a dog. That is unless they were driving a pickup, which most people were. However, he was surprised when he opened the passenger side door, that the driver of this pickup was not one of the people, but a white man.

"Need a lift?" asked Will Dawson.

Manuelito looked at Dawson curiously. He was not used to getting rides from white people. And the truth of the matter was he did not really think that much of white people. His view of whites was not that they were all bad because of what they had done to Native Americans historically, rather that they were simply out of harmony. This was how he thought of most of them, except for Father O'Donnell. Somehow Manuelito did not see Father O'Donnell as either native or white, he simply was and his inner harmony was apparent.

"Where are you heading?" asked Manuelito.

"Well, I've been on the road a long time and don't have that far to go now. I am going a few more miles down this road, then I turn off to the monastery. I can take you as far as the turnoff if you would like."

This was indeed curious, thought Manuelito. This white man is going to the same place that I'm going. I wonder if he has had a vision quest that told him to come see Father O'Donnell. He felt some reluctance to ride with a white man. However, it seemed to be outweighed by the fact they were heading for the same destination and Ooljee needed water.

Dawson spoke again, "I'm Will Dawson," he said sticking out his hand.

Manuelito ignored the hand. "You may call me Man," he said, "and I will go with you to the monastery. I am on my way to see Father O'Donnell."

Well, this is a coincidence, thought Dawson.

Man threw his backpack in the back of the pickup and motioned for his dog to jump onto the front seat. Man followed the dog and closed the passenger door.

Dawson was a bit taken back, thinking the boy would put his dog in the back of the pickup. However, it didn't really matter in this old clunker. Besides there was something different about this dog that fascinated him. The dog sat in the middle of the front seat with real dignity. It wasn't just the animal's strange brindle color; somehow the dog combined qualities of gentleness and fierceness at the same time.

Dawson pulled the shift lever into first gear and the three of them headed down the road.

CHAPTER 10

Dawson had done his best not to leave any tracks. He caught a flight from Richmond. Virginia to Las Vegas using his new Godfrey Adams identity. To avoid renting a car, Dawson bought an old Ford pickup from Jimmy's Auto Plaza, a used-car dealer on the south side of Las Vegas who sold well-worn vehicles primarily to Mexicans and Indians. Dawson paid cash for the car and he got a temporary tag for the vehicle. He had no intention of ever registering it. Dawson's only concern was whether the pickup would make it as far as the Four Corners area. In an abundance of caution Dawson did not even communicate with Father O'Donnell to let him know that he would be coming.

Dawson reflected that it was easy to move about undetected if you simply put yourself in the mindset of a poor person traveling in the 1950s. Dawson kept his new iphone and Mac Book turned off.

As he drove the final miles to the monastery, Dawson experienced a vague feeling of apprehension that Father O'Donnell might not be that happy to see him. Maybe the chance opportunity to give the young Navajo a ride to the monastery would allow Dawson to be received favorably.

Nothing about their arrival at the gate leading down to the monastery gave Dawson any reassurance that he would be warmly received. The gatekeeper was nowhere to be seen. Dawson and Man waited for a few minutes and the gatekeeper still did not appear.

"I wonder where José is," said Dawson.

"Maybe I can find him," said Man, and with that he opened the pickup door and slid out, followed immediately by his faithful dog. Together they slipped under the fence and went around the corner of the gatekeeper's house.

Less than a minute passed and Man re-appeared from around the corner of the gatekeeper's adobe hut with José. They were laughing and talking in Spanish.

José went straight to the gate and pulled it open. Man opened the passenger door of the pickup and he and Ooljee jumped back in. Dawson waved at José as he drove the pickup through the gate. José gave him an impassive stare.

Dawson turned to Man. "I am glad you are with me today. José has never been happy to open the gate for me. What did you say to him?" asked Dawson.

"Nothing particular. We are old friends. He took part in my coming of age Sing. He is part Mexican and part Navajo, and I think the Navajo part is greater because he has a real sense of the harmony or disharmony of people's energy. It is not that José dislikes you, it's just that he feels disharmony in your energy and he doesn't like people bringing their disharmony to Father O'Donnell. José is very protective of everybody at the monastery."

Dawson was stunned. After all he had learned years ago from Melissa about people's energy fields, here was a young Navajo who seemed to understand this complex subject intuitively. Man's understanding held a mirror up for Dawson. He was deeply stressed, running undercover and not sure from what, nor sure where he was going.

Soon they pulled up to the old farmhouse that housed the monastery and served as a base camp for the hermitage. Dawson got out of the pickup. Man and Ooljee got out the passenger's side and followed along behind. Dawson went up to the front door and knocked.

After a few moments the door opened and there stood Brother Will. He smiled in recognition. Dawson felt relieved.

"I have come to see Father O'Donnell. Well, I guess we both have. Man has lost his parents and believes he is supposed to come here. And, now that I think about it, I pretty much have lost my way also. We would be very grateful for the opportunity to stay and see Father O'Donnell."

Brother Will nodded and gestured for them both to come on in. They walked down the central hallway to the kitchen. Brother Will got out some peanut butter, honey and bread and a large container of cold water from the refrigerator. He gestured for Dawson and Man to help themselves. Then Dawson remembered from his first visit that most of the time the brothers keep silence.

Dawson recognized his own tendency in the face of Brother Will's silence to also remain silent. Funny how silence could be catching. Was that another energy field thing he mused to himself. He realized that for now his silence was not necessary. He looked at Brother Will then asked him, "Is Father O'Donnell here or is he up on the mountain in his hermitage?"

Brother Will motioned his head upward and pointed in the same direction.

"Can you take us up to see him?" asked Dawson.

Brother Will pulled out a small pad from a pocket hidden somewhere in the folds of his robe and wrote on it, "Tomorrow."

Dawson nodded. Brother Will and Man then disappeared out the back door. Looking through the kitchen window Dawson could see that they were getting a bowl of water for Ooljee.

Now that he had finally arrived at the monastery and hermitage, and even though he did not know what Father O'Donnell would say about his arrival, he could feel his body gradually begin to unwind and relax. He walked back down the hall and looked in the room where he had stayed when he visited before. Inside the room were two simple cots and a small table for writing. Dawson took a deep breath. Even on a small cot he would sleep deeply tonight for the first time in a long while.

CHAPTER 11

Blaine had been waiting for Rat for an hour. She was sitting in the small Turkish café that had become their favorite meeting place. Blaine had gotten used to the strong dark Turkish espresso, and she had fallen into the habit of sucking it through a sugar cube like she had seen some of the old Turkish men do who frequented the place. Being able to sit in the coffee shop for over an hour sipping at a thimbleful of coffee seemed to epitomize entry into another culture. She had never managed to sip at a cup of espresso for an hour, unless she had first downed one like she was throwing back a shot.

Now she was on her third espresso and was becoming more jittery and agitated as she waited for Rat. Just as she was thinking of ordering another espresso she glanced out the window and saw Rat coming up to the door. He wiggled his rat-like nose at her and, as always when she first saw him, some thin vein of childish delight, which had almost been crushed in her, bubbled up to the surface. She smiled back at him.

"*Liebste, du siehst schön,*" said Rat, greeting her as he always did with such delight that she felt her normal anxiety recede even further.

"You don't look too bad yourself," Blaine told Rat, "though you do look like you could use a little sleep. Were you up half the night again?"

"Yes, I was. How else can I treat you to such exquisite dining?" said Rat as he made a dramatic motion with his hand to encompass all of the dingy, Turkish café. "Someone has to earn a euro or two and, also keep the world in delicate balance between the evil barbarians and the corrupting influence of state power." He motioned to the man behind the counter who was already at work before the espresso machine making a cup for Rat.

Blaine tried her best to look pissed. She decided she best address her concern head-on. "Rat, tell me what you are doing with Conficter. Europe seems so civilized and genteel, but if you are involved with those Ukrainian guys and Conficter it is like being out in the lawless Wild West. I am afraid for you." It was impossible for Blaine to hold a suggestion of anger for long in her expression directed toward Rat. She felt an impulse to reach out and caress the top of his head, although that seemed literally impossible given that Rat had managed to get his hair to stick straight up like a forest of black needles.

"You needn't fret, *Liebste*," said Rat, "I was not involved in setting that worm loose. You don't have to worry about that. But the truth is the Conficter botnet is so potentially powerful that me and a couple of the other guys decided that we must find a way to wrest control away from its creator at the critical moment when it is unleashed. This botnet is powerful enough to shut down most of the world's infrastructure. I am not about to stand idly by," said Rat assuming a cartoon figure bravado.

Rat had confirmed all of Blaine's worst fears. And at the same time she could not help but be amused by his save-the-world hype. He really was a Boy Scout, she thought, and when he was behind the computer screen he certainly knew no fear. She could not bring herself to criticize Rat for doing what he thought was right. In fact, she would not be here except for Rat's sense of what was right and his loyalty and protectiveness toward her from the start.

She looked at Rat. He was looking at her with a dazed puppy-love expression. Okay, she thought, his interest in helping her was more than brotherly and more than simply his desire to be an Internet Robin Hood. She would have to try to return the favor by cautioning him as much as possible from showing any tracks to those Ukrainian gangsters who were behind Conficter. She smiled to herself. For Rat she would keep worrying.

"So are you making any progress with our conflicted American?" Blaine asked.

"Not much," said Rat, "I did get a message from Dawson saying that he had gotten our curiously strong message and had gone underground. The link is established now so I can stay in touch with him. Is there anything you want me to tell him?"

There was a lot that Blaine would like to tell Dawson. She wanted him to come to Berlin. She wanted more time with him to see whether two people, who were as emotionally self-protected from others as she and Dawson were, could possibly tear down their emotional defenses together. She didn't know if she was in love, however she kept thinking about that line from an old Joan

Armatrading song, "I am not in love, but I am open to persuasion." Maybe this was the reason for her feelings of uneasiness, even with the wonderful new life she was leading in Berlin. Despite the fact that she was very inexperienced in dealing with men, she knew it would be unfair for her to talk more about her feelings for Dawson with Rat. She simply shook her head no.

Returning to her immediate concern, Blaine asked, "What are you doing then to stay ahead of the Ukrainian mafia?"

"Right now we're simply trying to figure out how they programmed the worm, and we are trying to put a worm in the computers they have already infected that would get activated when a message is sent to the botnet. Putting this worm into the infected computers is rather difficult, since the worm they sent out closed port 445 behind itself after it had entered. So we have to go in another port, find their worm, and re-train it so that once it is activated we can take over control. Conficter had a way of disabling itself if the computer was using the Ukrainian language so we have to do our work with Ukrainian language computers and that has made it mighty slow going. But, I think we have perfected our counter-worm, although we won't know whether we have actually been able to infect the Conficter worm until an order is sent to the entire botnet. This is pretty high stakes poker."

"I'll say!" said Blaine. "Do you have any idea who is behind Conficter or what their objective is?"

"You hit on exactly the next item on my agenda. Somehow we

THE END OF DEMOCRACY

need to be able to read the minds of whoever is behind Conficter. We know the minds of the Ukrainian techies are bizarre. I don't just mean Ukrainians. All of those people who grew up in Eastern Bloc countries where people lived double lives under repressive communist regimes just don't think the way we do. Their approaches to creating software are automatically convoluted and surreptitious. I have a buddy who grew up in East Germany whose thinking is as screwy as anyone's I have ever seen. He is one of the guys I'm working with on this."

"It sounds to me like you may need Melissa's help," said Blaine. "After all, maybe there was a reason you went to that Enneagram conference? Surely you don't think you went just to see me?"

Rat stuck out his two front teeth and brought his hands up under his chin like two little paws and grimaced at her in his most rat-like manner.

Blaine laughed.

"You know, Blaine, that is a great idea. Let me see if I can find out where Melissa is and what she is doing and maybe get in contact with her. This will probably not be easy, seeing how she has been eluding the CIA for some time and whoever else has been trying to catch her. Of course what is impossible for others is every day business for the Rat."

Blaine laughed again. Rat was a cartoon character in his own cartoon strip in which he single-handedly waged a titanic battle against the forces of evil and oppression. She was just grateful to Rat that he was so freely letting her enjoy his role as the star in his own limited edition show.

CHAPTER 12

Dawson had forgotten how early they got up at the monastery. It was hardly good light when the knock had come on the door. Dawson and Man took turns using the bathroom before pulling on their clothes. Ooljee went outside for a morning pee.

In the kitchen were two other brothers and Brother Will. There was silence. A hearty breakfast of huevos rancheros was soon on the table. Dawson and Man ate hungrily.

After breakfast Dawson and Man followed Brother Will out to the shed where the all-terrain vehicle was kept. Brother Will brought along a large pack he had filled with supplies to take to Father O'Donnell.

The morning was beautiful. The air was crisp and cool. The sun was up but its direct light had not yet reached the valley floor. They all three piled into the ATV followed closely by Ooljee who did not seem above hitching a ride. In less than an hour they crossed the valley floor to the foot of the mountain. The vehicle's name was a misnomer. It would be of absolutely no help to them in climbing the steep mountain trail.

After about an hour Brother Will motioned for them to stop.

They were climbing now in the direct rays of the sun. Each was carrying extra water which they brought out. Brother Will, who was carrying a heavy pack, seemed to be breathing easily as did Man, however, Dawson could feel the altitude, and too many days of sitting at an office desk, pulling at his lungs. He was glad for the break. Despite feeling totally out of shape, Dawson was glad to be in the beauty of the high desert. The light sienna-colored rock cliffs contrasted intensely against the dark blue sky.

Almost two hours later they emerged onto a rocky ledge. Along the ledge, the mountain had been carved inward, leaving a long open cave. At the far end, the open front and one side had been enclosed with wood creating a cabin like shelter. Just outside the shelter door Dawson recognized Father O'Donnell putting a kettle on a propane gas burner.

Father O'Donnell gave Dawson a warm greeting. But he seemed most joyous to see Man. He gave the young Indian boy a great hug and almost danced with him in his arms. Man also seemed delighted.

"So what brings my two friends all the way up here?" asked Father O'Donnell. His smile began to wane as he saw the seriousness of the expressions worn by both Dawson and Manuelito. He handed them both a cup of strong Irish tea.

Dawson deferred to the young Navajo. Man silently drank his tea. He knew how to be respectful of Father O'Donnell by not launching directly into the story of his visit.

"I hope you have been well Father O'Donnell?" said Man.

"Yes, thank you, I have been well. I had not planned to go into seclusion quite so soon. While the trip to Turin and the conference were fascinating, I feel this real need to get deeply grounded again. It is like I am being told to go to spring training early, that the season is going to be starting earlier this year and I need to be spiritually in shape. I am glad that the two of you came when you did. I've only been up here for a couple of days so I can have a good visit with the both of you before sinking deeply into solitude."

Man let a decent interval of silence follow. Then he spoke. "I have come to you because of what happened at my coming of age Sing and the vision that I had. My father, as you know, was an alcoholic and last week he crashed the pickup into a tractor-trailer and killed himself and my mom. My mother's relatives offered to take me in, but it is my feeling that I should come to be here. Father O'Donnell, I need you to help me find out from the Great Spirit what is right for me now."

Father O'Donnell nodded. He did not hurry the conversation.

"I am afraid that if I stayed with my mother's kin I would soon get in trouble with my cousins and end up an alcoholic like my father. I know that you taught me that the Great Spirit never wants us to live our lives out of fear, yet I confess there is fear. There is also sorrow at leaving my people. My vision that I am to be one who walks in both worlds, the world of the *Diné* and the white man, pulls at me. I feel the truth of my vision. And I feel that it is time for me to walk on the path of that vision, and right now that path starts here."

Again Father O'Donnell let Man's words be honored by the punctuation of silence. After a while Father O'Donnell said, "I am glad you are here, Man. I believe that the Great Spirit wants you to be here. From this place we can pray to understand the direction for the path of your life. You remember the story I told you from the Old Testament about the sea parting. The sea did not part until someone first began to walk into the water. You have walked into the water of your life by coming here Man. We will wait and pray together to see in which direction the sea parts."

Father O'Donnell turned and looked at Brother Will, who was packing up trash from Father O'Donnell's hermitage, getting ready for his departure back down the mountain. "Brother Will, I want Man to be given all the privileges of a novitiate in our Order. Please see that he has a room of his own, that the brothers welcome him into the monastery and that he be given a place in the life of our community."

Brother Will nodded assent.

Father O'Donnell turned then to Dawson. Father O'Donnell's glance seemed to acknowledge that Dawson looked equally bereft and homeless. "You seem to have a heavy burden, Will. Tell me what is on your heart."

Dawson hardly knew where to begin. Finally he realized he must pick up where he and Father O'Donnell had left off. At Father O'Donnell's suggestion Dawson had gone to the Turin conference disguised as Father O'Donnell's monk assistant. Dawson hoped that he would discover Melissa at the conference, or at least some way to get in touch with her. Instead he had spent most of the days of the conference in the company of Blaine Astrid, a young research assistant for an American professor.

"I came back from the conference thinking that I had betrayed both Melissa and Blaine. I now know that Melissa was probably at the conference, although because of the CIA's surveillance of me, which I was oblivious to because of my interest in Blaine, she was unable to contact me. I feel guilty that I let her down. I may have totally run out of chances with Melissa. I let her down before when I failed to keep in touch with her after I got transferred out of Afghanistan.

"What I did do was spend a romantic week with Blaine, and at the end of the week, despite her invitation to pursue our relationship, I bolted and came back to the States. I am older than Blaine, but not old. I could have followed her to Berlin and given our relationship a chance.

"Since I've come back, Blaine's friend Rat has warned me that I am under surveillance by both the CIA and some other unknown entity. It took my best training to slip this surveillance and come out here to see you." He paused. "It's funny, the whole time coming out here it has felt like Blaine has been watching out for me, which only makes my regret deeper. I feel lonely and empty and don't know what to do. I am at an emotional and spiritual bottom."

Father O'Donnell let a few moments pass. "Would you like a little more tea?" he said, picking up the teapot off of the rock that doubled as a serving table.

"You have come to the right place, Will Dawson. What there is that is decent about the church specializes in being the place for the downtrodden and disconnected. How did you find wearing a brother's robe, anyway?"

"It wasn't too bad," said Dawson. "You can keep an awful lot of stuff in the pockets of those folds, except the damn thing is awful scratchy."

The priest chuckled. "You could sign on just like Man. Be a novitiate here for a year or two. This would give you time to get connected with yourself and God. To use the language that your friend Melissa would use, this would also give you the opportunity to practice connection with your own energy field and thought field. If you are ever going to have an intimate relationship with any woman you are first going to have to learn how to have an intimate relationship with yourself, and in my humble view, with God."

Dawson looked over his cup at the stark southwestern landscape rolling away into the distance. Father O'Donnell's hermitage might be primitive, but it had a startling clear and daunting view. Maybe if he spent time here, like Father O'Donnell, then he too would speak as direct and clear as the magnificent terrain spread out below.

"You have met in your life two remarkable women. If you ever hope to have something meaningful with Melissa, or with Blaine, you will have to develop a greater level of consciousness. Both of these women have spent a lot of time doing practices to develop their consciousness and understanding of their energy and thought fields. It's not likely that you could ever have a relationship with one of them unless you catch up a bit.

"There is also the possibility that you might find in this brotherhood the kind of meaning and connection with self and others that you long for, and the absence of which keeps your life lonely and empty. Either way, it seems like spending time here is a good place for you to start, Will, and I am more than happy to have you. You will have to live the life of a brother and spend the time which we spend daily in prayer, silence, work and devotion. Do you think you are up for that?"

Dawson ran his hand through his hair and looked off into the sky. He got up from the rock where he was seated then sat back down again. Father O'Donnell did not rush him—the seconds, then minutes slowly ticked by.

At last something in Dawson surrendered and he was once again able to look Father O'Donnell in the eye.

"At this stage, I am out of answers. I guess I am up for most anything," said Dawson. "The way I have been living my life for the past twenty years has totally not worked. I know that you and Melissa, and even Blaine, have some connection which I don't have that makes your lives more vibrant. I don't know what it is, but I'm willing to do whatever you tell me to try to find it."

Father O'Donnell looked at Dawson for a long moment. He knew that this was exactly the depth of surrender that was necessary if there was ever to be a meaningful chance of a spiritual journey toward consciousness. His face relaxed into a deep smile. "We're glad to have you, Will. Welcome."

"Now I think it's time for me to get back to some silent meditation. I expect to be up here for at least thirty days. That will give you time to settle into the monastery and we can talk more when I get back down. Oh, and you will have to decide on a new name as a brother. You know we already have one Brother Will and we like to keep it simple. Traditionally when a monk takes vows, he takes a new name to represent a new way of being in life. Your new name will symbolize the new state of consciousness and connection to others which you aspire to. You can let me know what it is when I return and we can celebrate yours and Man's novitiate initiation into the Order at that time."

With that, Father O'Donnell rose and gave another hug to Man and Dawson. Then they parted, with the younger men heading back down the mountain. Father O'Donnell turned and walked back to his hermitage. *Now*, he mused, *the real work begins.*

CHAPTER 13

Gordon Slade was having a hard time concentrating on work. *Maybe*, he thought with a grin, *too much Joy*. And just maybe, he was making up for lost time.

Whatever it was, his mood was buoyant. All of a sudden, he had lost his appetite for the chase. The chase at work on behalf of his clients trying to locate a missing person or catch an offending spouse in the act. The chase in his personal life, pursuing attractive women until he could get laid and then move on.

Still there was one chase he did not want to give up on. He was haunted by Will Dawson's unexpected visit. When Dawson visited Slade, the night Slade found him sitting on his doorstep, Dawson told Slade that if Slade was able to find out anything about what was going on, he should e-mail it to Blaine. Slade met Blaine in Turin when he was there with Peter Wagner. Every time Slade had turned around she was there with Dawson. Slade thought she was a little weird, though he believed she would be a reliable conduit to get information to Dawson.

In his visit, Dawson had not exactly begged Slade to try to find out what the CIA was up to, however, he'd come as close as he dared to ask for as much of Slade's help as Slade could possibly give. If the CIA really was on Dawson's tail, he was going to need Slade's help big time. The help would have to be proactive. Dawson needed to have a bigger picture to understand exactly what was going on if he was going to survive, and he was the last person in a position to try to sort through information to figure out what that picture was.

Because Joy had been so much on Slade's mind and in his life, and because he did not know what to do anyway for Dawson, Slade had done nothing. Suddenly he realized that the least he could do was to confront his old client Peter Wagner. Slade ought to do this for his own self-respect. Wagner had fired him in a short written note and left in the middle of the night to return to the United States from the Enneagram conference in Turin. Slade decided his best approach would be to simply act as if Wagner owed Slade an explanation, even though he knew, in his profession, he was owed nothing more than his fee—not even common courtesy. But before he talked to Wagner, Slade wanted to talk over this dilemma of how to help Dawson with someone smart and trustworthy.

Slade picked up his office phone and gave Joe Carroll a call.

"Hey Joe. Slade here. Are you going to Fenway tonight for the ball game?"

"Well, dude!   Does the Pope...."

Slade interrupted before Carroll could inject his usual coarseness. "Joe, can I meet you before the game starts in that bar we usually go to after the game?"

"Slade, your timing is perfect, or I should say your suggestion to meet in a bar is always perfect timing for me. I haven't gotten a thing done all day. I bet I can meet you there in forty-five minutes."

"Joe I haven't gotten a thing done today either. I'll be there in less than an hour. Thanks, buddy. See you shortly." Slade put the phone down.

In a town full of academics, Joe Carroll was the only one that Slade had found he really liked. Since he'd been hanging out so much with Joy he had not seen Carroll recently. The two had spent a good bit of time drinking single malt Scotch in various Boston bars and chasing women together; but more than anything else, challenging each other with quirky ideas and quick wit. Carroll was an assistant professor in the creative writing program at one of Boston's many universities. Both Slade and Carroll were proud of their backstreet upbringing and their rough-and-ready manliness that was attractive to women. However, while it was easy for Carroll to carry on in his good old boy, girl-chasing persona, Slade knew that Carroll was really smart, and sometimes just talking with him would give Slade the lead that he needed for a case.

Carroll was the first to get to their ballpark local. He corralled a corner booth that offered a good view of the comings and goings of the baseball crowd. It was Beer-for-a-Buck night, but when Slade sank down into their booth opposite Carroll, Carroll was already sipping on the single malt Scotch that both men preferred.

"You poking that little librarian yet?" Carroll asked, in his typical start-every-conversation-bluntly fashion.

Although he was used to Carroll's coarseness, the question made Slade bristle a bit. Characteristically, Slade did not let his feelings show and in his typical evasive fashion, avoided the question. "Hey Joe, thanks so much for coming to meet with me." He turned and nodded toward the barmaid who was approaching the table. She registered his nod and turned and put in his usual order.

When the drink was on the table, Slade took a long slow sip of the single malt.

Joe could tell that something was eating at Slade more seriously than usual. "What's going on, Slade?"

"I am in a quandary. I need some background about why people pursue a quest for consciousness. What are the twist and turns? What is quantum consciousness? And, I have something for you." With that, he reached in his pocket and pulled out a fortune cookie and pushed it across the table to Carroll.

Carroll was surprised. He quickly recovered, tore open the cellophane, put the cookie in his mouth and unrolled the strip of paper that was inside.

"'*The last apostle will be first; follow her.*' is what it says," said Carroll. He stared at the words. "Wait a minute," said Carroll, "if I hadn't gotten such a bizarre fortune, I could have covered all those questions without you even having to buy me another drink.

"Let me put the fortune cookie message aside a minute and just start talking, and maybe I'll say something helpful," said Carroll with a grin. "Whenever humans have had some basic sense of security, that is, when they are not hunter-gathering all the time and they have some time to think about life, there emerges this compelling drive to take the experience of life to a deeper level. They get in touch with something about their essential nature. Socrates called it a *daimon*, Plato named it psyche, and the medieval philosopher Duns Scotus named it 'thisness'. The poet Shelley, because he located this 'thisness' in his head, called it genius. Bernard Shaw called it the life force.

"How am I doing?" Carroll was really in an expansive mood tonight. Either that or he had been drinking much longer than Slade thought. "You probably already owe me a couple of drinks just for all that. Anyway, you get the idea. A poet or a philosopher tries to describe the essence of our beingness as a human and then tries to imagine ways to sink deeper into the richness of beingness. If you are the Buddha you do this through meditation. If you are a serious Christian you do this by giving up your ego self that masks beingness. Experiencing God's deep and abiding love can only truly be done from a place of greater consciousness. Conversion, contrary to many religious notions, is really about being converted to a higher level of consciousness. If you weren't such a lapsed Catholic you would remember that Jesus always referred to himself in the Gospels as the Son of Man, not the Son of God. By Son of Man I believe he meant the next generation of humanity, the generation he predicted would come into his Kingdom, which is when people are living with more consciousness, living with more beingness."

Slade let out a low whistle under his breath. Carroll was indeed on a roll and when this happened Slade was always fascinated.

"If you are lucky enough to be a man like you or me, or say like Jack Nicholson, you chase the experience of that beingness beneath the skirts of attractive women."

Carroll paused, waiting for some affirmative comment from Slade. When nothing came, Carroll continued.

"Commentators would describe this effort as a kind of individualistic primitivism. We try to find the essence of beingness in the sensual world. In this respect it remains largely an ego project, which by its very nature is never going to be completely satisfying. However, as you very well know, Gordon Slade, it is a damn fine place to start.

"I'm afraid this individualistic approach to life is currently eclipsed by more collective notions. Christianity was probably the start of these. The collective approaches bring forward the notion of paradoxical truth."

"I am not sure I follow you," said Slade.

"Well, for example, the paradoxical idea that you have to lose your life in order to find it. Or, you only find true joy for yourself by helping others. These notions are very current in our culture. But, for the most part, simply as nice sounding ideas, not lived truth. What is currently completely absent in our culture is a faith or creed that is compelling enough that people would be willing to lose their life for it, to live the paradox." Carroll couldn't tell if Slade was following him or not, but he was paying intense attention.

"In other words, the quest for greater beingness is as driving a force as ever in our world, however we are hamstrung by a lack of a belief structure that will allow us to get out of the thorny grip of our own egos. Or, to describe it another way, we are too jaded and cynical to let go of our attachment to the alienation of modernity. I, for one, have given up the struggle and decided that the individual narcissistic pursuit of romantic primitivism is not all that bad. Would you like another drink?"

Slade nodded affirmatively. He loved how all you had to do was push the right button with Joe and he was off and running on some intellectual rant. "There's more, I take it. Proceed, professor."

Carroll continued. "So the history of religion, philosophy and poetry is strewn with individuals who have sought access to a greater level of beingness from different directions. There are three principal starting directions depending upon whether the person is primarily a mental type, emotional type or a body/somatic type."

"If you are a mental type, then you are going to pursue this greater level of beingness from your mental center through philosophy or mathematics; that is, through some type of mental exercise. I must admit I admire these guys though I can't really hang in there with them.

"The emotional types experience life from their emotional centers and their approach is often best expressed by the poets. These people are trying to find a connection with their beingness by connection to nature, or to another person, or if you are a great mystical poet like Rumi, to God. Poetry is a way to try to describe a mystery that cannot be described.

"Then there are the Jack Nicholson types like me, who are living from a body-centeredness and are pursuing beingness by chasing beaver. Okay, some of these body-centered types are respectable. They might be great yoga or aikido masters.

"A person of any type usually stays trapped in their individual narcissistic pursuit of life through their predominant way of connecting with life. Those who don't stay trapped in the ego move into paradox. In paradox, the first big surrender is you give up the dominant way you experience life. You begin to experience life more from your repressed center, or at least your experience begins to be modulated by a consciousness that is experienced through all three centers. This is the beginning of transitioning out of a self-centered consciousness. Only when there has been the experience of self, not as a separate being, but as part of a larger beingness does the process of enlightenment begin. From this perspective we are not really separate narcissistic beaver-chasing guys at all, but simply the part of some larger beingness that we don't yet perceive. We are simply caught for the time being in a Jack Nicholson inspired, bird-dogging chicks trance. Could be worse, huh? By the way, you still haven't told me about what has happened with that librarian friend of yours."

Slade reminded himself that in solving a case for a client, things often had to get murky before there was clarity. He could make some sense out of what Carroll was saying. His exposure to the presentations at the Enneagram conference also tied in to a bigger picture. The picture was not yet clear, but he was able to see some new outlines. He thought Carroll's ribbing him again about Joy meant the lecture was over. He was mistaken. Carroll was still on a roll.

"What we see in the history of art and literature and philosophy is that the culture at different times also is predominately an expression of one of the three different centers. The expression of art, poetry and philosophy springs from whatever the dominant center of the culture is at the time. For example, back in the Sixties along came the hippies and the country turned and connected with a more emotional center. Then we had a generation, when I first started teaching, that was very intellectually focused. They were not interested at all in the emotional experience of poetry but focused entirely on techniques of the craft. And today we are back to a more somatic, bodily focused cultural expression. Go to the library and look in the psychology section and you can pick up literally hundreds of books about the importance of being in the body. Yoga has gone mainstream.

"So while we are all chiefly affected by our own dominant center, we are also very much influenced by the dominant center of the culture at any given time. Caught between these forces, it is extraordinarily difficult to live a life out of all three centers in a balanced way, which seems to be necessary for the beginning of the process of enlightenment. So the promise of enlightenment continues to be elusive.

"Slade, I need another drink. Are you ready for another?"

Slade looked up. "I think I get it. Do you think this force of consciousness, of enlightenment, is so powerful that if someone controls their consciousness, they could control humankind?"

"Students in my class don't get to ask questions until the lecture is over."

"This is my dilemma, Carroll. What if there are people who understand how to control the life force, the desire for beingness of our collective unconscious, all of this dynamic power of the drive for beingness which is in the world? It makes sense that, in order to get to a place of higher consciousness, you have to be a good person who has sought enlightenment for altruistic purposes. However, maybe there are people out there who see the power of all this and are set on capturing it."

"Like who?" mused Carroll.

"One of those groups is your traditional bad guys, I expect. And what if the other is our government?"

Carroll looked his friend directly in the eyes. "Gosh, you do need a drink." The bar was quickly emptying. The game was about to start. "It's time for us to run if we're going to be there for the start of the first inning." Carroll grinned. "I hope I explained everything that you need to know."

Slade got up from the table and threw down a couple of bills. He felt like Carroll had told him nothing helpful. But then again, maybe he had.

CHAPTER 14

Redmon closed the file containing the most recent report on Dawson. The trail had gone completely cold. There was no sign that Dawson had been at his apartment in Alexandria in weeks. Redmon felt a kind of grudging admiration. Dawson was being a good officer. This did not make Redmon's life any easier. Especially given that they had also run into a dead-end trying to find Melissa Dowling.

The Company was keeping Melissa under surveillance for some time prior to the Turin Enneagram conference. The hope was that she would provide them some evidence of collaboration with a foreign government or terrorist organization at the conference. She did neither. Much to their surprise, she did not even contact Will Dawson while they were both at the conference. Instead she gave the Company the slip. She took a flight back from Rome to Boston and then disappeared from sight.

Redmon had thought it would be easy to pick up her trail again because they were wiretapping her mother's phone. However, as far as they could tell Melissa was having no contact with her mother, at least not by phone.

Redmon was able to see some good news in this. If Melissa was

THE END OF DEMOCRACY

not working for a foreign government or terrorist organization, then there might be a chance that they could enlist her aid. They would want to have some leverage first. With Dawson seemingly out of the picture for now, that left but one alternative: Melissa's mother, Mrs. Dowling. The Company never made a request of a citizen to help their country unless the Company could also put something in jeopardy the citizen valued. This wasn't fair, Redmon realized. However, the Company did not operate on fairness, it operated on what was efficient.

Even though they did not know Melissa's whereabouts, Redmon figured he might as well put the squeeze in motion. This might cause Melissa to surface. Redmon clicked on the Dragon voice recognition icon on his computer and dictated a message to the Wisconsin office. The result of his memo would be that a road crew would shortly be doing work in front of Mrs. Dowling's house. The crew would make sure the house suffered structural damage so that the floors in the house sloped precipitously. He would add to that an IRS tax audit and weekly random hang-up calls. This might put the old lady over the edge, but maybe that's what it would take to get her daughter to show up and cooperate.

Redmon sighed. It was a tough job. How else was the Company to keep American democracy safe? Then he remembered the 1776 report. There wasn't going to be anymore democracy, or maybe it had ended years ago.

*   *   *

Redmon picked up another file. Code name Shackleton. The Company never put all its eggs in one basket. If they could not figure out from others how to control people's thought fields, then they would learn how to do it themselves. At least the more the Company learned about this, the more adept they would be in dealing with those individuals who appeared to have this ability.

Thus the Shackleton Project was born. Two officers had been selected for the project because of their uncanny ability to walk in a room and immediately discern who in the room were armed and dangerous.

Although Redmon had several officers at the Turin conference conducting surveillance on Will Dawson and Melissa Dowling, he neglected to have the officers gather information about what was presented at the conference. He realized that this was a mistake. As an afterthought, after the Shackleton Project was formed, he had the two selected officers screened for their type using the Enneagram. Both were sixes. While Redmon knew nothing about the Enneagram, he did know a good bit about the various psychological tests that the Company used with their officers. Both of the two officers selected for the Shackleton Project scored in the paranoid range using clinically established psychological instruments. The Company preferred officers like this. They tended to have intuitive abilities outside of the normal range, and their psychological abnormality often gave the Company an ace in the hole when it came to being able to control and put pressure on these officers if that were necessary.

Redmon's limited reading about the Enneagram had confirmed that this was the type which, at its lower levels of development, was most likely to exhibit paranoid features. Maybe there was some connection between the Enneagram and developing the ability to read people's thought fields. Redmon would not worry about that now. For the moment, he was putting his hopes on the Shackleton Project.

As soon as winter arrived, the Shackleton Project would get underway. Then it would be summer in Antarctica and the two officers would be flown down near the South Pole to undergo experiments in perception. The theory was that by taking people who were naturally talented in picking up signals of danger from the environment and placing them in a stark white landscape with very limited perceptual cues, their normally high perceptive abilities would increase further, and because there was very limited information that could be ascertained from the sensorily barren environment, they would be able to isolate cues that helped provide information about the thoughts of others.

Redmon continued to look through the file. At least this project was going nicely. All of the covers had been set up with the National Science Foundation. All they were waiting for now was the right season. The Project assumed that a person needed to learn how to read the thought fields of others as a prerequisite to controlling others' thought fields. Antarctica was the perfect environment to give these two talented officers a chance to see what they could do.

However, if reading the thought fields of others had nothing to do with simply narrowing sensory input so it could be sifted through at a finer level, then they'd be on the wrong trail. Redmon's view was that there must be some type of physical cues which certain people were able to discern that then allowed them to infer what the thoughts of others were. Once these cues were identified and learned, he hoped his officers would be able to figure out how to give off stronger sensory cues in response to the perceived thoughts of others, which would influence and control the thoughts of others.

Redmon made sure the file was in order. At least he would be able to report to his superiors that the Shackleton Project was on track. He was glad for that. One of his superiors kept saying that Shackleton and 1776 were the new Manhattan Projects. The United States had been the first to discover the secrets of atomic energy, and because of that had been able to dominate the world for the next seventy-five years. His superiors believed that it was just as crucial that the United States be the first country to discover the secret of being able to control the thought fields of others, that the fate of world history literally hung in the balance.

Redmon closed the file. The last thing the world needed was some mystic from some desert monastery running the world or worse than that, some mullah from the Iranian outback. He looked out his window at the polluted morning haze. The morning newspaper had reported a third consecutive week of an extremely unhealthy pollution index. Redmon shook his head. Sometimes it was hard to tell what they were saving, and for whom. Those details, he often joked, were above his pay grade. His job was simply to keep the machinery of the Company turning.

CHAPTER 15

Rat and Blaine were in the habit of often going to the same Turkish café to eat. It was Friday after work when Blaine walked in again. The proprietor greeted her with a wave. She was a regular now. It was good to feel some sense of community living in a foreign country. It was strange how in a foreign country often that sense of community comes from being in community with other foreigners.

Rat had told her that he would have to work late and it would be a good while before he could join her. Blaine had texted Rat that she would go ahead and eat since she was hungry and for him just to send her a text when he was ready to come meet her.

Since it was early in the evening, there was almost no one in the café. No one except a young woman sitting in the back corner. Blaine had often noticed this same woman in the café. She always sat at the same table in the back corner as if she wanted to be as far away from other customers as possible. The woman was always dressed the same way. She wore old-fashioned long sleeved blouses with collars up around her neck regardless of the weather. Her clothes did not fit well and were muted earth tones.

Blaine had told Rat recently that she was beginning to feel lonely. This was a new experience for Blaine, since she had always thrived on withdrawing. In fact, withdrawing had been the only way she had been able to survive early in her life. She told Rat his company was wonderful, and she also longed for the company of a woman friend. All of her women co-workers at the software company where she worked appeared to have frenetic, over-scheduled lives. They were friendly to Blaine, but their lives seemed to have such velocity and global orbits, that there was no space in them for Blaine. Rat had encouraged her to try to reach out to make new girlfriends.

So as she stood in the doorway of the restaurant, returning the proprietor's wave, she paused. Rather than heading to the table that she and Rat usually occupied in the corner next to the window up front, maybe she ought to reach out to the woman in the back of the café. She looked like she was probably in her late 20s, just a little older than Blaine. This was not something Blaine did easily, but surely there was no downside. Why not give it a try?

With that as the last thought in her head, and before a new thought popped in to change her mind, Blaine headed to the back of the restaurant. She had been in Germany now long enough that she was not afraid to try to start a conversation in English or the German she was fast learning.

"Hello," she said in English, "would it be okay if I joined you for dinner?"

The young woman looked up, frightened. Clearly, she did not

know what to say. There was a long stunned pause. Finally without ever looking directly at Blaine, she motioned her to take the other chair at the table. Blaine sat down.

"I see you in here often," said Blaine, "so I thought it might be fun to meet you. I am an American and I am a little lonely in this country. My name is Blaine."

The young woman appeared to make an effort to gather all her strength. Finally without looking at Blaine she said, "My name is Aasia. I do not speak English so good. Thank you for making your hello."

There was a long pause. Then the young woman reached for her water glass with her right hand. As she did the long sleeve of her blouse pulled up her arm just a bit. Blaine could see the white rope of a scar going back up her arm. The scar was thick and knotted. The cut must have been vicious, and first aid to sew it up a long time in arriving, if ever it had.

Despite the difficulties Blaine had always had in reaching out to others, all of a sudden she felt a release in her chest. Her breathing relaxed. She looked again at Aasia. This time there was a kindness in Blaine's gaze that she did not even know she had the capacity to express.

There was another long pause. This time it was a gentle pause, without tension. Their conversation began gradually. About places they shopped in the neighborhood and what it was like learning about a new country. At the end of the meal the two women agreed to meet again.

Gradually a pattern emerged where the two new friends met for dinner, particularly on those nights when Rat was working or had to be elsewhere.

Slowly, ever so slowly, Aasia's story began to emerge. Aasia was a Muslim from Bosnia. She had been resettled in Germany by the United Nations refugee agency after the Srebrenica genocide in 1995. Blaine was surprised that Aasia would feel so much like a newcomer to Germany since she had been in the country a number of years. Clearly Aasia did and, gradually the two women began to become fast friends.

During the Bosnian war, Serb forces conducted sexual abuse terror on Bosnian Muslim girls and women. Blaine learned that more than 25,000 systematic rapes of women and girls occurred in Bosnia-Herzegovina, many of them in the Srebrenica region before and during the Srebrenica genocide. Women and girls were kept in various detention centers where they had to live in intolerably unhygienic conditions and were mistreated in many ways, including being repeatedly raped.

Aasia had been in one such camp. She had been twelve years old at the time. In her camp, the Serbian soldiers left their literal mark on each woman they raped by cutting the woman's body. The psychological mutilation was much worse. Aasia had been relocated to Germany after it had been determined that her entire family had been exterminated in the genocide. She had years of counseling through a German charity, though on some days, she confided to Blaine, she felt as if she was barely free from the camp. The sizable Turkish Muslim community in Berlin rejected women like her because she was an unmarried Muslim woman who was not a virgin. Aasia was stigmatized by the very community that should have embraced her. The proprietor of the Turkish café, where she and Blaine often ate, was one of the few members of the Turkish community in Berlin that did not mind having Aasia as a customer. She trained at a Berlin nursing school and now had a good job on the nursing staff of a major hospital where she worked in an emergency room trauma unit. Her experiences in the rape camp had anesthetized her from feeling any emotional response to trauma. She told Blaine that she was able to work on the most grossly disfigured accident victims without feeling anything.

Blaine began to realize that the physical and emotional abuse that she had grown up with paled in comparison to Aasia's experience. And, there was another difference. Somehow Blaine had always felt deep within herself that she would have some way to fight back. She might have to wait. The opportunity might be long delayed. However, Blaine never gave up hope that she would be able to strike back in her own defense. The Serbian soldiers not only raped and mutilated Aasia, but they also destroyed an inner hope about the goodness of life. She was left with that kind of will to live that only survives within a hard shell of hate. Aasia had grown weary of living in the hard shell of hate, but she felt if she did not have the hate she would simply disappear from the earth.

When Aasia met Blaine, Aasia had been surviving for years in a virtual purgatory between wanting to take her own life, because of the agonizing guilt she felt that she had escaped, and being captured in that shell of hatred that kept her from reaching out in this new country to discover a new life. Aasia had been unable to move in any direction. The new country was a refuge, but it was not inviting to her. Only the steroidal stimulation of the hospital's trauma operating room allowed her to feel alive inside of her shell of hate and fear.

As Aasia's friendship with Blaine grew, Aasia gradually began to change. Aasia began to relax a little more in her own life. She actually enjoyed meeting Blaine for dinner at the Turkish café. Her diet which she had kept exactly the same as it had been in Bosnia, slowly began to have more variety. Blaine could tell that her friendship with Aasia was having a positive effect. What Blaine could not see was that her friendship with Aasia was allowing Blaine to develop a capacity for compassion that she had not known before.

However, Blaine's capacity for compassion was not gained at the expense of her anger. As her compassion for Aasia grew so did her anger and outrage at what her new friend had been through. Much of the rape and genocide in Srebrenica had occurred in spite of United Nations Dutch soldiers being stationed there to protect the Muslim population. Genocide in Europe, which the world had hoped ended in 1945, had reared its ugly head right under the nose of civilized authority. Blaine knew that if there was ever an occasion for her to direct her anger on her friend's behalf, she would not hesitate. She would use the one instrument that she had learned to wield like an aikido master wielding his jo—her hacking skills.

CHAPTER 16

Dawson had never seen Brother Will so upset. In fact, Brother Will was so disturbed that upon meeting Dawson in the hall, he had immediately started talking. Dawson tried to calm him down.

"Just take a deep breath, Brother Will," said Dawson, "and then start over again and tell me slowly what is going on."

Brother Will took a deep breath, and then a second one, and slowly began to get some control. "Brother Issac," he said, addressing Will Dawson by his new name, "this letter came from Mother Mary, who is a very close friend of Father O'Donnell's. She is the abbess at a convent in Minnesota that is a sister order to our order. It was marked urgent so I thought that I better open it immediately to determine whether or not to take it up to Father O'Donnell in his hermitage."

"What I learned from Mother Mary's letter is that your old friend Melissa has been staying there in the convent. Well, not really in the convent itself, but the convent sits on over 1000 acres of land and Melissa has been somewhere out on the land in a self-made hermitage."

"Hold on there," said Dawson. "Say that again. Are you sure the letter said Melissa was found?"

"I don't know about found," said Brother Will, "but yes, the letter said Melissa was there. And it also said that just the other day some police officers showed up with a warrant for Melissa's arrest. Mother Mary is very afraid that they will come back and start searching in the wilderness around the convent for Melissa. She asked Father O'Donnell what she should do. I'm afraid I should not have opened the letter without taking it to Father O'Donnell first."

Dawson was still not quite able to take it all in—could it possibly be true that the woman for whom he had been searching for months on end, the first love of his life with whom he had been head-over heels in love in his twenties—was alive? She was where he could go to see her. His back slid down the hallway wall until he was seated on the floor. Finally, Dawson looked up at Brother Will's anguished face.

"I am sure you did the right thing, Brother Will," said Dawson. "Obviously we need to immediately do whatever we can to help Mother Mary and Melissa. Please take the letter up the mountain to Father O'Donnell. In the meantime, Man and I and Ooljee will start for Minnesota. That way, by the time Father O'Donnell decides what we should do, we will be in a position to be of some help. Since the temporary tag on my old pickup has long since expired it is probably best that I take the monastery van. We will call you from the road to let you know where we are. Any instructions for us should probably be sent via this chat room, in order to avoid creating a trail. Brother Will, let me write down for you exactly how to access the chat room so Father O'Donnell can provide us instructions." Dawson knew that this method of communicating would also alert Blaine and Rat to exactly what was happening.

As soon as the directions for entering the chat room were given to Brother Will, there was a flurry of packing by Dawson and Man, their few clothes and some sandwiches for the road. Soon, along with Ooljee, they were in the monastery van heading down the dirt road on the way out to the county highway. At the gate, José waved for them to stop to receive his personal blessing. José also insisted that they take certain things with them for their journey, including corn for tortillas, a rattlesnake skin and the skull of an armadillo. Dawson was in too big a hurry to protest and accepted the gifts. Man and Ooljee seem quite pleased with these gifts for their journey.

Dawson had been at the monastery for only a couple of months. This was the first time in his life he'd ever done any work on his own consciousness. It was hard work. Having the chance to hit the road on a new adventure came as a flood of relief. He'd enough training in becoming more conscious to see how powerful the relief was when he allowed his ego more control. The realization hit him that all his life running projects for the Company, over and over again, he had used his ego to control and to manipulate people and information. He could feel this surge of ego urging him to get control, to be the hero, to find and save Melissa. This revelation was frightening, as it slowly settled in upon him beneath the hypnotic motion of the van heading north. How in the world would he be able to hold the non-dual stance that Father O'Donnell had been talking to him about in their spiritual direction sessions and also be the action hero of his ego's own imagination?

Dawson could see both Man and Ooljee were also pleased at the opportunity for new adventure. Ooljee was sitting in the back seat with his nose at the window taking in the sights with his acute sense of smell. Man's hair had grown longer over the past few months and today for the first time he'd pulled it back in a ponytail. He looked more Indian to Dawson than he ever had. He sat there at ease in the front passenger seat slowly sharpening his knife against a whetstone, as the van took them north through Colorado. The distant peaks of the Rockies were covered in snow, but the roads were dry as they headed towards Nebraska.

"Hey that is a fierce looking blade you have there, Man." said Dawson.

Man folded the knife up and slipped it back into his boot where he always kept it. "Was a gift from my father," he said, "like Ooljee it came from a poker game. I have such mixed feelings. I miss my dad and I am very angry at him. My older cousin told me that as things go on the rez sometime that is a lot for a father to give a son—a good dog and a good knife." Man turned slightly in his seat toward the side window signaling the conversation was over.

After thirteen hours, they made it to a little northern Minnesota town just a few miles from the convent. The radio reported thirty degrees and there was now a light blanket of snow on the ground. There was one motel in town, an off-brand, called Sleepy Tyme Inn. Dawson went to the small office to check in. He left Man and Ooljee in the car. Dawson could tell he was back in Company mode. He would sure stand out in this small town if he checked in with a young Indian boy and a handsome Plott hound. He paid in advance for his room in cash and parked the monastery van close to the door of the motel room.

The next morning Dawson awoke disoriented, momentarily unsure of where he was. He had slept hard. He looked across the motel room. Man was already up. He was doing his morning Navajo warrior practice. The practice took about thirty minutes and involved different postures and breathing techniques. Dawson was used to watching Man do this practice in the morning and could tell he was almost finished. Ooljee sat patiently on the floor next to Man. Dawson rolled out of bed and headed for the shower.

As much as Dawson's stomach wanted him to cross the street to the family restaurant opposite the motel, Dawson instead pulled the monastery van into the nearest service station. He left Man and Ooljee in the van while he went inside to see what was available that would pass for breakfast. He came back with a couple cups of coffee and several granola bars and a bottle of water for Ooljee. It wasn't much, and it would get them out to the convent.

They had gone only five miles out of town when Dawson saw the sign on the right pointing the way to the convent drive. He swung the van right and proceeded up a long driveway threading circuitously through birches and pines before finally coming to a stop in front of a low-slung rambling building. It was early, and Dawson assumed that the nuns kept similar hours as the brothers did in his monastery. Dawson looked at his watch. It was about time for the nuns to be returning from chapel to breakfast.

Just then he saw a figure emerge from a building that must be the chapel. She was followed by another person, then another and so on. Dawson rolled down the van window, and he could make out a mosaic of sound like birds chattering early on a spring morning. Clearly this Order did not have the same rules regarding silence as were obeyed in his monastery. Dawson watched the trail of women enter another building. That must be the dining hall. With a little luck, maybe they could get a real breakfast.

Dawson opened the van door, stepped down and stretched his legs. He headed for the closest building, which had a small sign out front that said Office. He walked inside. No one was there. He pushed a small button on the counter and faintly could hear a bell ringing somewhere way off in the distance.

After a few minutes there was the sound of movement in the hallway behind the counter. A woman appeared. Even though she did not seem to be dressed as Dawson thought nuns dressed, there was something about her that told him immediately that she was a nun. It was not that she presented some rigid persona, a nun stereotype from a bad movie, rather it was about the lightness of her bearing and the clearness of her eyes. Dawson immediately knew that something important was happening at this convent. He suspected that these nuns were engaged in the same practices that he had been learning from Father O'Donnell.

The woman who stood before Dawson was, more than anything

else, extraordinarily present. Dawson tried to stay grounded in his fact-discerning Company mode, however, his traditional analytical fact-sorting was not computing well for him. He had no idea whether this woman was 30 or 50. He would spend time later wondering whether she was strikingly beautiful when he first saw her, or whether what appeared to be beauty was simply her clear and unconditional presence. She stood before him, with a half-smile on her lips, waiting patiently.

"Hi, well, good morning," said Dawson fumbling for words. "I am... I mean I hope I'm not disturbing you just now." He stopped, unsure what to say next.

The woman before him simply waited. The power of her presence had him tongue-tied at first, then he tried again.

"My name is Brother Isaac. I come from Father O'Donnell. I would like to speak with Mother Mary."

"Well, you are at the right place." The woman said. She did not move. Her eyes continued to dance as she looked at Dawson. "You must be one of those cowboy brothers down there in New Mexico. Do you get to wear cowboy outfits all the time?" she said surveying Dawson in his blue jeans, boots and cowboy shirt.

Despite the urgency of his visit, and his uneasiness, Dawson found himself relaxing almost against his own will. He was about to make a comment about Minnesota nuns' habits looking like schoolgirl outfits. Before he could speak, she said, "I bet you are hungry, and it looks like you have somebody with you who may even be hungrier."

Dawson followed her gaze out the window where Man was leaning against the monastery van patting Ooljee.

"You may be right, and I don't know who is hungriest. However, we would be glad to see if we could find out for you."

Much to his surprise, she leaned toward him across the counter and extended her right hand. Her eyes were light blue and had the same mystery as the sky directly overhead on a clear spring day. "Welcome, my name is Sister Theresa," she said and paused, "and be on your best behavior. These girls don't get to see a lot of men, especially cowboys."

Dawson reached and took her hand. Immediately he realized that she had extended it, not for the purpose of engaging in a ritual handshake, but for the intimacy of feeling his energy. Dawson could tell it was the kind of thing Melissa would do. It was as if Sister Theresa was taking his energetic pulse with her fingertips. He could feel the startling clarity of her energy running down his arm. Gently she removed her fingers from his hand. He was certain that he had been put through some test. He wondered if he had passed.

"Come to breakfast," she said. "We have been waiting for you. Mother Mary will meet with you as soon as you have eaten."

CHAPTER 17

Blaine and Aasia had become fast friends. When Aasia was not working in the trauma unit at the hospital, and when Blaine was not at work at her software job, the two women were most likely spending time together. In a strange sort of way, their lack of trust of others brought them closer to each other. Blaine realized early on that the best way to treat Aasia was the way that Rat treated Blaine. Rat had never asked Blaine to disclose anything about herself. Rat always just treated Blaine as if she was a very special friend. Gradually his unconditional acceptance of Blaine allowed her to become more open to him. And now Rat knew more about Blaine's inner life and thoughts than anyone else. Almost as much as Blaine herself.

Fortunately, Rat welcomed Aasia into the time that Rat spent with Blaine. And Rat welcomed Aasia as he welcomed anything that Blaine was interested in. If Blaine liked Aasia, then automatically she was okay by Rat. This was good news, because any time Aasia got down and depressed, Blaine was not nearly as successful at lifting her spirits as Rat was. All Rat had to do was show up and wiggle his nose and both of the women were soon in hysterics. Blaine thought she'd figured out why. No matter how much a woman was distrustful or fearful of men generally, a super techie like Rat, who looked like a mouse out of a Disney movie, did not trigger that amygdala fear-of-men pattern in a woman's brain.

* * *

It was only by accident that Blaine and Aasia discovered how scarred they each were. Aasia had come over to Blaine's apartment after she got off her shift at the hospital. Blaine was in the process of doing her laundry. At the last minute, she decided she wanted to wash the slacks and top she had on, and she pulled them off in the hallway where the clothes washer was located. Aasia was in the kitchen fixing tea, though not so far away that she missed seeing the many vivid knife cuts on Blaine's body. Even the fact that many of the scars were incorporated into glowing tattoos could not disguise their origins.

When Blaine returned to the kitchen buttoning up a clean top, after having pulled on a pair of jeans, Aasia was sitting stock still at the kitchen table, her eyes wide, her mouth agape. Finally Aasia spoke, "Blaine, is it okay for me to ask you? Can I ask you what happened? How you got all the cuts? I mean part of me does not want to know anything about it. Nothing. Nothing at all. You are my only friend. Would you tell me what happened? Is it okay for me to ask?"

Blaine smiled and Aasia could feel relief wash over her body as she started to breathe again.

"Aasia, I know this looks terrible, but it's not nearly as bad as what happened to you. All of the knife marks you see I made. I know it looks crazy, however, at one point in my life the only way I could get relief from fear and terror was to cut myself. Thank God I did. I am sure I would've killed myself otherwise, if I had not been able simply to cut myself and feel for a few brief moments the warm flow of relief the cutting gave."

"What happened to me by my own hand is even hard for me to imagine now. It is not something that is so horrible, though I know it looks that way. I look at the scars now and just see scars. I don't see all the pain and terror that made me slice my skin open again and again. I know you have scars. And you don't need to show them to me. It is possible to have scars from something horrible and brutal made by something outside of you as you have and to have scars from something that is horrible and brutal inside of you as I do. Either way, the task is to get rid of whatever was outside or inside that was horrible and brutal.

"It's taken me years to begin to get beyond my internal self-hate. I think I have Rat to thank for a lot of the progress I have made. He has helped me feel that I could relax in my own body and that life would be all right."

There was a long pause. Then Aasia slowly began to take off her long-sleeved blouse. White corded knots of scarred flesh zigzagged across her arms and torso.

"Is it okay to show you more?" asked Aasia. Blaine could feel a red-hot anger rising from the base of her spine, but she nodded yes. Aasia reached behind her back and unfastened her bra strap. Blaine could not help note that at one time Aasia must have had nearly perfectly formed full breasts. Now they were a lattice work of white knots and red scars. The nipple on her right breast had been severely disfigured. It looked as if the men who had raped her had especially tried to disfigure the elemental parts of her womanhood.

Blaine's whole body winced. She realized that she had never considered taking a knife to her own breasts.

Blaine got up and reached for Aasia and wrapped her arms around her friend. The two women sobbed together in each other's scarred arms until weak in their knees they both sat down at the kitchen table.

Suddenly Blaine's cell phone rang. She glanced at the phone to see who was calling. She looked at Aasia. "It's Rat," she said, "Do you mind if I catch it?"

Aasia shook her head no.

"Hey, Rat," Blaine said, "your timing as always is perfect. Aasia and I were just exchanging deep personal stuff."

"Well, personal stuff it is," said Rat. "Let me get right to the point. Dawson has been in the chat room. He is afraid Melissa is about to get caught. If we can figure out some way to get her to Berlin, are you willing to hide her out?"

"Holy cow! I don't know," said Blaine. "Can I take a little while to think about it and maybe talk to you and Aasia?"

"Sure, take a couple of nanoseconds. Wiz and I are trying to get her out of the U.S. via Canada. I'll keep working on that and we can talk more about this later. Shall I just plan on meeting both of you at the kebab café as usual for dinner?"

"Okay," said Blaine, "that would be great. We'll see you there in about an hour."

Aasia was putting her blouse back on. Blaine knew that Aasia would eventually be haunted by the same question that had haunted Blaine ever since she had fallen for Will Dawson in Italy. How in the world would any man who Blaine would be interested in going to bed with, want to go to bed with her? Even if he did, one glimpse of her scarred body would change that forever.

"Aasia," Blaine said, "our bodies carry the scars of our past, but that does not mean that we have to let these scars dictate our future. You know I love Rat. He is my best male friend. I don't love him though in a romantic way, but if I did, I often wonder how it would be to sleep with him. This is so worrisome and nonsensical. And I know even harder for you to imagine. Plus how in the world could you want to have an intimate relationship with someone of the gender who has caused you so much pain? Still, at some point, we may want to bridge that gap. I hope you will want to. Don't let the fear of the problem of bridging the gap keep you stuck in your life at a place where there is never the chance to step over the gap. I did that for a long time. We have already been robbed of much in our lives. Aasia, will you commit to me that you will not let fear rob you anymore of what life has to offer you?"

Blaine held Aasia's gaze for a long moment. Finally, Aasia nodded and almost inaudibly said, "Yes."

"Good for you," said Blaine, "us scarred girls have to stick together. Let me go put the washed clothes in the dryer and then we can head over to the kebab shop."

"Yes," said Aasia, a grimace of intense anguish crossing her face, "I will try with your help not to be robbed by fear, but I never want to sleep with a man. The thought is repulsive to me and even if I did, the thought of any man's repulsion from seeing me would be too humiliating for me to bear."

Blaine turned back to her friend. "Don't worry, Aasia, I love you just the way you are."

Aasia looked at Blaine. She felt her body tense as she tried to smile. When her eyes met Blaine's, she began to relax. Now that her only friend knew her secret, it was not that hard, after all, to smile.

CHAPTER 18

Godfrey Adams found himself placing each foot carefully in the middle of a steppingstone as he followed the path to the side door entrance to Father Hay's office. Godfrey had been anxious for his monthly meeting with Father Hay for spiritual direction to roll around. In fact, he was more than anxious. He was angry. Maybe it was his anger that caused him to regress emotionally as he arrived for his appointment. But, his anger was such that he hardly noticed he walked in like a fretting child.

As always, Father Hay's warm smile made Godfrey relax. The momentary relaxation freed his anger and it began to roll out.

"I just don't get this whole crucifixion, resurrection thing," said Godfrey. "I mean I am no dummy. I know the ancient Greeks for hundreds of years had the practice of releasing a goat into the wild to bear away their misdeeds. I thought Jesus was supposed to bring about a new level of consciousness in the history of world religion. Yet this whole scapegoat thing seems to be the central crux of what most Christian churches want to talk about. I thought we had gotten beyond animal sacrifices! Jesus! Give me a break, no pun intended! Even the great church I go to, which welcomes gay men like me, is focused on this theology of 'some guy dying to take away my sins.'"

Father Hay remained calm, but beneath his attentive expression he was excited. His directee was off on an unorthodox path, but Godfrey was caring passionately about his beliefs. This boded well for the possibility of real spiritual progress. He didn't speak. He waited on Godfrey to continue. He didn't have to wait long.

"I like the Greek version better. I would much prefer to buy a goat and let it escape. And what makes me even madder is I don't know why I am so mad about this archaic theology. You have told me over and over again that what is most important are not head beliefs, but the beliefs or values of the heart that precipitate action in the world. I know all this scapegoat stuff is head stuff. Somehow I am just trapped in anger at being a part of a religion whose central premise is no better than letting a goat go out the back gate."

"So tell me, Godfrey," said Father Hay, maintaining his warm, curious, spiritual director demeanor, "is there anything in particular that has triggered your anger about this particular piece of Christian theology?"

Godfrey paused. He had been so caught up in his anger that he had not even begun to consider where it might be coming from. He realized he had once again missed the first step of the spiritual practice he was learning—awareness.

"All right, I'll tell you, Father Hay. I have been talking to my partner Jeff about my spiritual journey and the work we have been doing. I get excited about this. I feel in the past year or two of our work, I have turned a huge corner. I am more at home in my life than I have ever been. And I know that is hard for a gay man anywhere in this culture. I feel a sense of serenity about my life and my partnership with Jeff. I am not sure what has shifted, but something major has changed.

"When I try to explain to Jeff about my journey and my beliefs he throws this scapegoat theology up in my face and, well, it just pisses me off. It pisses me off that somehow my life has been changed by my spiritual journey and that the theology, at least theoretically, which underlies my spiritual path is totally hollow. I mean really absurd. Yes, I know the practices you have taught me, that I have begun to make a part of my life, like centering prayer and welcoming prayer have changed me, but for what real purpose?

"Gosh, you know how Jeff is. He's a great guy, and he is not the questioning kind of person about what is the purpose of life, like I am. Yet when I try to share with him about the journey I am on, I keep getting jarred—no really embarrassed—by what the church believes." Godfrey paused. "I had not thought about it before, but that's where my anger is coming from."

Father Hay let the silence settle in. He could feel that Godfrey's anger had dissipated. And, he needed a period of silence so that he could discern the best way to guide his directee. There were several ways to go. On the psychological level, Father Hay knew that for Godfrey shame was a big issue. There would be value in exploring this issue separate and apart from the theological conundrum which triggered it. Shame is a powerful emotion that can separate a person from themselves and from the experience of God's love for them.

Father Hay also knew that he could step out of his role as a spiritual guide and put on the hat of a modern Christian pilgrim and talk to Godfrey about how he had found his way through the theological thicket that was charging Godfrey's anger. After a few more minutes it became clear to Father Hay that this was one of those special times when it was appropriate for him to take off his spiritual director hat and talk about the modern day problems of Christian theology. Father Hay knew that an intellectual understanding of how to get through the thicket was not something that contributed to one's spiritual growth. However, it did seem to Father Hay that, on balance, at this moment the need for mental clarity was compelling. While anger has its spiritual uses, it was not helpful here to Godfrey as a way to stay on his path or increase his intimacy with Jeff. Sometimes intellectual insight could put the utility of anger in perspective.

"Godfrey, I'm going to step out of my role as spiritual director for a moment, if that is okay. As your director it is my role to help you discover the direction you are being called in your own life, not to offer information or judgment. However, it seems like the questions you raised could be illuminated just by more information, to get as broad a view as possible of the theological lay of the land. What do you say?" Godfrey nodded his assent.

"I want to explain my own understanding of some of the theological issues that are so troubling to you. It doesn't mean that my way of seeing these issues is something I am suggesting you need to agree with. To the contrary, I think there is value for each of us in struggling to find our own way with our beliefs.

Anger is often the thing that provides the energy to allow us to get through this struggle. And, you are exactly right, there have been centuries of distortion of the central message of Christianity, so I think a little overview is important. It is important because I don't want the theological distractions to sidetrack you from the spiritual journey that you are on. Too much progress has already been made," said Father Hay with a sigh.

"There are two fundamental psychological issues that the Christian gospel message was designed to cut through and clarify. These two issues are gender and projection. If we go back and study the message of Jesus in the canonical Gospels as well as in the Gospels of Thomas, Philip and Mary Magdalene, we see that Jesus' message tried to teach us how to address these two fundamental issues. It is safe to say that while the message has been preserved by Christian mystics and saints who have reached a level of consciousness where they could experience the truth of Jesus' message directly, for the most part the church has been caught in the cultural biases of gender and projection and often bent the gospel message, or at least the tenor of that message, to conform to these biases.

"This is woefully sad and woefully human and understandable. We know from the Garden of Eden story that God's creation was good. Later, humankind developed a sense of self-conscious I-ness, that we equate with leaving the Garden of Eden. The ability of us as human beings to have a sense of self is fundamentally tied first to our sense of gender, of being male or female. Historically, men have asserted this sense of identity by diminishing the feminine. In addition, as you are acutely aware, the historical track record is vividly clear that straight men have engendered their sense of male identity by denying a sense of identity to gay men and putting women in subservient roles. This staggeringly profound shadow aspect of the search for male identity has been just as destructively pervasive in the church as it has been in the rest of Western culture."

Godfrey nodded. "As you say that, I recognize how I have felt embarrassed at the misogyny of some of my gay friends." Father Hay knew the blessing of silence and he waited as Godfrey experienced the sadness underlying what he had expressed.

Then Father Hay continued, "The other primary way by which a sense of self is established by human beings is through projection. You will remember the ad campaign: 'Be like Mike.' By stressing that Michael Jordan was a hero for many young boys to project upon, Nike made millions of dollars selling shoes.

"We grow and develop by projection. We see a person who is really good at doing something we would like to do and we are drawn to that person, because they allow us to experience our own desire to be proficient at the same task. Projection is also a common part of our spiritual development. As a young person we project God to be a father-like figure up in the sky. This figure has all the aspects of a human father and then some, and that projection initially provides us security and a sense of being looked after. It provides enough security for us to get started on our journey.

"At some point in time, everyone on a spiritual path has to give up the need for security which is found in an over-identification with their gender role, and the need for security found in the easy projection on what a father God is like. Many young people have tremendous difficulty ever becoming interested in religion because their issues with their human fathers are so great that they have never had a sufficient loving experience with a father to be able to imagine the possibility of a loving father God.

"When things are going well for a child, it seems we have a biological need, certainly a psychological need as we grow up, to feel comfortable with our gender identity and to experience projection on those individuals whom we would like to be like. So without denying the age appropriateness of these processes early in life, the message of the Gospels is that as mature adults it is time for us to put aside childish things, that is the ways of defining ourselves through projection. We must accept that we are not only predominantly male or female, but we have both feminine and masculine qualities. We must stop looking out there both to find God and to find a likeness of ourselves and look instead inside to connect with ourselves and with God.

"If we don't begin to find the things within ourselves that are our most fundamental identity, then we continue to try to find them externally, and the more we push to do that, the more the shadow aspect of our diminishment of the other gender occurs and the more we project and give away our power to others. Either way, when this occurs human beings build structures of prejudice and bigotry in order to feel secure because they have failed to connect with themselves and the security of their God within. Unfortunately, the church has built projective structures just as easily and pervasively as such structures have been built by other institutions in our culture.

"The good news of the Gospels is that we are all richly and abundantly loved by God. It is this love which cuts through the structures of prejudice and bigotry that we build when we are disconnected from God in order to feel secure. Just like the rest of the culture the church has for the most part been content to build structures that diminish the role of the feminine and created an external male priestly authority.

"Godfrey, I am glad you are angry. If you weren't, you would not be getting the true message. The question for all of us is what do we do with our anger at the church, at the very institution that should have protected the reality of Christ's message. I do not believe there is one easy answer for all of us. Rather, the challenge for each of us is how do we channel the energy of this anger in a constructive way to move us along our own spiritual path." Father Hay paused, took a deep breath and looked intently at Godfrey.

"Well, I am relieved and disheartened," said Godfrey. "I am relieved that you understand the anger and frustration that I feel, and I am disheartened that the church has created such a state of alienation from its core principle of the creative force of love. And I know this thought is totally out of the blue, but I am also wondering: what, if anything, does being gay have to do with all this."

Father Hay took an audible deep breath and then waded in. "Godfrey, this is just my belief, and I offer it to you for what it's worth. I believe God loves diversity. All you have to do is look around in nature and see that this is true. The evolutionary process which creation has set in motion and is always unwinding thrives most of all on diversity. The greater the number of plants, animals, kinds of peoples, religions, ideas, the more things thrive; all of these are the way of nature and of reality. This is the order of God's creation and I believe that it is good. If you take the Darwinian idea of survival of the fittest, it is only true at a microcosm level. At the macro level—the systems level—survival depends most of all on variety. Looking through a biological lens we see that life thrives on diversity. And, I include gender in that understanding. Being gay may be the gift we bring to the rest of humankind to help free people from the idea of a monolithic idea of gender and to free people from the idea that authority in the natural order is innate in the male gender. Maleness, femaleness are all spectrum concepts emotionally, physically and spiritually. Regardless of a person's gender orientation, the challenge for each person is to integrate all aspects of being human."

"Holy cow! You think being gay is a gift to humankind?" said Godfrey. "After all the shame I have carried for years. You have got to be kidding me. Father, I really respect you and all the help you have given me, however, this is too much of a stretch. Don't do a smoke and mirrors thing with me."

"I know it's little personal solace," said Father Hay, "but from a bigger perspective, yes, all the groups that have suffered because of their minority status in our culture, either due to their gender, sexual orientation, ethnic background, race, religion or other beliefs have carried the burden of being different so the majority group could justify its authority. These minorities have all perpetuated diversity. Nowhere have these different groups folded up and become like the majority. Despite their burdens they have persevered. God must truly love diversity."

"Okay," said Godfrey, "I get the idea. I am going to need some time to think about it. And I get your concept that gender identification and projection, two of the key psychological processes for growing up, are also the two twin pillars that sustain the power of a majority over those that are different. But I don't see how this exonerates the church from its misogyny and abuse of power."

"I am not suggesting it does," said Father Hay. "Only the starting point here was your desire not to be burdened by the crucifixion theology of much of the Christian church, which I grant you is, for many Christians, simply a scapegoat projection. I am saying that you can look at the broad stream of our Christian theology and see preserved in it the golden threads of truth that are not affected by the need to augment gender identification or infantile projection."

Godfrey shifted in his chair so that he was sitting straight up. He was enthralled by what Father Hay was telling him.

"Take, for example, the Franciscans. They have always believed that the birth of Jesus was the redemption, because Jesus' birth was a statement that God is in this with us, that God is on the side of creation. Of course the Franciscans, like all the other celibate male religious orders, carry the shadow of their unintegrated feminine. The truth is, if you look for the light of Jesus' message of love as a way to conquer all, you will find it gleaming in many places. If you look for the places where the church has distorted that message, and particularly if you look at church institutions whose structures reflect distortions of that message, then you will also find those in abundance."

Father Hay took a deep breath. "Let's sit in silence for a few minutes." And the two men did. Sunlight came through Father Hay's office window and danced on the floor around the two men as their heads bent in silent prayer.

CHAPTER 19

"What do you know about our Order?" said Mother Mary, "the Sacred Order of the Sisters of Mary of Magdala."

"Not anything, I guess." said Dawson, recovering a bit from the abruptness of Mother Mary's question and the gigantic amount of food that he had just consumed for breakfast.

"The Sacred Order of the Sisters of Mary of Magdala, or SOS as the girls call it, was founded many centuries ago to honor the first apostle, Mary Magdalene. In fact, it is our belief that Mary Magdalene was the apostle to the apostles. You probably have not heard of our Order because the hierarchy of the Christian church is so male-dominated. For centuries a group of sisters has kept alive our belief, and our experience of our belief, that Jesus and Mary Magdalene were soul mates and that the Christian faith is about learning to experience Christ consciousness in the same way Mary Magdalene learned from Jesus. Though its central principle has often been obscured or misplaced, the Christian religion is above all else a religion of love. Our sisterhood believes that the depth of Christian love can only be forged in relationships. We believe that Jesus could never have experienced complete incarnation—known the depth of human love, where human love becomes divine love—without being in relationships that allowed this to happen.

Dawson began to squirm in his seat. Why in the world was he getting this lecture on the history of her Order, when all he wanted to do was find out what this lady knew about Melissa? However, the authority of her presence kept Dawson from interrupting.

"I will get to the part you are interested in about Melissa in just a moment," said Mother Mary, as if she had read the discomfort in his mind. "First, I want to give you the context. You perhaps, of all people, need to understand this context. Most of Western understanding bought readily into the Greek idea that because there were different words for love that these different words described distinctly different ideas. You remember on one end of the spectrum was *eros* and on other end was *agape*. We do not believe this is a Christian understanding. Rather our belief is that agape is simply transformed *eros*. Love starts with *eros*. You might say *eros* is the booster rocket that gets love launched, and, if we are lucky, takes us to the sublime regions of celestial love."

"Thank goodness for the Sufis. It is wonderful to read the poetry of Rumi, so richly full of the energy that *eros* provides us to love God. Are you familiar with this poet, Mr. Dawson?"

"Just a little bit," said Dawson. "I remember Melissa quoting him years ago when we were in Afghanistan. And now he seems to be quite popular."

"Yes," said Mother Mary. "His poetry has caught on because it taps into a huge longing people have been unaware of, their desire for their beloved. We believe that Mary Magdalene and Jesus were pilgrims into the depths of human love from its erotic quality to where it becomes divine. For that reason our Order is somewhat unique in that it is not a celibate Order. So while we do not doubt the authenticity of the path of monastic celibacy as a way to experience a God-centered life, we believe that Mary Magdalene taught us that the truest way to the deepest love of God is through God's love mirrored to us in human relationships.

"Don't misunderstand, this is not some romantic notion. This is not an easy path. Nor is it readily understandable by most of the Western world that in its shadow fears the feminine. For that reason the practices of our Order have for centuries remained esoteric. You can understand why. We live in a society that is both sexually excessive and sexually anorexic. Traditional Christian teachings have been afraid to give women equality, and therefore Christians generally have always been leery of sex as an expression of deep religious feeling. True love always is an expression of equality, and true love is always mutual. There is no power relationship in true love and this is the kind of relationship that Mary Magdalene had with Jesus."

Dawson took a huge breath. What Mother Mary was saying was more than he could take in, and his body was reacting by gasping for air.

"I can see this is more than you asked for. I know you are chomping at the bit to find out about Melissa. I am just about to get there. I say this with great compassion, Mr. Dawson. This discussion is necessary because it was in part because of your failure to be able to respond to Melissa's love that brought her first, and now you, to our convent.

"True, her path was circuitous. However, after Melissa's enlightenment experience at St. Issa's pond in Afghanistan, her course was set. She experienced the greater reality that connects us all, and she became a spiritual warrior on a path."

Dawson sat there stunned. Mother Mary had unleashed a bombshell in his emotional being. He felt wounded and fragmented. Yes, he had fallen in love with Melissa years ago in Afghanistan. And he knew now, with deep regret, that he had not followed his heart. However, he had followed his love for his country. Admittedly, this idea of love of country is a somewhat abstract idea that comes from the head and not the heart. Still, he had convinced himself that he should put his patriotic duty before personal considerations. It had only been recently that he allowed himself to even consider the idea that it was not love of country he had put first, but fear of an intimate relationship with a woman that had driven his decision.

"Do you mean that the reason Melissa did not meet with me in Turin, Italy at the Enneagram conference is because in some way I was spiritually inadequate to meet with her?" said Dawson incredulously. "I was told that she was at the conference to meet me and didn't because she was aware that I was being followed both by the CIA and some other organization, and that her not meeting with me was really an act of love to avoid getting me into her troubles. What do you really think was going on, Mother Mary?"

Mother Mary sighed. "Mr. Dawson, one of the things that you

come to realize when you lead the kind of spiritual life that we are called to in this Order is that there is a multiplicity of meaning in almost every event. Our goal is to be sufficiently spiritually centered so that we can experience even contradictory meanings at the same time, as well as the larger knowing that everything is held in God's love. Yes, there is no doubt that Melissa acted on your behalf at the conference by avoiding direct contact with you. And, there is perhaps another reality which explains the reason why this meeting did not take place after almost twenty years, some larger meaning which suggests that the time was not ripe.

"What I am suggesting, Mr. Dawson, is that perhaps neither you nor Melissa controlled whether you would have met. If you are to have the chance to meet in the future, it is more likely to happen if you have done some deeper work on your spiritual path. I am so glad that you are now working with Father O' Donnell. He is a man of deep insight and connection with the divine Presence. Follow his lead. Perhaps at some time in the future you will meet Melissa in this reality, or some other."

Dawson was irritated and perplexed. For twenty years as a CIA officer he had been mission focused. He knew what a mission was. His mission right now was to find Melissa.

"Mother Mary, I appreciate everything you told me, and I would still like to know where Melissa is right now." He said this with as much force as he could muster looking directly at Mother Mary. She seemed totally unfazed by the urgency of his entreaty.

"Mr. Dawson," said Mother Mary, "as you may know, through the beneficence of one of our patrons, the convent grounds are situated on over a thousand acres of land, much of it wilderness, and a portion of which goes up and over the border into Canada. This has a certain convenience. For a good while, Melissa has been living in a hermitage off in the wilderness area. When it became apparent that those seeking to apprehend Melissa were closing in, she simply crossed the border and is now on her way to a safe haven. I'm afraid, for the safety of everyone, that is all I can tell you at this point.

"You see for us, Mr. Dawson, geopolitical boundaries are simply lines on a map, signposts of the status of tribal thinking. They really mean nothing. Immigration is a non-issue for us. We are all God's children. There is just one earth. We know that there is huge resistance to accepting this fundamental reality of life, however, if humankind is going to evolve and avoid destruction, then we all must come to terms with this greater reality."

Dawson could again feel the anger beginning to grow inside of him. Here was this woman telling him that he had spent the last twenty years risking his life for something that was just imaginary lines on a map, that he was not a patriot defending his country. Before he could respond, she continued.

"Brother Issac," said Mother Mary, referring to him by his new order name, that he was not even aware she knew, "I have not meant to offend you. I am simply trying to help you understand the worldview of the woman you are trying to find. I am suggesting to you that your chances of finding her are going to be much greater if you give your own perspective a chance to broaden."

Mother Mary got up from her chair as if to indicate that their conversation had reached the point where movement in thought would only follow movement of the body.

"Let's go see how that young man you brought with you and his dog are faring with the sisters," she said with a twinkle in her eye.

As they left the room where they had been talking and walked down the hallway toward the refectory, the volume of noise coming from the other end of the hall got increasingly louder.

When they entered the dining room, Sister Theresa was sitting on the floor next to Man. Scattered around them, also sitting on the floor, were eight or ten other sisters, all of whom looked remarkably young to Dawson. In the middle of the circle with Sister Theresa and Man was Ooljee. Dawson stopped to observe. They were playing some kind of game. He couldn't quite figure out what it was. It seemed crazy to him, although it looked like a giant Ouija board tableau. One of the young sisters would ask a question and then Man would whisper it to Ooljee in Navajo and then Ooljee would in some manner act out the answer. When the answers came the girls would break out in riotous laughter. After two more rounds it became apparent to Dawson that the young girls' questions had something to do with sex. Exactly what, he was not sure. Clearly, the subject matter was what led to the excited spontaneous laughter.

Just then, Mother Mary, who had been standing in the back of the room with Dawson, cleared her throat. The young women looked up immediately.

"Sisters, thank you so much for welcoming Manuelito and his dog to our home. It is now time to finish up the chores so that we can all be in the chapel in thirty minutes for our mid-morning prayers." She turned to Dawson.

"Brother Isaac, you and Manuelito and Ooljee are welcome to visit with us for a few days if you would like. Sister Theresa will show you where you can sleep and provide you with a schedule. We encourage visitors to participate with us in our practices of work, prayer and, yes, even a bit of silence."

Dawson knew that what he wanted most was to get out of there as quickly as possible. His conversation with Mother Mary left him quite uneasy. He came to find Melissa and had been told that if he wished to find Melissa, he needed to do a better job first of finding himself.

He turned and saw Sister Theresa standing before him ready to show him to the guest quarters. Struck by the sight of her, he hesitated. He remembered one time in college, as a non-credit course, he took a photography class with an instructor from France. A young model posed for the students. She was relatively plain looking. However, by the time the instructor placed the lighting in its proper place around her, she was extraordinarily beautiful. Maybe, Sister Theresa was a rather ordinary looking young woman. Except to Dawson, she was illuminated by an inner light and was startlingly beautiful. He turned and nodded to Mother Mary and followed Sister Theresa out of the room and down the hallway.

CHAPTER 20

Blaine and Aasia were at the Turkish café deep in conversation when suddenly Rat burst through the door. He started to talk, then stopped. Then he started again to speak. Blaine laughed. She was not used to seeing Rat confused.

"I have some good news. Or, maybe bad news." Rat looked at Blaine perplexed. "Well, I'm not sure what it is. For me as a hacker, whenever we help anyone escape from the stealthy, manipulative hands of the State, we are elated. However, I don't know how you will feel about this, Blaine. We got Melissa out. She left Canada a few hours ago and should be arriving in Iceland shortly. I think we will be able to take care of her there. Iceland is a hotbed of hackers. Either you stay up all night and drink or you find something to do on the computer. Anyway, I've got a good buddy in Iceland who should be able to help Melissa. At least, I think he's in Iceland. He operates out of a proxy in Eastern Europe but he is always making jokes about reindeer and stuff like that."

Rat was rambling on, and at the same time he was paying close attention to Blaine. He didn't want to make a love triangle into a square. All he knew for sure was that whatever Blaine wanted in this situation would be what he wanted too.

Blaine sat digesting the information. She was not, as she might have been in the past, either frozen in anxiety or triggered into rage. She was simply allowing things to sink in. Aasia was watching her just as closely as Rat.

Blaine could feel herself starting to react in an old defensive way. And she could also feel herself soften. Maybe it was being with Rat and Aasia. Maybe it was assimilating something from all the research she had done for Professor Gallagher that reflected an Enneagram template in Jesus' teachings of transformation. Finally Blaine said, "Melissa may be my enemy when it comes to Will Dawson, however, she may become a friend for other reasons. This is new work for me holding the possibility of two different outcomes at the same time. Good work, Rat."

"Oh, one thing I forgot," said Rat, "she did not tell me this directly because I have not directly communicated with her. However, she did provide a message inviting you and Aasia to meet with her some place later after she leaves Iceland. She didn't say exactly why, just implied it was some sort of sisterhood thing."

Blaine began to frown. Then her face began to relax and she started to smile. "You know," she said, looking at Aasia, "this is a strange thought at first, however, the more I consider it, the more possibility it seems to have. I think we may need to go see Melissa. It could be that the next level of healing will come about in visiting with her. Do you think you might want to go?"

Aasia pondered the question. Finally she replied. "I am not sure what I want to do. I am tired of being in Germany. Yes, I know it is a refuge. I could not have done without this place to escape to. But, somehow I need to move on. Being with you, Blaine, has been the most important thing in my life since I got out of the hospital after first coming to Germany. Something is still missing. I don't mean missing in our friendship. I mean missing in me. I feel I have to travel to find what the missing piece is, even though I know it is inside of me and not out there somewhere."

Blaine nodded and put her arm around her friend.

Rat let Blaine and Aasia off at the airport in Berlin. Both women were nervous. Blaine still hated going through immigration and customs. Despite all the growth in recent months, she still feared someone finding out who she really was. Aasia had agreed to go with Blaine to meet Melissa in one of those rare moments when she was feeling self-confident. Now she was not so sure. Aasia knew nothing about Melissa, and she had had her fill of therapists and other so-called helping professionals. Sweden lay ahead. Each woman traveled with her own ambiguous feelings and a sense of both danger and opportunity in what might lie ahead. Whether they knew it or not, the two friends were ready.

CHAPTER 21

Officer Walker leaned across Officer Norris, who was seated next to the window, to get a better look at the sheer, jagged peaks of the Andes as the commercial jetliner made its descent into Santiago, Chile. The tallest peaks were still covered with snow even though summer was beginning. Officer Walker pulled himself back upright in his own seat. The South American continent looked more rugged than he ever imagined. Not only did the mountain peaks look razor-sharp, there was a primitiveness about the landscape that grabbed him. He had been a little uneasy about this assignment from the start, and he began to feel an old churning in the pit of his stomach.

Soon the plane was below the mountain peaks as it made its final descent for landing. Although the Santiago airport is a good distance from the center of the city, in no time they had their gear and were headed toward the Grand Hyatt on Kennedy Avenue where they would overnight before the last leg of their air journey. Tomorrow they would be in Ushuaia, Argentina, where they would catch a research ship to Antarctica.

The trip to Ushuaia would be longer than Officer Walker had initially expected. The flight was over four hours. He had encountered this problem before, of under-estimating vertical distances on a map. A vertical map distance never appears quite as long as a horizontal distance of the same length. He was glad for the extra time from a longer than expected flight. He needed to spend more time boning up on his cover story.

Their destination was Palmer Station on Anvers Island on the Antarctica Peninsula. To get there they would catch a boat in Ushuaia and proceed down the Beagle Channel that separated Argentina from Chile in the scattering of islands off the southern tip of South America. The real fun would come when they got out past Cape Horn into the Drake Passage. It is a 500-mile crossing of some of the potentially most turbulent water on the globe. Officer Walker was used to benefiting from worrying about things in advance, but there was nothing he could do by worrying now about their crossing. He opened his briefcase and began again to study the details of his cover. Supposedly they were coming to the Palmer Station to study the Ross seal. Walker began to read the background report.

The history of the mammal population in Antarctica is a classic example of the delicate balance of ecosystems the world over. A variety of seals thrive on the icy continent because of the rich aquatic menu available for them. The fur seal was what originally brought human predators to Antarctica. The Antarctica fur seal population was being totally decimated in the late 1800s, but recovered to a relatively stable level by the 1950s. More recently there have been significant increases in the fur seal population. These dramatic increases may be due in part to the fact that there is now less sea ice and more open water. This species of seal is a canary in the coal mine in the context of global warming. Because fur seals spend their winters not on ice, but primarily in the water, their recent population growth correlates with a warming trend as their habitat increases with ice melt. Even now, there is so much ice in Antarctica that if global warming were to cause the Antarctica ice cap to melt completely, sea levels worldwide would rise by approximately 330 feet.

There has also been a significant increase in the number of crabeater seals. The name is a misnomer. Crabeater seals do not eat crabs but krill, the small shrimp-like creature which is one of the vital links in converting plankton into food for Antarctica whales, walruses, penguins and seals. The increase in the population of the crabeater seals is probably due to the continuing decrease in the whale population. In Antarctica, blue whales feed almost entirely upon krill and a large blue whale may eat as much as four tons of these tiny animals a day. With much of the Antarctic whale population reduced by commercial harvesting, there is more krill available for the crabeater seals and their population has been increasing.

The southern elephant seal has also made a comeback in recent years. This is the largest seal species in the world. These creatures are even bigger than the walrus. The male can weigh as much as four tons. Before international restrictions reduced their human predators, elephant seals were killed and their fat reduced to provide as much as a hundred pounds of high quality oil per seal.

While much is known about most of the seals that inhabit Antarctica, little is known about the Ross seal. This solitary animal is rarely seen because it inhabits thick, treacherous ice packs along the edge of the Antarctica continent. The species was discovered by the British explorer Sir James Ross during an expedition he led to Antarctica in the late 1830s and early 1840s. Their incisors and canine teeth are sharp and curved for catching squid, which is their main source of food. Their breeding habits are unknown.

Walker kept looking at his briefing papers for some explanation of why the research they would supposedly be engaged in on the Ross seal was important. Apparently this information vital to their cover had been overlooked. He also needed to catch up on the research being done at the Palmer Station. Walker knew that ozone was found in significant amounts in the stratosphere around the globe, and that it was important because it shielded the Earth from solar ultraviolet radiation. Atmospheric studies at both polar regions have shown that there are vortices at the poles during the coldest months.

Studies at the Palmer Station showed that increases in ultraviolet radiation in Antarctica had caused the hole in the ozone to become larger. The hole formed in the ozone above Antarctica was now about the size of an area equal to the continental United States. As a result, the level of photosynthesis in plankton, the vital food for krill, was significantly reduced.

While the enlarged ozone hole was apparently not healthy for life in Antarctica or the rest of the planet, secret research was being done at the Palmer Station seeking to utilize the opening in the atmosphere for experimenting with vortices and with certain types of lasers using the energy of the vortices. The U.S. military was hoping that these experiments would lead to new weapons which could destroy the satellite communications of other countries during a time of war.

Hell, thought Walker, one man's ozone hole is another guy's gold mine.

These experiments were highly classified because of the underlying legal structure governing Antarctica. Antarctica is historically claimed by seven countries. Under a treaty ratified in the 1950s these territorial claims are all held in abeyance, and the continent is governed by a collaborative mechanism set up by the treaty. Probably the only reason that the treaty was successfully implemented—with land claims being held in abeyance—was because neither Russia nor the United States had any such claims. The treaty mechanism requires that Antarctica will not be used militarily and will be nuclear-free. To comply with the treaty, the United States dismantled its nuclear station at McMurdo Bay, which was developed to provide electricity there. The success of the nuclear disarmament and verification process in Antarctica was the precedent that led to the later adoption of the SALT treaties by the United States and the former Soviet Union.

The type of governance established for Antarctica is in tune with the ideas of many native peoples, who believe the land belongs to no one. For traditional countries, based on land sovereignty, the governance of Antarctica represents a special form of collaboration and unique innovation by humankind.

Walker put down his briefing papers and elbowed Officer Norris dozing next to him. Norris, as usual, was inattentive to beefing up on the background story. Norris had the extraordinary ability

THE END OF DEMOCRACY

to be totally present in any situation, particularly in emergency situations; however, he never seemed to do anything to help prepare himself to know how to act. He simply showed up ready and his actions always seemed to unfold appropriately. Walker did not appreciate his buddy's seemingly chronic inability to prepare the back story for a mission.

"Huh, what is it?" asked Norris, obviously irritated at having his nap interrupted.

"Oh, nothing really," said Walker, pleased to have interrupted his buddy's siesta. "I just wondered what you thought of this cover story and what you are going to tell these guys at the Palmer Station about your expertise in studying Ross seals?"

Norris looked at Walker. The two men had known each other for at least fifteen years as fellow Company officers. Over the years, they had often been assigned together to work cases. This was the first time they had received such an intimate assignment. They would be spending many days together out on the ice with no one else around.

Norris looked at Walker. Norris was not someone to pussyfoot about, with Walker, or anyone else. "I think I'll tell them that when I was getting my Ph.D., some asshole kept waking me up, so in my sleep-deprived state, I never really learned anything. Anything else on your mind?"

Walker stared back at Norris. He realized their time together could be a long time or a short time. Which it was would depend on their ability to work together, not so much on a professional basis, which he was sure they could handle well, but on a personal basis. No point getting off to a bad start. "Sorry old buddy," said Walker. "I guess I was just getting a little anxious about the holes in this cover story we've got."

"Yeah," said Norris, "those guys back at Langley never do really get the whole picture. Here's the way I usually handle it: I just try to ask more questions about what the person asking me questions is doing, than giving answers to questions about what we're up to. It works about eighty percent of the time. If I get some really curious bastard, I usually just aggravate him enough so he spends more time fuming about what a jerk I am than worrying about what I'm up to."

Walker had to admire Norris. Walker tried to stay ahead of trouble by figuring out in advance where the land mines were. Norris never worried about what might happen. He was just good at sizing people up and figuring out how to work around them in the moment. Maybe this was the reason the two had been given this assignment together, and the guys at Langley were not all melon heads after all. Perhaps they would make a good team.

"You are right," said Walker, "sounds like a perfect way to play it. Sorry I interrupted your nap. Looks like we'll be touching down in Ushuaia shortly."

Norris nodded in acceptance of the apology. They both glanced out of the window. They were descending rapidly and all they could see was water. Just as they were about to touch down, land seemed to appear out of nowhere. They taxied down a runway just a stone's throw from the water's edge.

CHAPTER 22

It seemed impossible that a month could have gone by since his last visit. However, here Godfrey was, heading back up the walkway to the entrance to Father Hay's office.

"Good morning," said Godfrey to Father Hay, "It's good to see you again."

Father Hay took a long moment to take in Godfrey's presence. "It is good to see you too," said Father Hay. In that moment Father Hay assessed Godfrey's energy and determined that his spiritual directee was doing much better than he had been doing at their last meeting.

"You know," said Father Hay, "a lot of people, both in the therapeutic world and the world of spiritual direction, think that it is inappropriate to spend much time talking about our search for meaning in ideas. This is a reaction to the overly intellectual pursuit of meaning that has characterized Western culture for the past 200 years. Well, really since the time of Descartes. My view is you don't throw out the baby with the bath water. While it's next to impossible to access wisdom with just one of the three centers of intelligence, I think it is very important for us Westerners to pursue our intellectual journey to the point where we can let go of it. In other words, information itself is not the enemy. Rather, it is our attempt to process life just through our mental faculties that is the problem. Was the exploration in our last session helpful, when we looked at how the fundamental growth processes of gender identification and projection have distorted an authentic understanding of the Christian message?"

Godfrey loved the fact that even though he had not seen his spiritual director for a month, they were immediately connected right back to the vital threads of their last discussion and time together. He could feel himself begin to relax inside.

Yes," said Godfrey, "it was a great help for me to begin to understand how the distortions of the Christian message have emerged over the past 2,000 years. I guess I still have real problems with what the Christian message really is. Fortunately, I am not all tied up in knots worrying about trying to figure that out. The compulsion to have to know in order to feel okay has subsided. I still have a lot of curiosity, but I am not as entangled as I was in the anxiety of uncertainty. And the good news on the home front is that I am not so reactive to questions from Jeff about this spiritual experience that I am living through."

"Curiosity is good," said Father Hay. "Even a certain amount of anxiety is not necessarily a bad thing. What we don't want to have happen is for the anxiety to be at such a level that it overwhelms us. We always have something to surrender on this journey and it is good to practice surrendering our low-level anxiety on a daily basis. Sometimes an intellectual map of the terrain of the spiritual journey is helpful to us so that our big emotional blocks to moving deeper in our journey can soften."

"So what will it be, Godfrey," said Father Hay, "is there some spiritual or emotional disconnect in your life right now we should pursue or do you want us to have a more discursive conversation about what Jesus' message really was?"

"Well, I'm not sure," said Godfrey. "I understand what you're saying about not developing an over-reliance on mental intelligence as a way of knowing. I know I have a tendency to want to figure out everything so I will feel comfortable. I would like to explore Christian theology in more depth with you. Is there a way we can do that without reinforcing my tendency to want some kind of intellectual certainty?"

"Absolutely," said Father Hay. "We just need to be attentive to your somatic and emotional experience as we talk about these ideas. The truth is that theology is not just a mental subject. We can encounter theology on a somatic level and emotional level also. So as our discussion progresses please pay particular attention to what is happening in your body and what feelings you might be having. This way, we can keep our discussion on track to provide us some wisdom rather than simply reinforce your over-reliance on your mental faculties as a way to feel less anxious in this world. Does that sound okay to you?"

"That sounds great," said Godfrey.

"Okay," said Father Hay, "take a moment to get in touch with yourself inside and tell me where you would like to start."

Godfrey took a deep breath and let out a long exhale. He relaxed. "What is coming up for me is what we talked about a good bit last time, and that is this idea that Jesus was the scapegoat, sent as a sacrifice to provide us with a heavenly afterlife."

"You are getting to one of the core distortions," said Father Hay. "This was not the belief for early Christians. Jesus was not seen as the savior for a future life, but rather the life-giver for the present life. For the focus of salvation to be about something in the future, there has to be something wrong with the present. What the church has presented as wrong with the present has had more to do with the distortions of a monastic celibacy system, that repressed the expression of normal male sexuality, than Jesus' message. The repression of the feminine caused by the celibate monastic tradition created a perception that humankind was basically evil. Do you follow that Godfrey—if humankind is evil then something is wrong with the present?"

Godfrey nodded.

"There is a long history of the repression of healthy human sexuality that started with Paul and continued later with people like St. Augustine of Hippo, which led to the development of a theology, which has been maintained by the church for centuries and is totally at cross-purposes with Jesus' actual message.

"Let's get to what Jesus' message really was about. What he brought to humankind was a path to freedom. An inner freedom that only occurs with a shift in consciousness. So despite centuries of distortion by the church, the true message Jesus brought is still right there in the Gospels. Regardless of what you might choose to believe or not believe about Jesus, the primary task of the Christian is not to get to some particular theological belief, but rather to put on the mind and heart of Christ. Christ being the term that is used to distinguish between the human person Jesus, and the state of consciousness he achieved, and which he came to show is accessible to us all. Jesus' ministry on earth is really about understanding the path that he walked to achieve this state of consciousness and the guidance which he provides to us on how we too can walk that path. In fact, Godfrey, you are on that path right now. How do you experience the reality of being on that path in this moment?"

There was a long pause. Godfrey smiled slightly. "When you say it like that, I feel this warmth in my chest."

Father Hay nodded. Then he continued. "One of the things that jumps out at any student of Jesus' message is his constant referrals to the Kingdom of Heaven. He often says the Kingdom of Heaven is like a certain thing. And most important, he says the Kingdom of Heaven is within you. And that the Kingdom of Heaven is at hand. It is not that you die to get there, as some church teaching would suggest, but rather you wake up to arrive there. The Kingdom of Heaven is a shift in perspective brought about by a change in consciousness. This change in consciousness is what we talk about nowadays as 'non-dual consciousness' or 'unitive consciousness.'

"The most salient characteristic of this consciousness is that it perceives both the duality of our existence and our unity with all matter and energy at the same time. Jesus speaks of this in the Gospel of John in a beautiful way: 'I am the vine, you are the branches.' 'Abide in me as I abide in you.' These are very non-dual expressions of the idea that we are extensions of the divine and we are not the divine. There is a mutual reciprocity, a mutual indwelling, if you will. This flowing one into the other is a dynamic process, and this dynamic process is what Christians call love. This is the fundamental characteristic of the Christian religion. Its purest form is revealed in the interactions of Jesus' life, what he lived in those interactions was love—not as a noun, but rather as a verb, a process. Christianity is a religion of the process of unfolding love. This means any time you try to concretize Christianity in certain beliefs or rituals you commit idolatry."

Father Hay's face reddened and his hands moved back and forth through the air. "This means, in addition to sounding wonderful, that Christianity is a religion of dynamic relational interaction. It is not a religion of regret about the past or a religion of the future, but about living in the present and being present in our living. We, like the rest of the universe, are in an organic, dynamic relationship with God and with all life and matter, which is held together by God's love, which is also in us.

"In unitive consciousness there is both separation from God and no separation from God. There is both separation from other people and no separation from other people. The energy which allows for both separation and no separation at the same time is this dynamic flow called love. It is a little bit like Heisenberg's theory of uncertainty. From one particular viewpoint a particle can seem to have a positive charge, from another viewpoint it has a negative charge. From one point of view we are separate and from another point of view we are united. This is a dynamic process. The charge, if you will, the flow, is the process of love.

"Let me give you an example. One of the most recognized teachings of Jesus is 'Love your neighbor as yourself.' We usually hear this message in a dualistic way. We here: 'Love your neighbor, as much as yourself.' This is not what Jesus said. Loving your neighbor as yourself is his teaching about a shift from the dual perspective to the unity of a non-dual perspective. You love your neighbor as yourself because you are not really separate from your neighbor. Loving your neighbor as yourself is an acknowledgment of the unity of being."

"Holy smoke," said Godfrey. "I never had a clue that this was the meaning of Jesus' teaching about loving your neighbor. Always before I saw it as some huge task that the ego was given, which, frankly, I never believed I could ever achieve. For me, this commandment has always been a setup to feel like I'm a failure. You mean it is simply Jesus telling us that we can experience ourselves as connected as well as separate?"

"You got it," said Father Hay. "Not that it is all that easy to get to the place of consciousness where you readily experience that shift in perspective most of the time. Of course, we all experience it from time to time. We all have glimpses of the Kingdom of Heaven when we experience that unity."

"So are you saying that the term 'Kingdom of Heaven,' as Jesus used that term, is really a metaphor for a way we see the world?"

"Yes, a metaphor for our intellectual understanding. And also, not just a metaphor. Experientially when we see with the eye of unitive consciousness, just like Heisenberg's observer shifting perspective, we bring this new unitive reality into existence.

"This is the magic of greater consciousness. It brings into being a greater reality. It is a little bit like the old teaching story: if a tree falls in the forest, and no one is there to hear it, is there any sound? If you are in a place of unitive consciousness you both see the tree fall with no sound and you hear the sound."

There was a long pause. The two men sat in silence. Godfrey let Father Hay's explanations seep into his body and heart.

"Okay," said Godfrey, "I think you're on a roll. Keep going."

Father Hay looked at Godfrey for a moment. He wasn't about to let his directee off too easily. "Well," said Father Hay, "as you sit there just in this moment, tell me what else bothers you."

Godfrey thought for a moment. Then he said, "What is still bothering me is I don't understand the role of Christianity. All this stuff about unity of consciousness sounds like it could be any of the world's great religions. Why am I bothering with trying to be a Christian? Wouldn't it be better to be a Unitarian Universalist or a Buddhist? At least other people seem to like these folks better than they like Christians." He grinned.

Father Hay smiled inwardly. He was not at all disappointed with his student. He had tossed the ball to him, and, sure enough, Godfrey had hit a line drive right over the head of the second baseman.

"Yes, here's where many people get tripped up these days," said Father Hay. "Christianity seems so encrusted with old barnacles, that almost any other world religion seems a safer path. However,

Christianity never has been a particularly safe path. A religion of love is a radical departure. Prior to the time of Christ, the Greeks had experimented with first, on the one hand, Epicureanism, that is, just trying to enjoy everything in the moment as much as possible; and, on the other, Stoicism, that is, not trying to get too involved with life. Both of these Greek efforts were trying to deal with the problem that the Buddha sought to address, which was how do you experience life without getting caught up in attractions or aversions that cause suffering? Neither of the Greek paths seemed to work. The Epicureans were too caught up in their attractions and therefore suffered greatly. The Stoics were not sufficiently involved in life to have any joy. The Buddha found a solution of non-attachment to both the things you want in life and the things you seek to avoid. The Buddha did not suggest that one be withdrawn from life like the Stoics, rather that we be actively engaged in life, just not become attached to the people, ideas or institutions we are attracted to, nor attached to avoiding suffering, loss and other things which are aversions.

"Basically when Jesus came along he continued to build on this developing consciousness that Buddha had outlined. He advocated non-attachment to desires and non-attachment to aversions. You can see this in his teachings about being 'in the world, but not of the world'.

"The Buddhist approach can also be a pathway to non-dual consciousness, particularly when the focus is on such Buddhist practices as meditation. However, this was not the path that Jesus came to live and teach. His path was much more radical. Rather than just seeking to achieve a state of emptiness as the Buddhist path suggests, Jesus believed that underneath the emptiness found in Buddhist meditation, or Christian centering prayer, is this huge fullness which is love, and that the expression of the energy of this love and living in this dynamic of unfolding energy from God is the pathway to unitive consciousness."

"Wow, this is really exciting," said Godfrey. "I had always seen different philosophies and religions as being in competition, not as steps in an unfolding mosaic of humankind's evolution of consciousness."

"Thus, while the Buddhist path recommends non-attachment as a way to achieve emptiness, the Christian path goes one step beyond that and asks us to get in touch with the fullness, beneath the emptiness, and to live that fullness not from our ego, which would be attachment, but from that part of our essence which is connected to God.

"It may be that from Heisenberg's perspective the Buddhist path is a negative charge and the Christian path is a positive charge and that they both are part of the same energy. I don't know, Godfrey." Father Hay paused.

"It may be that the Buddhist path is simply the yin path, and the Christian path is the yang path, the path of action. Like I said, I don't know. I think there is more unity here than just two paths. I think the dynamic of love, whether it is receptive love or assertive love, is the energy field that holds the universe together. We get to decide whether we wish to seek to develop our consciousness so we can participate fully in that love flow or not."

"So how are you feeling in your body right now, Godfrey," asked Father Hay.

"Anxious, excited and uncertain. All kind of knotted up in my stomach," said Godfrey.

"Good, we are making serious progress."

CHAPTER 23

Walker awoke to the strange sound of metal and wood tensing and releasing. Then he immediately noticed the rocking motion. Light filtered through the drawn blinds over his porthole. On the other bunk Norris was snoring lightly. They had been at sea now a little over twelve hours and were about 200 miles south of Cape Horn in the Drake Passage. He lay in his bunk absorbing the rolling motion of the ocean. Not too bad, he thought.

He rolled over and put his feet on the floor. Well, on second thought, maybe not so good. He stood. He immediately realized that the more vertical he was, the more he seemed to be affected by the motion of the ship. He took three steps from his bunk and reached the bathroom. He stepped inside and looked into his toilet kit for the meclizine, which he had been given at the start of the trip for seasickness. He tore open an individually sealed packet and popped one pill. He hated being drowsy instead of being alert, but for the moment this seemed to be the best alternative. His seasickness threw off his focus anyway. He came back and fell into his bunk. Norris had not awoken. Soon Walker was asleep again.

*   *   *

THE END OF DEMOCRACY

Walker eased out of his bunk. He glanced across the cabin. Norris was gone. The movement in the ship had shifted significantly. He started to stand up, and the roll of the ocean sat him back down. Gingerly he pulled on his trousers and got dressed.

Walker eventually found Norris outside leaning against the railing on the starboard side near the bow. He seemed unfazed by the weather and the rolling of the ship. He was staring out at a wandering albatross dancing atop the lift from the waves.

"Norris," said Walker, "it seems to have gotten a little rough out here."

"Oh, it's not bad," said Norris. "We are not yet past the convergence. After that we will be in colder water and perhaps there will be a little more action then. How are you doing anyway, Sleepyhead?"

"Not that bad," said Walker, "I just cannot seem to get un-sleepy."

"Yeah, I know what you mean," said Norris. However, he seemed oblivious to the rolling seas and the kind of effect that they were having on his buddy.

Norris continued. "Yes, it is a good thing to see that albatross. You know, the albatross represents the soul of a dead sailor. In the kind of work we've got to do, it might not be a bad thing if we have guidance from someone who has gone before. Not like we're going to die," said Norris continuing in a talkative mood.

"However, there is some connection between death and this search for another level of consciousness that we have been tasked with. Maybe we really do need a hand from someone who's been to the other side. Do you know what I mean?"

Not really, thought Walker, suddenly feeling that the subject had turned serious. He moved to where he was beside Norris facing out along the railing. Maybe Norris was on to something. Maybe he has a better idea than I do why we are here. I could reply flippantly that what we're doing is for the birds, but then again given what Norris is saying about the albatross that might be the most serious thought I've had all day.

Norris looked at Walker for a long moment without speaking, waiting for Walker to reply. Walker continued to ruminate without speaking. Finally, Norris shifted his stance as if he were about to bring the conversation to a conclusion.

Then Norris pointed out to sea. "See that tiny little bird," said Norris. Walker peered out over the vast surface of the ocean and looked and looked. He was just about to give up when he spotted a little bird dancing on the water.

"Yes, finally, I see it," said Walker.

"A storm petrel," said Norris. "The name comes from St. Peter in the Bible. Notice how it faces into the wind with outstretched wings and appears to walk on the water. While it is doing this, it is also picking up tiny crustaceans and plankton-like organisms. An incredible little bird, out here hundreds of miles from shore."

Walker shook his head in amazement at the tiny dancing bird.

"Yeah, before this thing is finished," said Norris, "we may have to take a lesson from this little bird. I expect if we are going to succeed in this operation, we may both have to walk on water."

Just then there was a thud underneath the ship. The bottom of the boat, having lifted out of the water, had dropped down against a swell. It sounded for all the world as if a giant had swung a telephone-pole-size club against the boat's backsides. A chill went through Walker and he shuddered in the cold. Norris smiled.

CHAPTER 24

Will Dawson, Man and Ooljee had a long, hard trip. The van broke down twice on the way back from Minnesota. The first time, Man volunteered to hitchhike into town to get help. It was not like being on the rez, and no one picked him and Ooljee up. So Man and Ooljee spent all morning and part of the afternoon walking all the way into town. When they finally found a garage with a tow truck, the owner was unwilling to even consider sending out his tow truck at the request of an Indian teenager.

Finally Man got the tow truck owner to bet with him. The wager was that if Ooljee could count to ten successfully then the tow truck owner would send a tow truck out. If Ooljee failed to count correctly, then Man would go away and stop bothering the tow truck owner. It was a setup by Man. He gave Ooljee commands either in Navajo or by a slight gesture of his hand, and Ooljee obediently scratched his paw in the dirt however number of times Man instructed.

By the time Ooljee had gotten to eight, the man started laughing and told Man to get in the truck. The van was towed into the garage. Fortunately, Father O'Donnell had given Dawson some cash just in case such an emergency arose. The vehicle was up and running again by the next morning with a repaired transmission and the threesome took off again.

Later, halfway through Colorado, they had a problem with the van overheating. This time they were a little wiser about the situation, and Dawson hitchhiked into town while Man and Ooljee hung out by the vehicle on the side of the road. The radiator leak was repaired by pouring some viscous fluid into the radiator. Dawson wondered how the radiator could even function after that kind of cure, but it did the job well enough to get them back to the Four Corners area and to the monastery.

The long drive was made even more challenging for Dawson because he was unable to get Sister Theresa out of his mind the entire way back. He was sure that by the time he saw Father O'Donnell again he would have to tell him that his chances of successfully being a monk were close to nil.

When they got back to the monastery, they discovered that Father O'Donnell was still up the mountain in his hermitage. Dawson was disappointed that he could not speak with Father O'Donnell immediately. He was unsure of how he should proceed now that Melissa had escaped to Canada, and this uncertainty caused him great anxiety.

Dawson promptly volunteered to handle the next scheduled supply-run shift up the mountain to Father O'Donnell. Five days later Dawson hauled a loaded backpack onto the ATV and Brother Will dropped him and the backpack off at the foot of the steep mountain trail.

It was still cool at the beginning of the ascent. By the time he had been climbing for an hour, Dawson was soaked. He had not wanted to bring a lot of drinking water for the climb, because he was already loaded down. Still, he was glad he had two full water bottles.

A little past eleven o'clock, he finally reached the upper ledge of the mountain where Father O'Donnell's hermitage was. Father O'Donnell had seen him coming and had water heating on the propane stove.

"Welcome, Brother Isaac," said Father O'Donnell. Dawson was too winded to do anything except nod. Father O'Donnell indicated a seat on a rock opposite his own customary spot and gave Dawson a cup of strong Irish tea. Dawson gratefully sat and sipped it.

Finally, Father O'Donnell began their conversation. "Brother Isaac, it is good to see you." Dawson looked at the priest. There was a light in Father O'Donnell's eyes. Dawson thought this a good sign. It appeared Father O'Donnell's time in his hermitage was renewing and hopefully that meant he would come back down from the mountain before too long.

"Father," said Brother Isaac, "it sure is good to see you. I have been anxious to report in to you on the trip and to get your advice on what I should do next."

"I have heard from Mother Mary that you had a good trip. Oh, I know you didn't find Melissa, however, Mother Mary was very impressed that you stayed there visiting the convent for almost a week."

"Uh, well yes, it did turn out we stayed longer than I had expected to," said Dawson, a bit nonplussed that there was any way in the world that Father O'Donnell could've heard from Mother Mary up here in his hermitage. "Well, you know," said Dawson fidgeting, "it was a chance for me to learn a little bit more about this monastic life thing from the women's side. I have got to tell you I think the women are having more fun."

"You do, do you?" said Father O'Donnell, "very interesting. Tell me more about that."

"They have the same kind of pattern that we have here: work, prayer and silence; and they also just seem to have more fun. I don't know exactly why or what it is, but that was my impression."

Father O'Donnell sat looking at Dawson and simply nodded.

Dawson hurried on, his anxiety to unburden himself obvious. "I mean, I met this one sister, Sister Theresa, and she just seemed happy all the time. I don't know what it was. I couldn't get enough of her. I mean hanging around her."

"Tell me, what did you notice about her?" asked Father O'Donnell, not about to let the impact of this obviously significant meeting go unaddressed.

"I have thought about this a lot on the drive back. I'm not sure what it was, there was simply a quality of lightness about her." Having gotten this far in talking about Sister Theresa in Father O'Donnell's non-judgmental presence, Dawson began to relax.

"She seemed very open, but not in the way of some people who just regurgitate all their emotional stuff whether they know you or not. I just felt strangely warm when I was around her. She had a sense of serenity and calmness about her, and she was very lively at the same time."

Father O'Donnell nodded again.

"The truth of it is, I felt this huge attraction to her. You know, Father, I don't mean to be crass—I wanted to get her in bed. The instinctive urge to mate with her was so strong it scared me, and at the same time I was delighted to be experiencing it. In fact, I can't get enough of desiring this woman. Looks like I'm not all that much of a monk."

"Brother Isaac, it is the desire to love another that may make your being a monk possible. Don't give it short shrift and keep your pants on." Father O'Donnell paused.

"This may be hard for you to understand, Brother Isaac. Your sexual longing is one of the most important energy sources for your spiritual journey. You are not advanced enough in your training here to know exactly how to use this energy. For the time being, just be thankful you have it."

"I'm not sure what you're talking about," said Dawson, "however, if you'd like me to go back up to Minnesota to see Sister Theresa again, I would be more than happy to do that."

"What would you do if I did send you back up to Minnesota?" asked Father O'Donnell with a smile that crinkled all around his

THE END OF DEMOCRACY

eyes.

This seemingly innocent question from his mentor totally floored Dawson. He had no idea what he would do. In all the years of his life he had never been able to follow through on an *eros* urge to find a place in his heart from which to pursue a woman. He was now in the middle of his life and more confused than a fifteen-year-old. He had no idea what the answer to Father 'Donnell's question was.

"Great question," said Dawson, "I have to admit I don't have any idea. I guess I would just hang around and see what happened."

Father O'Donnell began to laugh in great big guffaws. He had sprung the learning trap on Dawson, and Dawson had fallen in, right up to his eyebrows.

"You have this desire for this woman," said Father O'Donnell, "and you would just hang around?"

Dawson could feel himself starting to get angry. It was anger at himself, but all he could sense was that Father O'Donnell seemed to be causing it. Yet he was in this bind because anger at Father O'Donnell was not something he would allow himself to feel. Dawson got up and kicked at a small rock and sent it skittering over the rock ledge. "Okay, okay! I don't know what I would do. I don't know what I have been supposed to do most of my life. I don't really know why I went to work for the Company, or why I got married or even why I got divorced. I have lived half of my life probably and I just don't have a clue. I know it's pitiful, Father, I'm just trying to be as honest with you as I can."

"Your honesty is appreciated," said Father O'Donnell, "and it doesn't get us too far. We will need to step up your awareness practices once I get back down to the monastery."

"Yes, I have been meaning to also ask you about that," said Dawson. "When do you expect to be back down the mountain?"

"Things have been going rather well." Father O'Donnell's light blue eyes seeming to go from a twinkle to a blaze. "But I don't conduct my hermitage time based on how subjectively well things seem to be going. No, I always do at least forty days. So it will be another ten days before I come down. Why do you ask?"

"What should I do?" said Dawson. "Do I continue to act like I'm a young monk in my 20s, when I'm not, and just stumble along here not knowing really why I'm here, or do I go back up to try to see Sister Theresa? Or, do I take some action to try to figure out what I might do to help Melissa? Or, even if I should try to find her?"

Father O'Donnell felt compassion for Dawson. Compassion in the spiritual world is not soft and mushy, it is tough. Not tough in the sense that one often thinks of assertive masculine energy as tough, but tough in the disciplined way Father O'Donnell knew a novice must be pushed to see reality clearly, even when it was painful.

"This place of unknowing you are in is a good place," said Father O'Donnell. "I know it is hard to be there without seemingly having a hand rail to hold on to for the journey. Actually, the handrails are all around you." Father O'Donnell nodded in the direction of the open space beyond the ridge. There, circling high above the valley floor, was a golden eagle. The sun glinted off its feathers.

"When I come down, we will approach this next phase of your spiritual work on two fronts. I want you to get some sense of what it means to love God from that energy that goes down deep in your sexuality. This next week read the Song of Solomon for your *lectio* practice and get Brother Will to give you a book or two of Rumi poems. On the other front, I'll give you some Scripture readings about Mary. Mary is the karate master of receptive energy. She is the model we all try to follow. From her we learn to strengthen our receptive energy, this energy source which is so necessary for our spiritual growth."

Father O'Donnell smiled at Dawson. "I know this is a hard place you're in. However, it is a wonderful place from which to more deeply let go and surrender your need to understand your life. For it is not really your life at all. And it is only by letting go of it that you have any chance to receive some inkling of the abundance that God is offering you. The longer you are able to live consciously in your unknowing without diverting yourself from it, the greater will be the emptiness carved in your soul. So it is time to excavate a little deeper. The deeper you go the more spacious the emptiness becomes that will be filled later. I know this does not exactly make sense to you right now, but if it did, you would simply grasp hold of a little scrap of meaning you thought was there, and that grasping would slow you up. Brother Isaac, you do not have time for that. Nor does Sister Theresa or Melissa or Blaine have time for any such indulgence by you, if any one of them are ever to be meaningfully in your life.

"I have packed up the trash over there," said Father O'Donnell after pausing slightly.

Dawson could tell that he was about to be dismissed. He knew there must be some other question that, if he could ask it, would illuminate his path.

"I guess you better be getting ready to go back down," said Father O'Donnell. "At least your pack will be a good bit lighter. There's not too much trash. I certainly appreciate you taking it with you." With that, Father O'Donnell rose and came over and put his arm on Dawson's shoulders. "Thank you so much for coming up to bring supplies and to visit with me," said Father O'Donnell. "I look forward to continuing our conversation and work together when I get back." With that, Father O'Donnell turned and walked back toward his cabin.

Before he got to the cabin door, Father O'Donnell turned and looked out across the ledge into the awesomely beautiful rugged landscape of the Southwest. He wasn't sure Dawson had the stuff to make the journey. Dawson seemed to be missing the link needed to use his erotic love energy to take him deeper to a place of unknowing. The wounded ego was never a sufficient source of energy for deeper spiritual work.

Father O'Donnell could tell that at the ego level Dawson wanted to make progress. But that, he mused, and three bucks would buy a cup of coffee. Still, the way of the spiritual path at an early stage was to allow the ego's energy to provide the fuel for the practices which diminished the ego's influence. Father O'Donnell remembered some of the mystical images for this phenomenon of a snake or lizard swallowing its own tail, as he gazed down the mountainside at Dawson making his way down the steep trail. Well, considering the man had been in the CIA for twenty years, an institution which thrived on reptilian brain energy and dualistic thinking, Dawson might not be doing so badly after all.

CHAPTER 25

Nobody had ever been able to explain adequately to Blaine and Aasia why this convent had been established so far north in Sweden, of all places. After the first week, Blaine and Aasia were getting used to being in such a cold climate. They were both a little startled when they first realized they would be living in a convent. However, it was a convent like none that Blaine or Aasia could have ever imagined. They had had an intense three weeks so far and the remaining three promised to be just as rigorous.

Their day was scheduled around the three energy centers of intelligence: the mental center, the emotional center and the somatic center. After morning prayers and breakfast, they got instructions on understanding personality theory from a spiritual point of view. They learned the basic theory of the Enneagram and their own particular Enneagram type. It took Blaine a little while to realize she was a counter-phobic six and what that meant for her. After she got it, there was an intense sense of relief to realize that somehow she fit in, in a world where she had always felt she didn't.

Blaine and Aasia learned the nine levels of consciousness that are set forth publicly in teachings about the Enneagram. They also learned that there were three additional levels, taught in esoteric mystery schools, and that they would learn something about these as they progressed.

The second part of each day was devoted to their trauma release work. The two women had very different trauma life experiences. Blaine had grown up in a severely dysfunctional household where she never had any sense of safety. Fear and wondering if she would survive were her earliest emotional memories. Aasia, on the other hand, had grown up in a traditional Muslim home, and within the safety of that home had a very nurturing and loving childhood. Aasia's trauma of rape and torture carried out by the Serbs occurred just as she was becoming a young woman.

While the timing and the type of trauma were different for the two women, the results were similar. Each had adapted to the trauma based on their Enneagram personality type. Blaine, as a counter-phobic six, had developed a level of paranoia that served her well as a computer hacker. Aasia, as an Enneagram three, was an achiever and she had been one in her early years. She had done well in grammar school and as a young healthy girl had felt a bit of pride in her winsome beauty and lovely, long hair. After she was in the Serbian rape camp, she had only felt shame. Her false self's natural tendency to perform and achieve in order to feel okay allowed her to function as a nurse in the emergency room setting of a large Berlin hospital, but always she felt shame beneath the image of competence. What she was learning now was that she had suffered irreparable damage to her false self. Therapy could not give her back a healthy ego structure.

She was one of the unlucky, or perhaps later she might say, lucky ones, who had no alternative. If she were to thrive, she had to learn to lead a life flowing from her essence. In other words, her survival, like many who have found themselves suffering from the chronic illness of alcoholism, depended upon her developing a spiritual life. Some people are just drawn to the spiritual path. Others get a choice of whether they will follow that route. Some, like Aasia, if they are to live, have no choice at all.

During the emotional trauma release work, whenever a memory came up for either Blaine or Aasia, the young sisters would simply arrange themselves around in a circle and allow their energy fields to transmit a palpable feeling of love. Thank goodness there was no therapy. Blaine hated the idea of therapy. Aasia had her fill of it in the German charity refugee system. As the two women were encircled with love and as they surrendered their traumatic emotional memories, slowly but surely each newly revealed trauma layer was peeled away and floated away like a dried leaf in the breeze.

Most of the rest of the day, each day, was spent working on energy practices. They were learning how to control their energy fields. How to be aware when their energy field was contracting and how to open up their energy field; how to expand and contract their assertive energy and how to expand and contract their receptive energy.

The toughest part of the exercises was learning how to open up instead of contracting when a painful memory arose. This part of the exercises was particularly difficult for both women. It was hard for Blaine and Aasia to get somatically in touch with their bodies at the level that their instructors desired without encountering huge emotional energetic knots that somehow needed to be released.

Blaine and Aasia were so glad that these nuns did not try to do talk therapy with them to deal with the almost continual emotional crises that happened every day in the first two weeks, even when they were not specifically doing emotional trauma release work. Whenever Blaine or Aasia would break down, regardless of the circumstances, two or three of the sisters would gather around, and while one of the sisters quietly encouraged her to let go into the pain, the other sisters would direct their warm healing energy directly to her.

At one point Aasia was in constant tears for three days. The young sisters did not seem to be fazed. They simply practiced this process of being totally present with her and acting as conduits for an incredible healing energy. At first it had been hard for Aasia to get past a re-occurring narrative breaking into her thoughts about the atrocities she lived through. It was very difficult for her just to stay with the somatic pain. Once she began to leave the story behind, she began to feel intense anger and rage. In the supportive container of the sisters' energy, her own energy began to move and she began to progress by leaps and bounds.

Blaine also had more than a few days where it seemed like she could not possibly cry anymore. Yet she was gently coaxed to continue to let go, and as her ability to trust increased, so did her ability to receive the healing energies of the sisters around her. For Blaine, the difficulty was her mind. Her mind had been her survival tool. Her mind enabled her to learn how to hack into computers. It literally saved her life. So it was incredibly frightening for her to let go of her mental processing about what had happened to her. Gradually, because of the loving energy she was receiving from the sisters, she began to let go of the need to understand.

For the first week both Blaine and Aasia had self-consciously worn long-sleeved turtlenecks to hide their scars, and for Blaine, also her tattoos. Their bodies were so different from those of the young blonde, blue-eyed women who surrounded them. In the middle of their crying—especially when the other sisters were directing healing energy toward them—it got very hot. At one point, Blaine forgot about her need to conceal the cuts and tattoos on her body, and later that day she realized this part of her story was out of the bag. The sisters didn't seem to be bothered by her revelation. Something similar had happened to Aasia and the ropey scars on her arms had been revealed. After that, both women decided not to worry about the tracks of their pasts cut into their bodies. They were too busy experiencing extraordinary healing, and to them it tasted like fresh spring water after spending years in the desert.

The only time that Blaine and Aasia got a real break from their study and trauma release schedule were the times each day that the sisters were all in the chapel for silent centering prayer. While they participated in all the other activities of the regular convent routine, they had been told by the Mother Superior that they would not be able to do centering prayer until more of their emotional trauma had been released. It would not be helpful to sit in silence until their inner emotional turmoil was taken off the fire of fear and rage. And taking it off the fire was exactly what their work was so intensely about.

It came as an inconsequential thought to Blaine that they had been there for two weeks and still not met Melissa. This was a bit strange since it was Melissa who had invited them to come. At first Blaine wondered if Melissa was even there. Blaine knew that Melissa's escape route plan was for her to travel from Canada to Iceland, and from there to have made her way to Denmark and then to the convent in Sweden.

Part of Blaine, the part of her that still had a longing for Will Dawson, was not so sure she wanted to meet Melissa anyway. When Blaine and Aasia finally met Melissa it was only briefly in a small prayer alcove that was part of the convent chapel. Their short time together was spent by Melissa simply thanking them for coming. After the meeting, Blaine and Aasia had not discussed Melissa, except Aasia had mentioned how amazed she was at the physical resemblance between Melissa and Blaine. In fact, Aasia commented that if Melissa had a few tattoos on her arm, she could easily have been mistaken for Blaine.

Afterwards, Blaine didn't give much thought to wondering why they never saw Melissa again, even though Melissa was the connection that got them there. If she had thought about it, Blaine would have to admit she was just as happy not to spend time with Melissa given that thoughts of Will Dawson still occasionally came to her mind. She and Aasia were both completely focused on the inner work they were being given this incredible opportunity to do. Blaine could tell something was changing in her with this work, something very significant.

At the end of the third week Blaine realized that Aasia had reached a turning point when she began teasing Blaine and, for the first time, Blaine heard Aasia laugh.

CHAPTER 26

Redmon was getting frustrated. It was about time he had a break in this case. Everybody gets sloppy after a while, even former Company officers. So far they had not been able to turn up any trace of Will Dawson or Melissa Dowling. They had broken into Dawson's apartment again, and this time figured out that he'd returned briefly without being detected and then apparently left town. They were going back over all the old aliases that Dawson had used at the Company to see if anything might surface under one of those old names. One of his old passports had turned up in Florida. The guy using it was shady enough, probably a member of one of the thriving eastern European mafia groups working with the Cuban exile mafia in south Florida, and clearly he wasn't Dawson.

Redmon was beginning to feel the heat from upstairs. He was always careful never to forecast what might happen on a project. However, his boss was after him for some facts which would indicate that they were making progress and where things might be going. Redmon had very little news to give him other than that the Shackleton Project had been launched in Antarctica.

One of the promising things about the Antarctica project was that there was a history of success there. Not with a Company operation, but with the Navy, and that counted for something. The Navy had gone to McMurdo in the mid-1950s and established a staging base for the building of a base at the South Pole. Operation Deep Freeze was initiated at the height of the Cold War. The first group of Navy personnel assigned to work on this mission was told that if nuclear war broke out between the United States and the Soviet Union it was highly probable that they would not be relieved for several years, if at all.

Fortunately, the threat of nuclear war with the Soviet Union receded. Cooperation between the United States and the Soviet Union in Antarctica under the Antarctica Treaty became a model that led to the successful conclusion of the SALT talks with Khrushchev. The story was that until the Russian scientists told Khrushchev about their cooperation with American scientists in Antarctica he had been unwilling to proceed with the SALT agreement.

An election was coming up and Redmon knew that the pressure for him to show positive results would only be increasing. The only thing he could do right now was to up the pressure on Melissa's mother. He made a couple phone calls. You didn't have to lock someone in Guantánamo to turn up the psychological heat. The old lady wouldn't be getting much sleep for a while.

He pulled out a cigar from a desk drawer and began to chew on it. There was no smoking in the building, but a little nicotine in the saliva would keep him from thinking of how he might feel if someone at the Company did to his mother what he had just ordered for Melissa's. He didn't want to think about that.

CHAPTER 27

Gordon Slade turned the key in the ignition of his Oldsmobile and his car sputtered to life like an old man with a smoker's cough. He quickly navigated his way from his home in Boston to the interstate and headed north toward Maine. His life had been diverted by having Joy in it. But he was a man who bore a promise like a grudge and he would not let it go. This was a promise that he had made to himself: to go back up to Maine and visit with Peter Wagner and find out exactly why he had been fired on the spur of the moment in Italy. Not that the termination of his job as a private investigator by Peter Wagner had anything to do with Slade's competence. Slade knew it was all about Wagner. However, in his business he liked to keep the loose ends wrapped up and this one was still flapping in the breeze.

He tried to call the lawyer who had initially hired him—indeed begged him—to take the job for Peter Wagner. The lawyer had never shown the courtesy of returning his call. Given that lack of response, Slade had not bothered to call Wagner to make an appointment. Better that he just show up.

He was glad there was a long drive in front of him. He needed time to sort things out in his mind and get clear about what he wanted to find out from Wagner and why.

*　　*　　*

Slade pushed his car door open after bringing his trusty Olds to a stop at the end of Peter Wagner's driveway. The day was hazy but the sun was still bright. A stiff breeze blew the salt air toward Wagner's castle-like home. Slade followed the precise stone pathway to the front door. He felt a surge of adrenaline as he knocked on the front door. He had no idea what kind of reception he would receive.

The front door opened just wide enough for Wagner's housekeeper to peer out. She recognized Slade immediately, hesitated and then asked him to wait a moment.

Several minutes went by before the housekeeper re-emerged. "Mr. Wagner was not expecting you." Her words seemed to be both a statement and a question. "He will see you for a few minutes. His health is not good right now. Please come this way."

Slade was taken into the sun room where he and Peter Wagner had their earlier conversations. Despite the tension in anticipation of meeting with Wagner, he could feel his body relax a bit as he again admired the beauty of the view looking out on the Maine coast.

After Slade had been waiting several minutes, Peter Wagner emerged in the doorway. Slade got up from his chair.

"I am not doing so well these days, Mr. Slade," said Peter Wagner. "But my memory is still fairly sharp, although at times I have been confused lately. I do not remember us having scheduled a meeting for this morning. Perhaps I am misremembering. Even if we had a meeting set, I don't believe I have anything to speak with you about."

Slade took a deep breath. Peter Wagner was looking all of his eighty-plus years. It appeared that Slade had taken a long ride for a very short interview. However, he would give it his best shot.

"Thank you for taking a moment to speak with me, Mr. Wagner," said Slade, not bothering to parse the question Wagner had thrown out of whether or not Slade actually had an appointment with Wagner. "It was a long ride getting up here. I wonder if there's any chance of your housekeeper having any of that fine English tea you served me before. The view out your windows has, if anything, gotten even more beautiful. I won't take much of your time. Can we sit for a moment?"

The taciturn Maine shipbuilder was not moved by Slade's easy manner. But almost in spite of himself, or maybe because of his physical weakness, Wagner turned and nodded at the housekeeper who withdrew and then he took a seat in his customary chair.

Slade sat down opposite Wagner. Slade could tell this was going to be a conversation where long pauses would favor Wagner, so without a better strategy, he continued with small talk. "I hope you have been able to get some rest since the trip to Italy. International traveling these days is very tiresome. How have you been?"

Peter Wagner ignored the question. Fortunately, the housekeeper quickly re-emerged with the tea tray. She seemed to take up the space of silence as she arranged the teacups and the teapot. Without asking, she poured a cup for Wagner and one for Slade. Slade realized that small talk was not necessarily going to get him any advantage with Wagner. He might as well cut to the chase.

"Mr. Wagner, I am not used to being terminated in the middle of handling a matter for one of my clients. I would respectfully like to know if I offended you in any way in handling your case?"

Wagner seemed suddenly to become weary from the weight of the question. Finally, he responded. "Mr. Slade, sometimes things in life don't work out the way you would like for them to. Don't take it too personally. Is there anything else I can help you with?"

"Well, yes there is," replied Slade. "You remember that I did not want to take this assignment at all, and it was only because of the very persuasive argument that you and your lawyer made to me that I took it on. For that reason, I believe I am owed an explanation. I found your daughter for you. We arranged to be at the same conference that she was attending. And you totally ignored her." Slade could see no reason to hold back. "Mr. Wagner, did you really want to be reunited with your daughter or was the whole assignment a sham because you were trying to find Melissa Dowling?"

Wagner stared intently at Slade. He seemed to be energized by Slade's question, which had been delivered almost as an accusation. Despite his feebleness, Wagner was accustomed to automatically asserting his own will and outlook.

"First of all, it is none of your damn business," said Wagner. He paused. "To tell you the truth, I am getting tired, and the doctor has told me I am probably not going to get better soon, if at all. You have lived long enough, Mr. Slade, to understand that most human endeavors are undertaken with mixed motives. Yes, I wanted to be reunited with my daughter. And at the same time, ever since my retirement I have been trying to provide some leadership to the efforts of the New England business lobby to get a nuclear power station up here."

Wagner paused a moment as if weighing whether he should go further. He hesitated, then he plunged ahead. "Mr. Slade, I am your former client. Does that keep information between us confidential?"

"If you want it to," said Slade.

"I guess, at this point, I really don't care," said Wagner. "What I will do is give you the big picture."

"A few of the top executives of the utility consortium that would develop the nuclear power station met with this young woman, Melissa Dowling, while she was working for that environmental group, and came back totally convinced that perhaps getting more nuclear power for our region was not a good idea, that we should be looking at solar energy and wind power. Don't get me wrong. These new technologies offer possibilities. However, the key reason to develop nuclear power is because it is a power based on fear. Nuclear power is dangerous. Nuclear power requires many levels of security. You have to have an elite group running a nuclear power station. Nuclear power allows for the concentration of control and authority. It creates exactly the right conditions in which voters feel fearful and dependent. When that happens, the electorate always votes conservative.

"Sure, it might be nice to get the price of solar cells down so that everybody could be off the grid. The people in Vermont and New Hampshire would love that. However, we are past the days of rugged individualism—that is simply an old myth that New Englanders cling to out of nostalgia for a more simple time. We are living in an era of corporate individualism. It is the concentration of power in corporations that allows our country, with its democratic façade, to be ruled by a conservative elite. Except for this, we would be living with a socialist government that appeased the mediocrity of the masses at the cost of constant runaway inflation. In other words, we would have economic chaos."

Wagner was obviously warming to his subject and, for whatever reason, was not holding back.

"You know, we stumbled onto this model of 'democracy by the elite' almost by accident. In 1886 a conservative Supreme Court stated in a case, with neither argument nor discussion on the question, that a business corporation is a "person" entitled to the protection of the Equal Protection Clause of the Fourteenth Amendment. In case you are interested the case was called Santa

Clara County v. Southern Pacific R. Co." said Wagner, with a whimsical smile.

"In fact, curiously, the case itself did not even hold that. The editor of the case notes just happened to include a line in the case summary setting this out as the holding of the case. What a wild stretch of the imagination to equate an abstract legal construct, a corporation, with a person, and therefore granting it all the rights that the Constitution gives to an individual. With this decision, the Constitution was changed from a framework of government for individuals into a framework of government by those who control corporate wealth. It is largely from Court decisions following this line of reasoning, including a fairly recent one during President Obama's administration, that the campaign finance laws passed by Congress have repeatedly been gutted by the Supreme Court. That case is called Citizens United v. Federal Election Commission, if you are interested in reading more; though I warn you, you may find it depressing reading about how the First Amendment applies to the legal fiction of a corporation.

"Sure, we go through the ritual of democracy in the United States. It is a ritual that helps keep people content. Don't fool yourself, Mr. Slade, money runs this country. I have worked closely with a few political campaigns. You do polling and focus groups. You find out what the most pressing issues on people's minds are. Then you get your best advertising and marketing agency to come up with media that will shape the voters' minds. It is logical and automatic. You put in x millions of dollars on the front end and you get y number of votes on election day."

Slade did not know if he actually felt the need to save Wagner from his own cynicism, however, he couldn't suppress the urge to speak up. "What about the Jeffersonian ideal of an informed electorate that makes decisions in the best interest of everyone?"

"Oh, come now," said Wagner gesturing demonstratively with his hands. "For one thing, we don't have a structure that could give us an informed electorate. Just the reverse. In the old days, when we had three major networks, we had a level of journalistic professionalism that delivered news to the American people, which was not grossly opinionated. Now we do not even have the illusion of that. All we have is spin information. You have to almost be a full-time researcher to actually know what's really going on and the vast majority of American voters don't even care.

"The American voter has surrendered his sovereignty to the control of corporate wealth. And though I can tell you that when I was young I would've thought this was terrible, I have come to conclude that it has saved us from something much worse. It comes and goes, but for the most part, the American voter is full of naïve optimism. The only way we can keep corporate control in place is to generate a certain amount of fear among the American people. Without fear, people will want to participate in their own destiny in a way that is simply unmanageable.

"International terrorism has been very helpful in keeping voters dependent on a wealthy elite. It helps cultivate a spirit of fear and dependency. Fearful people want more and more from their government and grow more and more critical of whatever their government provides. As long as government stays the villain, no one seems to care that corporate money is actually running the show.

"So when this Melissa Dowling woman got to the executives of the utility consortium, I realized there was more at stake than whether we simply build another nuclear power station. What is at stake is keeping our version of corporate democracy. I have worked too hard all my life to see the control of corporate America diluted. Strong corporate control of our government is the only thing that keeps us from being some kind of banana republic. Look at those countries which struggle. They are all countries that lack a strong corporate base and wealthy people to control things through their corporations.

"There is no question in my mind that this Melissa Dowling has the ability to change the thoughts of others. I expect she's some kind of Huey Long in a skirt. I don't know where she got her ability or how it works, but I do know we need to get her out of the way or get a better version of what she's got."

Slade was required to read Robert Penn Warren's novel *All the King's Men* for a literature class in college. At Wagner's mention of Huey Long, the image suddenly came to mind of Willie Stark's limo careening so close to a mule that it wiped the snot off the mule's nose. The memory of Willie Stark and his limo speeding through the night was an earthy image, but it perfectly mirrored the message of Wagner's tirade about the necessity of corporate political power.

"You see, it is not so much that I'm worried about her changing the thought fields of enough potential voters. I am just concerned that if the voters see that she has this ability, then it will become apparent to everyone that American democracy as being 'by the people, of the people and for the people' is a sham. Our version of democracy represents money—it is by corporate interests, for corporate benefit. Thank goodness. If people understood clearly what is going on they would probably not like it. When you have people in a dependency and scapegoating mode as exists in our culture, you do not want to become their target, you simply want to use their fear to control them.

"You have to admit, Mr. Slade, that when you combine the level of marketing sophistication we have in our country with the immediacy of electronic communication that we live in, whatever people buy at the polls, just like what they buy at the supermarket, is only what is up for sale. The beauty of corporate democracy is that at least people with some legitimate self-interest get to control what happens. Otherwise, I am afraid we would be adrift in mob rule."

Slade could not resist. "So you want to control people through fear because of your fear?"

Wagner did not take the bait. "I see the absence of any meaningful, deliberative way to make decisions in our mass media-dependent, instant-gratification culture. Given the mindset of most people, I want decisions to be made with some soundness. If that means this country is run by an elite oligarchy of corporate leaders, that is simply reality, and that reality is, in fact, the way political decisions have been made throughout most of history. I understand it sounds harsh to anyone raised on the pablum of democratic idealism. However, there is absolutely no foundation for believing that kind of democracy can operate practically or efficiently. The old-line liberals, who do control some wealth, win a few victories now and again and, because of that, preserve the illusion of real democracy, but even those Pyrrhic victories are starting to fade. The last major one was Obama, and even the liberals' enthusiasm for giving money to support him in the political process began to fade after he re-invented the war in Afghanistan. Spending to control the government spurred by idealism will never come close to matching what corporate spending can muster."

Slade had to admit there was a kind of logic in Wagner's thinking, and obviously there was no stopping his harangue at this point.

"Yes, I did hire you on something of a pretext. Yes, I would like to be on better terms with my daughter, despite the fact that she is off on her own ego trip developing her consciousness, whatever that is. It is for sure that it is all about her and not about trying to keep the fabric of our country intact. I may be a little hardhearted, but it's for damn sure it is not just about me.

"So I hired you, and I also hired a couple other private investigators, to help me get this thing sorted out. Unfortunately, none of you have done the job of finding this Melissa. However, it became clear to me that you misunderstood my reasons for being interested in that woman, and you did not realize how much was at stake. You turned out to be a bit more of a softy than I expected. That is why I terminated you."

Wagner paused and suddenly appeared to become very tired. "That's the whole story. It is more than you had any right to, but maybe I underestimated your ability to appreciate what is involved here. I'm not going to be around very much longer, my time is running out. Don't worry. The wheels will turn without me. I am not the Lone Ranger promoting the interests of corporate democracy. Far from it.

"So there you go, Mr. Slade. The people who run this country want to talk to Melissa. They will find her. She will not be allowed to ruin our country." He stopped. "I have gone on much longer than I intended and I need to go lie down. Good day, Mr. Slade."

With that, the elderly man gradually pulled himself to his feet and slowly walked from the room. In a moment the housekeeper re-appeared and saw Slade out the door.

As Slade returned to his car parked in the driveway, he took one last look at the gorgeous sweeping view of the craggy Maine coastline. He sensed that somehow Wagner had long ago lost the ability to appreciate the dramatic beauty that lay stretched out before him each day. Some of the best work he had done as a detective had involved wealthy, old men. Usually they were stuck at an impasse on a quest in which a younger woman was part of the answer. Peter Wagner was exceptional only because the desire of his heart was political. What was certain in Slade's experience was that age seemed either to give a gift of openness to other viewpoints or generated hard unmovable convictions. Either way, the later years of life provided an urgency and immediacy to see one's vision, whatever its source, completed. Wagner had a powerful vision. What, Slade wondered, would Wagner be up to next?

CHAPTER 28

There was not much spring in Godfrey's step as he walked into Father Hay's office. "Good afternoon, Godfrey," said Father Hay. "It is good to see you."

"Good to see you too, Father," said Godfrey. "I have been anxious to get here. I guess I am in a bit of a pit. You know for a couple of days after we talked last time my spirits were lifted. I had a wonderful vision of how Christianity is a reflection of the evolution of humankind. Do you know what I mean?"

"Yes, I think so," said Father Hay. "Would it be the idea humankind's consciousness is evolving and Christianity is the most recent step forward in that progression?"

"Yes, that is what I mean. I believe I understand this step forward from a theological point of view, and, at least for me, that is a big step," said Godfrey. "As you said, if I remember right, Christianity builds on the non-attachment of Buddhism, the idea of not having ego attachments. Then it adds this concept of love—not love from the ego, but from our essence, which is the conduit to God's love."

"Correct," said Father Hay. "Christianity is a theology which includes an energetic dynamic."

"Well, it sounds wonderful in theory," said Godfrey, "and I don't have a clue how to make it work. If I look at most of the biblical instruction about Jesus' message it all seems dual to me, even this new idea of unitive consciousness that you keep talking about. I'm down about the whole thing really. I wish I were more like Jeff, only interested in playing golf and not worried about this stuff. None of this bothers him in the least."

Father Hay paused allowing the energy of Godfrey's frustration to expend itself. What he did not say to Godfrey was that what one usually finds in Christianity—and especially in Scripture, for that matter—is a reflection of one's own level of consciousness. Scripture holds up to us a mirror, and what we see in it is usually what we are ready to hear and to integrate into our lives.

"Let's talk about a few tools," said Father Hay. "Then if there is a specific issue that is troubling you, we will see which tool might be helpful to you."

Godfrey agreed.

"Okay, let me set the stage," said Father Hay. "Just imagine that you are alive at the time Jesus lived. There is a foreign army occupying your land. The leadership of your people has been co-opted by this foreign occupier. There are a number of groups that are seeking a way to escape worldly conflict and political intrigue, and many of these groups have retreated to the desert. One such group are the Essenes. Most likely Jesus went to an Essene school when he was young, and this ascetic tradition had a large influence on him, but did not ultimately shape his approach to life.

"You are also aware from our earlier discussions that Jesus traveled widely, studied at the great centers of learning in Alexandria, and in Persia and India and was probably very familiar with Greek mystery schools.

"We also see in the canonical Gospels that Jesus was, above all, a student of human nature. He understood that there were nine different ways that people respond to life. I don't think that this understanding of these nine types was something that Jesus developed, rather I believe it was current knowledge in the spiritual foment of his times. And we see this pattern of understanding reflected deeply in his most significant teachings, such as the Lord's Prayer and the Sermon on the Mount.

"So the starting point for his teachings was his understanding that a person must first have the self-awareness to understand what his or her dominant way of dealing with the world is—in our terminology, knowing one's Enneagram type. With this awareness it becomes possible then to understand the source of energy by which we respond to life—whether that energy comes from our ego, our way of coping with the world, or whether it comes from our essence, from our connection with the life force of the universe.

"You with me, Godfrey?" said Father Hay.

Godfrey nodded. It had been a great revelation for Godfrey to realize that he was a type nine in the Enneagram system. He saw that through understanding his type he was more able to discern when he was simply responding to other people's priorities and not being in touch with his own heart values. This knowledge had been extraordinarily helpful to him. He wanted to know the next step, what tools he could use to move forward from this base of knowledge. Father Hay seemed to be wound up in his professorial role this morning. Hopefully, he would get to what Godfrey really wanted to know.

Father Hay continued. "So we have this starting point, which is where I believe many people probably were in Jesus' time. We can respond to life from our false self, that is, in a dualistic way (e.g., this person of this ethnic origin is not to be trusted or that way of bathing is not good, etc.), or we can respond from our essence, with a non-dual perspective that encompasses the duality of life and at the same time is grounded in something much larger and greater than who we are.

"So we see that the first practice Jesus taught was awareness. There are many scriptural lessons about this, how, as Paul says, first we 'see through a glass darkly,' then become aware. Once we get some awareness of how we respond to life through our ego, we can then begin to surrender that false part of ourselves that the ego's coping has built up, which we have begun to think is who we are. The two biggest components of this ego creation are our gender identification and our process of projection which separates, judges and defines.

"Building awareness is a practice that helps us develop the three centers of knowing: our mental intelligence, our emotional intelligence and our somatic intelligence. Developing these three centers is crucial because we build awareness by using all three of these centers together. In other words, you get some energetic feeling in your body, in your somatic being, that tells you how to respond to a situation. You also get some emotional response and mental activity. Our awareness builds as we learn to decipher from which of these sources our dominant response energy is coming. We then must learn how to balance it out with the other two centers of intelligence. A good rule of thumb is that when the energy is coming simply from one center—unless this is an emergency response situation—then the response is probably out of balance. The response does not speak the truth of who we are, nor does it allow us to tap into divine guidance."

Godfrey interjected, "Father, this sounds fine and very interesting but I am not sure how to get a handle on how what you are saying actually can be of help to me."

"Godfrey, I am going to get there for you, I hope. As a type nine, you know that although you are a somatic type, your somatic intelligence is repressed. What is going to be helpful to you are those practices which are going to get you more in touch with your somatic energy and intelligence so that you can balance your mental and emotional responses to life with this vital center.

"One of the tried and true practices for almost all spiritual traditions is meditation, or as it is known in Christianity, centering prayer. Because you are a type nine your false self's way of dealing with the world is often to withdraw. So for you, a meditation practice needs to be one that involves your body and gives you a dynamic centering. Many of the standard meditations practices would not be helpful because they would simply reinforce your false self tendency to withdraw from the world. Ironically, one of the ways withdrawal type people try to escape life is in the compulsive ego-driven pursuit of a spiritual path.

"So practice number one is awareness. An awareness that distinguishes between the response of the false self and the core essence. An implementing practice for awareness is a meditation practice, but the type of meditation must serve your type for it to deepen awareness."

"Father, I don't know whether this is what you are talking about, but it has always been easy for me to have a meditation practice. I just sit down and drift away for twenty minutes. I feel better afterwards but I never have any sense it is providing me real spiritual progress."

"Generally speaking, the purpose of a meditation practice is to experience periods during the day when the false self is not operating. These oasis points nurture us so that we can begin to distinguish the experience of being in the false self and the experience of essence that comes when all three centers of intelligence are equally on line. So what a good meditation practice does is allow us to get out of the grip of our personal emotional feelings, or overactive mental processing, or overdeveloped somatic responses. Which of those false self activities is going to be the most prominent is a matter of understanding our type.

"Meditation gives the person with an overly active emotional response to the world the opportunity to experience a deeper centering below the level of afflictive emotions, to experience serenity and equanimity. For the person who is an overly active mental type, it is the opportunity to experience what the Buddhist call Big Mind, a sense of clear seeing, without gerbil wheel type thinking. For the person whose instinctual response to life is overdeveloped, meditation is a chance for that person to get in touch with a quality of body knowing that lies beneath the automatic instinctive desires for food and sex.

"So the purpose of meditation is to still the mind, the emotions and the instincts so that the essence which is beneath each of them is touched. In this touching, the duality of the demand of our attractions and aversions fades and a greater experience arises by reason of our essence connection to the world, others and God."

"That is very helpful," said Godfrey, "just to have a better idea of the purpose of meditation." However, Godfrey's expression made clear that Father Hay's explanation had not touched Godfrey's deepest concerns.

"Practice number two is intention. We do not deepen our awareness without intending to do so. Intention focuses our energy. In centering prayer, it is our intention to abide in the Holy Spirit, in the pure ocean of God's love. This intention helps soften whatever the ego-defense is that might currently be driving us.

"The practice of intention is an interesting phenomenon, in that often it is our ego's intent to create more of a life lived from our essence. This is a fundamental illustration of how our ego is necessary and is not something that is necessarily bad. The intent of our ego can help us become less ego-driven. The false self's mental busyness in our head can be the exact cue we need to help us return over and over again to that deeper awareness of Big Mind. It is our intention which allows us to use our false self energy to become more whole and connected to God.

"How wonderful it is then, Godfrey, that your reason for being here is your ego desire to have a better relationship with Jeff, and perhaps your ego's desire to understand your own spiritual path better so you don't suffer. You are putting the energy of these ego-driven desires to work to allow you to be more connected with self, Jeff and God. It is a realization of unitive consciousness that the duality of existence does serve our greater being."

"At first that seemed a bit confusing, but I am with you," said Godfrey.

"What makes intention difficult for many Western Christians is that spiritual energy, our energy from our essence, is not something we manage with our assertive energy. Just as important to intention as our assertive energy (which helps us to do our daily practices), is our receptive energy. The bottom line is we can't manage or control spiritual energy. We can't have an intention simply to be more spiritual and assert our will to be more spiritual and have that bear any fruit. We also need to employ our receptive energy intention. This is an intention to let go, to surrender to the dynamic life force spiritual energy that is available to us when we are connected to our essence. The gradual letting go of attachment to our false self is the way we develop capacity for opening to incoming energy.

"How best to understand our receptive energy? The energy is best symbolized in the Bible by Mary, mother of Jesus. She did not assert against being chosen to give birth to Jesus, rather she was receptive and open to mystery. There is a way to work to develop our receptive energy, and that leads us to the supporting practice I wanted to talk to you about. We must practice our ability to access our receptive, feminine energy in order to know God's will for us so we can then use our more masculine energy to try to carry out that intent. Strong energetic receptivity is sadly lacking in the West. Without it we are adrift at sea in our assertive energy with lots of rowing power but there is no opening for the entry of God's Grace to tell us in which direction to head.

"An implementing practice for intention for us as Christians is *lectio divina*. Just as a meditation practice serves awareness, a *lectio divina* practice serves intention."

"I don't understand what *lectio divinia* is or how it might serve me," said Godfrey.

"*Lectio* is a how process. Let me circle around from the why. There is an utter simplicity in Jesus' message of transformation, or conversion as we church types call it—let go of your will, the false self we would call it, and follow my will. However, actually applying this message to our lives is difficult. On the one hand, as Christians we know that our job is to follow God's will for us, and that is straightforward and simple. Then the question is how to discern that will? How do we know what to form our intent around?

"As I have talked about earlier it is important to be aware that we can use our ego, false self or ego false self—they are really different labels for the same thing—to help us commit to practices that move us toward our essence. Our ego false self will help us have the discipline to do the practices that move us along our path. However, our ego false self will not give us any insight into what God's will for us is. In order for us to gain that perspective, we need to develop our heart knowing. Sometimes this is called three-centered knowing: where our somatic intelligence, our mental intelligence and our emotional intelligence meet, at our heart center. It is a way of knowing that comes, not from our analytical thinking, but from the intelligence of being incarnate, from being real, and from those deepest values of our heart. So while I like to refer to it as heart-centered knowing, it is the integration of all three centers of intelligence that leads to this heart knowing.

"*Lectio divina* is the process by which we exercise the muscle of our heart-centered knowing. It is a practice that has been used in the Christian monastic tradition for centuries. Before you leave today, I'll give you a pamphlet that explains *lectio divina*. No need to go into that now. We've spent too much of your time in this session with me talking rather than you expressing how you are currently experiencing your life. So let me wrap up.

"After awareness and intention comes a third practice, the practice of presence. This practice involves learning to experience the quality of your energy so that you are aware when you are triggered into contraction. We cannot be present in an openhearted manner when we are contracting. Only when we are fully present do we have access to our three-centered, integrated

THE END OF DEMOCRACY

knowing and by this integration to the open channel for connection and guidance from God. You might say the first four levels of consciousness in a human being correspond to the four layers of the human mammalian brain. The first, early brain is known as the reptilian brain. It is our survival brain. When we are motivated by fear or anger, this brain takes over and runs the show. We cannot connect with higher levels of consciousness when this brain is the software operating us. When this brain takes over we move into a contracted state physically. A presence practice involves learning to be aware of the physical cues that tell us we are in or moving toward this contracting state.

"The second brain is the emotional brain, often described as the midbrain. It controls our needs for water and food and our reproductive urges. It controls those types of activities that send neuro-chemical messages that we interpret as drives and instincts.

"The third brain is the neocortex, where we do our analytical reasoning and thinking. This operating system has been driving Western civilization for the past three hundred years.

"The fourth brain is the prefrontal lobes. This area of the brain integrates the whole field of our soma, our emotions and our thinking and is often also referred to as the God brain. Biologists of faith believe that this is the part of the brain which is open to receiving divine guidance. This is the part of the brain which has a large neuro-chemical antenna, which may open us to a larger energy field, a field full of divine energy.

"We experience the fifth level of consciousness when we move into a unitive state of mind, that is, into this larger field which includes the divinity in everything. This level is outside of us so it is not actually physically represented in our brain. The key point for now is that you can't get there when you're operating only in the reptilian survival brain, or primarily in the emotional brain where all the afflictive emotions such as anger or dislike operate, or primarily in the cognitive brain of the neocortex which is only able to perceive and process data that can be understood analytically.

"When the operating system of any of these three lower brains is running the show, we cannot be totally present and open to the energetic life force of the divine. So presence is about learning how to operate from the fourth and fifth levels of consciousness."

"I hear what you are saying, Father, but I have to tell you it all seems a little beyond me. What you are teaching me is both exciting and discouraging."

"I can understand the feeling of overwhelm. Certainly, Godfrey, the spiritual journey would be impossibly frustrating if it were about willfully getting anywhere. The true spiritual journey is about giving up the ego's need even to be accomplishing the journey. This is why the focus on the practices that bring about awareness, intention and presence are so important. Let me mention one other practice which supports the practice of presence: the practice of welcoming prayer. This prayer functions to disengage the operating systems of the three older parts of the brain. When an afflicted emotion comes along, this prayer welcomes that emotion and surrenders it. You can't surrender an emotion by trying to figure out what it's about. That is a little bit like wrestling with the tar baby. The key focus of welcoming

THE END OF DEMOCRACY

prayer is to welcome the emotion without judgment and then, regardless of how much you may think you dislike experiencing the emotion, you allow yourself to let go into the process of experiencing the emotion and in the process of experiencing it in an uncritical way it dissolves.

"Again, I don't need to go into any more detail with you about welcoming prayer, as we have talked about it in some of our early sessions and I know you are incorporating it into your spiritual life. I just wanted to mention it here to put it in the context of the practices we have been discussing, specifically a practice that supports presence.

"One final set of practices that I will mention now and we will come back to later comes under the heading of love practices. As you know, first and foremost, Christianity is a religion of love. There are practices that help us learn how to give love and to be receptive to love. The most well-known of these practices in Christianity is the Eucharist. Most Eastern traditions, like Hinduism and Buddhism, have methods by which the guru will transmit energy of healing and consciousness to his students. These are examples of energy love practices for conveying energy that is tangible love. Jesus did this all the time when he healed. For us as Christians, this divine energy transmission comes in a communal experience of Christ's love through the Eucharist. Our goal is to practice our receptive energy to be able to receive that love. You would use what you have learned about intention, awareness and presence to open your receptivity.

"Okay, I have talked way too much and you have not had any time to really tell me what this is bringing up for you. We are already over time. Let's figure out a way we can schedule another session before our regular meeting next month to plow this ground a little deeper. Will that work okay for you, Godfrey?"

Godfrey smiled. He loved it when Father Hay was on a roll and expressed the love that he had for the process by which he was leading Godfrey. His animation was tangible and present in his voice and the light in his eyes. "That would work great," said Godfrey. Even though he had felt down when he arrived, that negative energy was gone. Somehow the experience of being with his spiritual guide, being in Father Hay's energy had completely changed how he felt. Maybe he thought as he rose to leave, it had something to do with love.

CHAPTER 29

Norris was shaking Walker in his bunk to wake him up. "Come up on deck, Walker, you got to see this." said Norris.

Walker stuck his head above the blanket. Norris did not appear to have gone to bed all night.

"What's going on?" said Walker.

"We are going down the Gerlache Strait and there are about a dozen killer whales right in front of the ship. Come up to the observation deck above the bridge."

Walker got out of his bunk and pulled on pants and a shirt. Not enough clothing, he would discover later. He grabbed his coat and headed for the observation deck. There was Norris with a cup of something hot in his hand. When he saw Walker, Norris pointed. There they were right off the port side, announcing their presence with a hissing spray of exhaled mist, rising in a rhythmic arch and then disappearing beneath the dark Antarctic water.

So many killer whales were coming up at one time it was difficult to count how many whales and whale pods were actually surrounding them. Walker guessed Norris' estimate was low. There were at least fifteen killer whales, maybe as many as twenty-five.

The grace of these animals was mesmerizing. Walker almost didn't notice the jagged mountains totally covered with snow except for the sheerest vertical surfaces. Every now and then, they would see a cove that was the home of a small glacier. It was spellbinding. The scene was such an overwhelming sensory overload it was almost impossible to take in nature's grandeur for more than a few minutes at a time. Killer whales and the tops of the Alps transplanted to this ice-strewn ocean. As much as Walker hated Norris telling him what to do, he was glad he'd gotten him up, even though by now, standing on the observation deck with a stiff Antarctica breeze blowing across the icy mountains and the frigid water, he was freezing.

Later back in their cabin, Walker asked Norris "Do killer whales always school in such large numbers?"

"No," said Norris. "That was probably a super pod. Killer whales stay in matriarchal groups and hunt together like wolves. The sons and daughters stay with the mom. Sometimes a son or daughter will also have a calf, so there may be three generations of killer whales in a pod. Of course, nature does not want there to be breeding within a family group. So at breeding time various family groups will get together so that there can be cross-family breeding. It's that time of year. We're just on the verge of a major whale fucking frenzy." Norris smiled and seemed to be enjoying himself for the first time on the entire trip.

How in the world does Norris know such stuff, wondered Walker. He heaved himself back into his bunk to make up for lost sleep. They should be at Anvers Island shortly, and then the real work would begin.

CHAPTER 30

"You know," said Aasia, turning to look at Blaine as the two women were packing to return to Berlin, "I have been thinking that when I get back I might see a plastic surgeon. It was a turning point when I was able to tell the sisters about the scars on my breasts. And, it was an even more amazing experience for me when they wanted to see them, and then how they giggled with delight and told me how beautiful my breasts were. Do you think it's possible a man might feel the same way about my breasts?"

Blaine started to respond in her usual off-the-cuff manner. She paused, remembering all she had been learning. What Aasia was asking was asked in a light tone but was extremely serious. Now was the chance to put her new learning to use. She took a deep breath, and focused her attention on her heart center in order to let her response arise from there. She could hear her head wanting to reply something like 'Aasia, my suggestion is you ought to get some cool tattoos on them. Or, maybe those young sisters have been in the convent too long.' However, she waited and let these thoughts pass. "Aasia," said Blaine, "your breasts are beautiful. The right man will know that. He will know that because of the flaws from the past it is possible to more deeply appreciate your beauty in the present."

Aasia looked at Blaine somewhat amazed. Blaine felt this welling up within herself. Wow, she thought, so that is what it is like to speak from your essence.

Aasia had removed her blouse and bra and was examining her breasts in the mirror. Blaine recalled what a milestone it was when Aasia was first able to do that two months earlier in Berlin.

"Blaine, I am not as spiritually advanced as the sisters are. Maybe there is a compromise point. Perhaps just a little cosmetic surgery would help. It is still awfully painful for me to look at my naked, scarred body. Maybe I just don't want to be reminded of what happened. Those sisters don't have to live in my body, I do."

"Aasia, you are right. Fortunately or unfortunately, we don't live in a convent. Nor have I attained any higher level of consciousness. What sticks in my mind that the sisters stressed is that even our old ego survival defense mechanisms are okay to have. You have been injured enough by war and fear. We don't need to be at war with anything, not even our own thoughts and feelings. I realize now that spiritual growth is about learning new ways of living in the moment in the world. We have to become aware of the old automatic responses in order to do that. When we have that awareness then we can use the energy of those automatic responses as the very fuel for our progress. I think you deserve to have the most beautiful breasts possible, that is the way you were created with a beautiful body, and if that's an ego trip, your essence is just going to have to learn to live with it," said Blaine with a grin.

Blaine was aware that Aasia had advanced more rapidly than she had in the past six weeks. She knew that by her judging, she was hindering her own process, though sometimes she could not help it. Aasia's wounding had been so direct and brutal, that she had almost no false self left to surrender. The emptiness within Aasia had been so huge that when the sisters poured their love into her, Aasia began to blossom in an amazingly short period of time. Once Aasia experienced this energy pulling her beyond the confines of her contracted self into the field of her essence, she didn't want to leave. The ego that would normally fight essence for control was already almost gone. Even in her judging mind, Blaine was so grateful for her friend's progress.

Blaine realized that though it was hard for her to get out of the comfortable observation post of her head, she had also made amazing progress. And with that realization she too began to take off her own blouse and bra. The degree of self-loathing she had experienced was dramatically displayed across her body by the scars and tattoos within scars by which she had tried to blot out the scars. Yet underneath them, she could appreciate in a new way her lithe firm body and the supple, smooth curve of her unviolated breasts.

The two half-naked young women looked at each other and laughed, and slowly began to touch themselves. They had learned from the sisters that their bodies were the way they plugged into the life force, to be experienced the same way they experienced a beautiful sunset, with humble gratitude and amazement.

"Aasia, I am beginning to feel this tingling at the base of my spine, like I did after we had those two long days of meditation last week. I can feel this heat from it. The quality of the heat is like its excited heat. This doesn't make any sense, does it?" said Blaine.

"This is all so new for me, too," said Aasia, "I have been feeling tingling at times during our meditation for the past couple of weeks. Like you, I feel it now. It rises a little farther up my spine each time. I talked to Melissa about it. She assured me that it was completely natural and that this warm flowing energy would come all the way up to the heart eventually. When that happens, she said the heart opens. I am not sure what that means. I do know that my heart is feeling the best it has ever felt since I was in the rape camp. I feel like life is possible again. And, I owe so much of it to you, Blaine."

With that Aasia reached toward Blaine. Blaine stepped toward Aasia. The two bare-breasted women embraced. They both felt surges of electricity up their spinal columns and incredibly vivid sensations as their skin touched. The light coming through the window that a moment ago was gently diffused now seemed to sparkle. For a moment everything was true and totally real. The intensity of realness was not something they were yet able to handle for long, and their self-consciousness quickly returned.

The two women separated, still looking deeply into each other's eyes. "Holy cow," said Blaine, and she slipped her hand inside her pants. "I'm wet. I think I must have been about ready to come." She looked at Aasia embarrassed.

Aasia looked at Blaine and smiled. It seemed their roles were reversed. "Yes, it started happening to me a good bit of couple of weeks ago in those long sessions of centering prayer and it was one of the things I talked to Melissa about. Melissa was delighted. She said that because I have been emotionally and spiritually dry for so many years, my body is responding literally to the release of the fear contraction I have been holding for so long. I was afraid because I didn't understand what was happening. Melissa assured me that the more flow, the better." Aasia smiled, and tilted her head back. "So I have tried to surrender to the flow and it comes easily now. I was also worried about whether this meant I was a lesbian, since we were all women in the centering prayer sessions. Melissa laughed at me and said that I should not confuse the juice of the life force flowing in me with being gay. She said that gender orientation is something that I would know in my heart eventually with the fullness of time, and for now I needed to allow myself to be open to the erotic nature of everything, the breeze on my skin, fragrances, tastes—well, just everything. That includes you, Blaine, my most precious, life-saving friend."

Blaine was astonished. Not only at the wisdom and depth of what Aasia had to say, but that she had spoken so directly and honestly. For that matter, it seemed like the longest paragraph Aasia had ever spoken.

Blaine looked at the clock. "Gosh, Aasia, we better finish getting packed, it is about time to get to the airport."

*   *   *

Rat was there to meet them at the airport. Right at the spot where he had been the first time he had met Blaine, when she had first arrived in Berlin. Rat never seemed to pay much attention to anything that didn't have a monitor or keyboard, however, he immediately sensed that something was different about his two friends. As soon as they were out of the airport, Rat began to feel a dynamic energy coming from both Blaine and Aasia.

"Well dudes," said Rat. "What's the deal? I can feel something going on." He smiled his Disney-animated smile at them with amused curiosity. "It's like you guys have changed your frequency a bit. Clue in the Rat."

The young women giggled spontaneously. Then, as if in silent conspiracy, they focused their energy even more directly on Rat.

"Hey, I don't know what you guys learned up in Sweden town," said Rat, blushing with pleasure, "whatever it is, keep it coming." He twitched his nose and smiled his rat-like smile and endeared himself even more to Blaine and Aasia.

After being away for six weeks, both Blaine and Aasia were busy catching up at their jobs. For the first week or two back, they hardly had a chance to meet for dinner at their regular Turkish café.

Blaine and Rat made time to catch up with each other. Rat let Blaine know that, as far as he could tell, Will Dawson had not yet been located by the CIA or the other group that was trying to find him. Dawson was still checking on a regular basis the Internet chat room that Rat had set up. There was no real news from Dawson at this point. Dawson was aware that Melissa had escaped from the United States into Canada. He did not know where she had gone from there, and Rat had only told Dawson what Blaine had agreed that he be told.

At Blaine's instructions, Rat told Dawson that Melissa was safe in Europe. Blaine had told Rat, however, not to tell Dawson that she had seen Melissa. Maybe, she told Rat, it would be okay to tell Dawson later, but right now she wanted to see what Dawson would do. Would he take off and come to Europe in pursuit of Melissa? If he did, this would tell Blaine a lot about his reality. So far, despite her invitation, he had not come back to Europe to see her. Naturally, he had a good excuse with the CIA trying to catch him. If he came anyway looking for Melissa, that excuse would be hollow.

Blaine questioned Rat closely about what he was doing with the Ukrainian mobsters who had set up the Conficter worm. Rat told her that he believed he and Wiz had been able to set up a way to wrest control of the botnet from the mobsters once it was activated. However, there was no way to know for certain if their program would work until the creators of Conficter activated the botnet out of its latency. Rat told Blaine that he had spent days programming ways to avoid having his insertion of a worm into the Conficter worm be detected and traced back to him. This was new territory for Rat, and Blaine was worried about him. Unlike her hacking, where she went into somebody else's computer or network and then got out, Rat's hacking activities were like a giant computer game that never stopped. The processes by which he was interacting in the criminal Conficter scheme were ongoing and constantly changing. She knew that if he ever slowed down, the chances of him getting caught would increase drastically. Thankfully, right now he showed no signs of slowing down. He was as frenetic as ever.

In their conversations Blaine practiced opening her heart center to Rat. It was still not easy for her, despite all the practice at the convent. It was very difficult for her not to fall back on being able to rely on the quickness of her mind, rather than wait for a response from her heart center. Whenever she was able to respond confidently from her heart center, the effect on Rat was palpable. He would begin to feel more emotion than his body was used to handling and he would engage in some activity to dissipate the energy. Usually that meant jumping up and going to get coffee or run some errand.

The impact of Rat's behavior, in responding to Blaine as he did, was a very significant lesson for her. For the first time in her life she was coming from her essence and she felt emotionally empowered in human interactions. She also could see that being real was more than most people could handle. Even her beloved Rat. And, of course, herself. She remembered when she and Aasia had both taken their blouses off and how intense that experience had been. Living life from a place of realness was extraordinarily difficult. However, the door of possibility, of being able to do that was opening for her. She knew that now that this door of realness was being opened, she would never let it shut again.

Blaine was not sure that all of the new developments in her life caused by her consciousness training in Sweden were that helpful. She was now on a much more disciplined schedule, being sure that she had time for centering prayer twice a day and time to do her energy practices. Unless she kept her energy pulled in tightly around herself, she was getting much more male attention at work than she wanted. This time it was not just coming from the geeky guys, but from some of the best-looking young men in her department. Men were paying attention to her now who just a few months ago would pass her in the hall as if she weren't there.

Fortunately, she was able to be in e-mail contact with her mentor, Sister Maria, at the convent in Sweden. She needed guidance on how to respond. She could just respond with her quick witted one-liners like she would have in the past. Or, she could try to respond more from heart center. She was afraid if she responded more from her heart center that this would simply encourage the advances of these young men and she simply did not have time to deal with them right now.

Sister Maria gave her good advice. She pointed out to Blaine that one of the symptoms of her being unbalanced in her energy centers was when her mind went to an all-or-nothing perspective. Blaine had been thinking that she either needed to be entirely open in a heart-centered way, or entirely protected. Sister Maria's advice was to be in the middle. Sister Maria advised her to practice being more heart-centered and open with one or two people each day who she thought of as friends. Only those people who are very spiritually conscious can practice being open to the whole world all the time. For most, Sister Maria advised, it is important to learn discernment in your energy interactions. This is a practice of openheartedness to yourself. If you are centered in your own energy and connected to God, you will be led to know with whom to be most openhearted.

THE END OF DEMOCRACY

But Sister Maria told her the cat was out of the bag. Unless Blaine consciously cloaked her energy, other people would be unconsciously attracted to her higher level of resonance. "So get used to it," Sister Maria had told her. "You won't be able to keep your light under a bushel all the time now."

Aasia was even more shocked than Blaine by the effect that she seemed to be having on the men around her. Often in the emergency room fully gowned with a mask on, she would be approached by young interns and residents whenever there was a break in the triage process. She was not by nature a shy person, however, she had become one. The shyness of her responses did not seem to decrease the new interest men had in her.

Aasia talked with her mentor at the convent, and after that discussion, Aasia decided that she would work on learning how to respond to the attention of men in a gracious but deflecting way. Aasia wanted to spend as much of her spare time as possible working on developing consciousness. She was glad to have men attracted to her for a change, and she was not interested in them right now. She was even thinking, she confided to Blaine, about joining the SOS convent.

CHAPTER 31

Norris shook Walker's shoulder. "Let's roll out, buddy," said Norris, "we're almost there."

Norris was already dressed and ready to head up on the observation deck. Walker quickly pulled on his clothes and the new fleece-lined parka he had been issued and followed behind Norris.

Norris turned and pointed, "There on the right is Weinke Island. Just beside it is a little spit of land in a protected area called Port Lockroy. That's where a British research station once was, which is now restored as a historical site under control of the British Antarctica Trust. During the Antarctica summer, the trust opens the museum there which has a little gift shop. Rumor has it that several extraordinarily beautiful young women are staffing the place during the summer. The good news for you, Walker, is that with the short summer here, winter will be coming before you know it, and the young ladies will be closing up shop and heading home.

"Coming up on our right is our destination, Anvers Island where Palmer station is. You can begin to make out the layout of the station as we get ready to dock up against those two big fenders protecting the pier. Just past that on the right is the boat/dive house. Behind the boat/dive house is the main building for the station. On the first floor is the mess hall, on the second floor offices, including the office of the station manager, and on the third floor berthing. You will see there is a boardwalk going from the main building to another large building, called the GWR. Those initials stand for garage, warehouse and recreation. The upper level is also a berthing area and the lower-level is the power station. Though these two main buildings are connected by a boardwalk, you will note that it is not covered."

Walker couldn't help but smile at the depth of Norris' knowledge about their destination. The detail was better than anything in their briefing paper, which he was fairly sure Norris had still not read because he had seen it last night laying sealed on the table in their cabin.

Norris continued. He enjoyed being in the role of instructor for Walker. "Back up on the hill to the right is the Terra lab, which is a lab for ongoing monitoring of the Antarctica environment. The National Science Foundation is responsible for running Palmer and they subcontract the maintenance and upkeep of the facility to Raytheon Polar Services. Currently, while we're still in the summer season, there are forty-five people here, twenty-eight support staff and seventeen scientists. They're probably more than half a dozen scientific research projects going on at any given time in the summer. So we are a little less noticeable now coming in the summer.

"In the wintertime, most of the scientists leave. This past winter only one scientific project was being conducted—a biologist working on a project involving bone density in Antarctica fish. Because fish in Antarctica do not have swim bladders, evolution has solved the buoyancy problem for them by giving them less bone density. The research biologist was studying how lesser bone density has evolved in these Antarctica fish in order to see if this mechanism of change might provide better understanding of how to deal with osteoporosis.

"The Palmer Station manager this year is a relatively young woman with a lot of experience in Antarctica. She is a tall brunette with good people skills. She is a good planner who knows how to stay on top of whatever problems emerge and has no problem making decisions. Her name is Theresa Shaw. Everyone calls her Terry, although I understand some call her the Dog in reference to the rat terrier tenacity with which she deals with details. She manages by being in the middle of things so she knows everything that is going on. She is by necessity a Jack-of-all-trades, but above all, she has to be good at dealing with people. You get these academics down here who have to work and live together with others, and at least one or two act like five-year-olds. I don't envy her that part of her job. Last year they had some significant generator problems and had to go on blackouts part of the day. She does a good job rolling with the punches and keeping the whole operation moving. From everything I understand, we're lucky to be down here on her watch. She does not know that we are undercover, but if something screws up out there on the ice, she will be the one to figure out a way to bail us out. I think she is probably astute enough that she will figure out after a while that we are phony scientists, and I don't think that will bother her. As long as we follow her instructions regarding our safety—so she doesn't have to send us home in ice cubes—I expect she will let us do our thing.

"The U.S. has two more stations here, one at McMurdo and one at the South Pole. The McMurdo station is really the staging and supply station for the South Pole station. It is easy to forget how big Antarctica is. McMurdo is south of seventy-five degrees and is still 1000 miles from the South Pole. Up on the Antarctica peninsula where we'll be, is only about sixty-four degrees latitude. As best I can tell, there's not a lot of scientific overlap between the projects being done at Palmer and what is happening down at McMurdo and the South Pole. The guys at the Company simply picked out the less prominent site as the place for us to work.

"Before we start, we will get some survival training for these climate conditions. Then the station manager should be able to assist us getting ashore on the peninsula where we can get this experiment underway. I have to admit, this country is so awesomely beautiful I'm beginning to look forward to being here."

Walker never ceased to be amazed by Norris. He seemed to know the entire background for the operation and then some. For the first time it occurred to Walker that maybe Norris' ability to know stuff was the reason he had been assigned to this project. Begrudgingly, Walker was beginning to be pleased that he had been assigned to do this project with him.

CHAPTER 32

Blaine could not imagine why Sister Maria was coming all the way from Sweden to visit her in Germany. Blaine was pleased to have a mentor like Sister Maria for guidance on the spiritual path. She had not expected such diligent attention, especially since she and Aasia had so recently returned to Berlin from the convent in Sweden.

Sister Maria's e-mail came that morning, saying she would be arriving in Berlin that night for a visit. For some reason Blaine could not figure out, Rat was anxious to meet Sister Maria. So Blaine decided that they would all meet at the Turkish café for dinner and she gave Sister Maria that address. Aasia would join them as soon as she got off work at the hospital.

Rat was always on time to meet Blaine when they were going somewhere. Today was no exception, and he was standing outside the entrance to her office building when she emerged after work. They were not sure what time Sister Maria's flight would be getting to Berlin, so they decided to head on over to the café to be sure they were there when she arrived.

It was good they went directly to the café. They had not been there five minutes when Sister Maria came through the café door.

THE END OF DEMOCRACY

She was not dressed like a nun. She wore blue jeans, a University of Stockholm sweatshirt and no makeup. Her casual attire did not diminish her attractiveness.

Blaine rose from the table to accept Sister Maria's warm embrace. Rat also stood up, and much to his surprise, also got a big hug.

"I have heard much about you, Rat," said Sister Maria as she fully uncloaked her energy for Rat to experience, "and I am so glad to have the chance to meet you."

Rat was beside himself. He could hardly talk. Sister Maria reached out her hand and put it on his arm and he immediately calmed down. "Rat, I look forward to getting to know you better, and I have urgent matters to discuss with Blaine. Do you mind if we talk privately?"

Before Rat could reply, Blaine interrupted. "Sister Maria, you can talk about anything with Rat here. He knows me better than any person in the world, even you. I trust him with my life."

Sister Maria looked concerned. And automatically she went inside to discern what she should do in the moment. Her eyelids fluttered above her clear gray eyes as if they were receiving Morse code.

"Okay," said Sister Maria, "I guess it's all right. Rat, I need you to hold our conversation in the strictest confidence."

"No problemo, dude," said Rat.

Not very reassured, Sister Maria nonetheless continued.

Blaine interrupted, "Why don't we order some food first? They have great kebabs here."

Sister Maria smiled a tight-lipped smile. "I need to explain some things to you before I can possibly eat. And if you are agreeable, you will be hustling with me to catch an airplane later tonight, so we all might have to skip food for a while."

Blaine was suddenly serious. She nodded at Sister Maria.

Sister Maria began. "Melissa's mother has just died. Melissa would like to go back to the United States for the funeral. After much prayer and guidance about the situation, she believes she has to go back to be there for her mother's passage to the next world. As you know, if she were to travel in her own name, she would be picked up by the CIA. That is why I have come. To ask your help."

At first Blaine did not understand. Rat didn't get it at all. Then it suddenly began to dawn on Blaine what she was being asked to do.

"Sister Maria, I know some of the sisters commented about how much they thought I look like Melissa. Do you really think I resemble her so much that this could work?"

Sister Maria nodded. "I don't think there's any doubt about it. Just keep those tattoos covered up. Though you are younger, you two could be identical twins. Here is the plan. You fly with me back to Stockholm tonight. Then in the morning you switch passports with Melissa. You will fly to Milwaukee, Wisconsin by a direct route. There is no question that, as soon as you get on a plane headed for the United States, you will be followed. We do not think they will stop you until you get to Melissa's mother's house or the funeral home in Racine. If they have any humanity, they probably will not try to detain you until after the funeral. As soon as you get to Wisconsin, you will be picked up by two nuns from our sister convent in Minnesota. They will take you out to the convent. Even if the CIA shows up at the convent, the sisters will be able to hide you until Melissa arrives.

Melissa will make her way to Wisconsin by a more circuitous route. As soon as Melissa is met at the airport, another sister will obtain your passport from her and bring it to you. Once you have that back in hand, there should be no problem for you to leave the U.S..

One of the sisters will take Melissa during the night to visit her mother at the funeral home in Racine so she can give her mother a transmission of energy for her passage to the next world. Regardless of what happens to Melissa, we will pass you through to Canada so you can come back to Berlin from there. It may not be a perfect plan, and I think it will work."

Sister Maria reached inside her sweatshirt and pulled out an airplane ticket and pushed it across the table to Blaine. Our flight back to Stockholm leaves in two hours and forty-five minutes. We have clothes and everything packed for you in Stockholm for the trip to America." She paused. "Some are Melissa's clothes."

Blaine was stunned. She had no idea what she should do. Here she was getting a plea for help from some of the people who had helped her most in her life. Maybe it should be an easy choice, but it wasn't.

"So what happens if I get detained in New York or after I arrive in Wisconsin before I get to the convent?"

"We are working on that contingency," said Sister Maria. "I can't tell you that it is perfectly worked out. We have legal resources and lawyers in New York and Wisconsin that will be immediately available to you should you get detained."

Rat's nose was twitching. "Well, I could go with you," he said. Sister Maria looked aghast. "Oh, I don't mean literally," said Rat, "I mean I could go with you virtually and monitor everything that's going on. Do you think that would help, Sister Maria?"

Rat wiggled his nose in his most beguiling rat-like manner.

Sister Maria was a little bit unsure about how to take Rat, but she had no doubt that the more precautions, the better. "Sure, that would be great, Rat," she said as she turned her energy directly on him.

"All righty, Sister dude. The Rat will do it."

"What do you mean, go with me 'virtually'?" asked Blaine.

"I'll wire you up with a nice little necklace with camera and microphone included. You will be able to talk to me anytime in a low voice. I will be able to see and hear everything going on around you," said Rat.

"That is amazing. Can you really do that?" asked Sister Maria.

"Is the Pope Catholik?" quipped Rat. "Whoa, I didn't mean to get carried away, no offense, Sister, but I would do most anything possible to look after sweet Blaine. Plus, I'm kind of looking forward to checking things out when she goes to the bathroom," Rat said with a huge grin.

"Oh, Rat are you ever serious?" Blaine said as sternly as she could, smiling at Rat the whole time.

"Well chickos, if you are going to catch that flight, we better get rolling, especially since we need to go by the storage unit and get the necklace first. I think I can have it ready to go in about five minutes."

"Not quite yet," said Sister Maria. "Blaine, discern. See if you really are willing to do this?"

Blaine closed her eyes and allowed her focus of attention to go to the center of her chest as she breathed a deep relaxing breath, then another, then a third. She felt a warm energy in her heart center and she could see a greenish glow beneath her eyelids.

"I think the life force says it's a go," said Blaine.

"Then let's do it," said Sister Maria, visibly relieved.

The three got up from the table and started toward the door. Just then Aasia walked in. A big smile broke out on Aasia's face and she stepped into Sister Maria's warm energy and embrace.

"Aasia, it is so good to see you. I am sorry that there is no time to visit. This is an extreme emergency. Rat will fill you in on everything I am sure," said Sister Maria.

Aasia looked perplexed. However, Sister Maria's love for Aasia kept her from feeling any anxiety about the rush they were all in.

Aasia looked at Rat. "Rat, I want all the details and as soon as possible,"

"You will have them pronto, most lovely Aasia," said Rat. "Just give me about an hour to run by the storage room with Blaine, and Sister Maria and I will be back here to give you the whole scoop and, hopefully, finally get something to eat."

"Yes, tell Aasia everything, and absolutely not a word to anyone else. Is that clear?" said Sister Maria.

Rat looked at Sister Maria and wiggled his nose. "Yes, of course, your Popeness," he said. He could hardly contain his glee. Finally she smiled. With that, Aasia and Sister Maria embraced one more time, and they all headed out the café door.

CHAPTER 33

Rat decided it was better to seek forgiveness than permission. Without talking to Blaine, he decided he would go ahead and notify William Dawson about the trip that Melissa and Blaine were making to Racine for the funeral, and to the convent in Minnesota, just in case they needed somebody on the ground to help them with the CIA. Who better than a former CIA officer? If Dawson did not check the chat room that Rat had set up, Rat would use the emergency phone contact number.

Rat was trying to figure out how to cover all the bases to protect Blaine, when he got an e-mail from Wiz, his hacking buddy. Conficter was about to roll.

Wiz had figured out their strategy. It was brilliantly simple. The Ukrainian mafia was essentially using their power to exact a ransom from the world. They did not need to send the world a ransom note. Instead they would use their power to generate fear, then their payment would come automatically from a fear-based world. The actual mechanics involved setting up a huge stock market play. They were taking short positions on many major American stocks and Exchange Traded Funds. They would then use Conficter to create a major military crisis on the South Korean border with the North, and in Iran with Israel, by using the huge power of their botnet to attack the military computer infrastructures of all four countries. Each country would assume it was about to be attacked and go on the offensive. At least enough on the offensive to create fear worldwide, which would create a major crisis. Historically, any time there has been a world political crisis, the stock market, faced with a threat to international trade, has dropped precipitously. The Conficter guys were not even rolling the dice. They were betting on a sure thing.

On one computer screen Rat could see the Conficter worm coming to life. Each little blue dot that blinked on the screen represented 10,000 computers being taken over. The screen was beginning to look like a galaxy of stars. Timing was essential. Rat and Wiz could not activate their anti-worm until the entire botnet had been brought to life. If they activated their anti-worm too quickly, then the Conficter guys might be able to keep control of those computers not yet activated. If they waited too long to respond, then the botnet would have already done its damage and a political and economic world crisis would be well underway. Their timing had to be like tapping a batter on the shoulder in mid-swing and asking him to pause just a millisecond before completing his swing.

On the next computer screen Rat could see the pictures and sounds coming from the tiny transmitter around Blaine's neck.

On a third screen was the chat room that Rat set up for Will Dawson. So far Dawson had not yet checked in.

On a fourth screen was a new operating system that Rat was

developing. The inspiration for this new operating system was his conversations with Blaine about her experience at the convent in Sweden. Rat's working assumption was that the more closely a computer's operating system mimicked the human brain, the more effective it was. Blaine had explained to him how dualistic thinking was the reason that human consciousness was stuck. To Rat that equated, in computer terms, to being stuck in a binary system, the system almost all computer systems operate on.

Blaine explained to Rat that if Sister Maria and her convent sisters were right, the next step for human consciousness was for people to move from dualistic consciousness to unitive consciousness. Rat figured if that was the next step for human consciousness he might be able to get there even quicker with a unitive operating system for a computer.

As Rat glanced at the fourth screen, a new thought entered his head. Maybe such a new operating system would also impress Sister Maria. He smiled and his nose twitched involuntarily. He thought of Sister Maria's sparkling, clear gray eyes, her wheat-straw blonde hair and magnetic energy. He began to wonder if he was having a dualistic or a non-dual thought, and then he turned back to the other three screens. This was not the time for thoughts of the Swedish sister.

CHAPTER 34

Redmon smiled. This was the break he had been waiting for. He had just been notified by secure e-mail that Melissa Dowling was on her way from Stockholm, Sweden to Racine, Wisconsin.

Redmon was trying to decide whether they should intercept her in New York or Racine and then he got a second e-mail saying that she was apparently returning because her mother, Mrs. Dowling, had died suddenly of a heart attack.

He felt a knot of repulsion in his stomach. He knew immediately that the old lady's death had been caused by the harassment he had ordered. Collateral damage was the euphemism that would be used in the official report. At the moment it didn't help much. The e-mail went on to note that the funeral would be on Sunday. Okay, he thought, we've got plenty of time to see about picking up Melissa. At the very least, I ought to let her go to her mother's funeral.

Redmon arranged for observation of Melissa as soon as she landed in New York until she left on the plane for Racine and then from her arrival in Racine until the funeral, which was scheduled for three o'clock Sunday afternoon. There was no way

THE END OF DEMOCRACY

he could allow more time for her to grieve. She might slip away again like she did before. He had no alternative except to pick her up right after the funeral. He sent out e-mails to get the proper resources lined up to have her under constant surveillance.

CHAPTER 35

Walker and Norris had been at it for several weeks on the Antarctica peninsula using the sensory deprivation of the natural environment as a way to sensitize and strengthen their abilities to read the energy fields of others. Their project's goal was to be able to sufficiently control the energy field of the other so that they could influence the other's thought field.

Neither Walker nor Norris was sure that they were making any progress. Fortunately, their campsite had worked out well and they were staying warm in their prefabricated snow hut. They were checking in daily by radio with Terry the station manager at Palmer and so far that relation seemed to be smooth. She was coming to make a safety visit with them next week. But other than simply enjoying the breathtaking beauty of the snow-covered Antarctica peninsular mountains and the ice covered sea around them, both men were wondering if the experiment they were engaged in was simply the harebrained idea of some guy up in Langley who was getting far too little sleep.

*   *   *

Walker and Norris, like most Company officers, were divorced. They were very different types of men when it came to women, but living the Company life had the same domestic result for each of them, as it did for most officers. Walker was of average height, and looked like a slightly overweight high school science teacher. He had achieved in his appearance the perfect CIA disguise of ordinariness. Walker was the prototypical family man, and if it had not been for his wife's unwillingness to put up with his long absences, he would still have been married.

Norris, on the other hand, had always looked like and been a bit of a ladies' man. He was only an inch or two taller than Walker, but he was lean as a rail and appeared tall. He hadn't lost any of his dark brown hair which was combed straight back, and he favored wearing worn, but expensive leather boots even when he was obliged to wear a suit. He carried himself with a down-to-earth cowboy kind of dignity that did not make him stand out in a crowd, but assured he would be noticed in a small group. Except that whenever he was with other people, he had this natural instinct to be on the outside edge of any group, appearing to be just about to leave. He had been married once for a brief time, and his divorce had happened so quickly it would be unfair to have blamed it on the Company.

The Palmer station manager's visit last week had broken the monotony of their work. Still, they continued to feel they were making absolutely no progress on learning anything new about how to interpret each other's energy fields or control the other's thought fields.

The day after Terry Shaw left their outpost, Norris admitted to himself that he felt some pangs of desire while the efficient, tall, dark-haired woman visited. Curiously, after Terry's visit he did much better on the scoring instrument in reading Walker's emotional state. This gain passed quickly and he was soon back to his old baseline.

CHAPTER 36

"Is Joy just a diversion in my life, or is she the meaning of my life?" asked Slade. It was only after the second round of single malt Scotch that this question formed fully in Slade's mind. Slade had been meaning to meet up with his buddy, Joe Carroll, ever since he got back from his trip to Maine to meet with Peter Wagner. The usual stuff of life kept interfering.

Now Joe Carroll sat across the table from Slade at their local just a few blocks from Fenway Park. Carroll was in his usual feisty mood, but for once he did not respond immediately to Slade's question. Carroll could see that Slade was at a crossroad trying to peel back a resistant layer to more deeply understand his life. Carroll's greatest skill was his ability to provide the exact barb to bring any of his friends back down to earth, whether they needed it or not. Having restrained himself, Carroll fell back on his professorial role.

"Let's try to put this in context," said Carroll. "As a solidly committed, lapsed Catholic I would like to offer an analogy. For the most part both the practice and theology of the Catholic Church throughout its history has been to put down women or, looking at this in more mythological terms, the feminine. This has taken the form of excluding women from the priesthood and insisting upon male celibacy for priests. What folly! Reminds me of the guy who committed suicide in order to hurt his family whom he felt had rejected him, as if to say: 'Let me hurt you by hurting myself worse.' Celibacy is the ultimate sexual suicide— 'We will show women who has the power, we will deprive ourselves of them, and the path to wholeness spiritual union of genders offers.' This attitude is a classic immature response to someone who is perceived to have more power. What a colossal fear response!

"This was not the context in which Jesus lived. Jesus lived in a time in which Judaism still was making its case for male supremacy, but things were much more in flux. One of the predominant themes of the Hebrew prophets was that God was the faithful bridegroom and that his chosen bride was the community of the covenant. Over and over again, the bride is unfaithful, and God keeps loving His people anyway. This theme in Judaism is a reversal of an earlier theme, seen in the great Goddess religions of the Neolithic cultures that preceded Judaism. In these older cultures God—or I should say—the Goddess was feminine. The chosen bridegroom was anointed by the royal priestess, the surrogate of the Goddess, just as later in the Christian church priests become the surrogate of God. The bridegroom became the king by being anointed by the Goddess' surrogate and we can assume also sleeping with her. The sacred union of the priestess with the chosen king was seen as essential to the regeneration and vitality of the community.

"In many of the Mesopotamian Goddess religions, after the priestess anoints the bridegroom and sleeps with him, he is ritually sacrificed to ensure the continued fertility of the land.

The planting of the sacrificed king was necessary to ensure the fertility of the crops which would allow his people to thrive. You can see how Jesus played out this mythological paradigm. In all fairness, maybe this is where the great fear of the feminine in the Catholic Church comes from.

"After the Indo-Aryan invasion into the Middle East, the idea developed of a supreme male deity whose anger and wrath had to be propitiated. Gradually, through the centuries leading up to the birth of Jesus, cults based on an angry male God of unlimited power displaced the worship of the bountiful Goddess. This transition also happened in Judaism. Evidence of the older Goddess connection is seen at the time of Jesus. Herod the Great, who died just before Jesus was born and whose son ruled when he was crucified, made his claim to the throne based on matrilineal lineage.

"Jesus came at the time of the waning power of the Goddess cults and the rising authority of the God cults."

Slade interrupted: "Are you saying Jesus was some kind of synthesis?"

"No, I don't think he was a synthesis. Rather he was a leap beyond these two mythological currents. And he came within the context of those currents. He was the Messiah, which means the anointed one. He was anointed by the woman from Bethany with the alabaster jar whom many scholars believe was Mary Magdalene. He in effect represents a new integration of masculine and feminine. Unfortunately, the religion that followed in his name has spent the past 2,000 years trying to propitiate an angry God and keep women subservient. Look around and you will see a lot of angry people, and they reflect the kind of religious zeitgeist that angry-God Christianity has given us. When the feminine in a man is repressed he becomes an angry old curmudgeon. The same is true of a culture."

Slade laughed, "Now don't make fun of my clients."

Carroll grimaced and threw back his glass. "Yeah, that's what I am talking about. There is change, and we see it coming primarily from movements in the Protestant church and progressive Catholic groups in the United States. There are probably now more women ministers, or, if you are like me, you prefer the old term priests, coming out of mainline Protestant seminaries than there are men. Membership in Christian churches generally is over two-thirds women. For the first time in 2,000 years within the past thirty years we see women returning to their roles as surrogates for the divinity in Christianity. I, for one, believe if we are going to have a male God, we need female priestesses; or if we have a female Goddess I am okay to go with male priests. Or, maybe a 'Don't ask, don't tell' approach. Hey, no one is asking me."

Slade enjoyed listening to Carroll, but he was not sure if anything he was saying had anything to do with Slade and Joy.

Carroll paused as if realizing he needed to bring his response back around to Slade's question. "So I hope my answer has not been too long-winded. It's really quite simple. You can either end up a cantankerous old man, wrapped up in your male mantle of authority living in the tiny well-defended castle of your head, or you can be anointed by a woman and live in joy. Oops, didn't mean to offend you; I mean live with Joy or, hopefully, both.

Slade seemed puzzled.

Carroll continued, "I don't mean to be confusing you with history. I am just trying to make it clear that it is not your fault. We are products of our culture. You are not responsible for the way we have been shaped by it. However, after a certain age, you are responsible for what you do about it. Just a little more history that moves into literature may help. And might suggest the form that your responsibility could take.

"There was an attempt in the twelfth and thirteen centuries to restore some balance of the feminine principle to Christianity. This happened in Provence, France among the Cathars, and other Christians, who may have been adherents to the heresy that Mary Magdalene was the wife of Jesus and escaped to live in France after his death where she had his child. Whether or not this is true, many holy places in the region are dedicated to her. In any case, the Cathars' ideas and spirit were captured by the troubadours, which gave rise to the Grail myth. While ostensibly about a search for the chalice that held Jesus' blood, the more probable explanation is that the Grail stories are about the need and search to re-balance feminine energy and imagery in the culture. In this view, the chalice refers to the feminine as the vessel for the bloodline of Jesus.

"Interestingly, a similar current occurred in Judaism about this time in Spain. This an effort to restore the feminine counterpart to Yahweh. In esoteric Judaism this feminine force is known as the *Shekinah*. She was the consort of Yahweh for the mystical Kabbalists. This effort dissipated when the medieval flourishing of culture in Spain died out after first the Muslims and then the Jews were run out by the Spanish Inquisition."

Slade interrupted in a voice mocking Carroll's inflections, "Carroll you are enjoying some of this way too much. Are you using me as the guinea pig audience for a new reality TV show— 'Another Great Moment for the Church?'"

"Hey, that's a great idea, but remember dark humor is my bailiwick, not yours. Let's get back to the Grail story for a minute. You will remember that the Fisher King is wounded. He is impotent, and his kingdom is a wasteland reflecting the state of its king. The legend does not state that the Lost Grail is the bride, but that is the idea. Either the literal bride, or the rejoining of the feminine principle in God, is necessary to give new life to the king and the kingdom. The Grail is only restored when the right question is asked. So you, my friend, are on the right track in asking a question, but I am not sure you have asked the right question yet.

"Oh, one other thing, there is only a certain time period to ask the right question, and you get only one or two chances in life to ask the right question. If you fail, then according to the myth, your opportunity is lost and your life will remain a wasteland.

"But wait." Carroll paused for dramatic effect. "There is one other alternative to ending up a misogynistic old man, or surrendering to a woman: single malt and chasing skirts. I like this third option because it allows me to keep one foot in both camps, so to speak. I get to be a feminist and an asshole at the same time, and that seems to fit me like a pair of old shoes.

"Think I will have another," said Carroll with a grin.

"Yes, please order me another too." said Slade breaking into laughter at Carroll in spite of his best efforts to remain serious.

Slade knew that in his own roundabout way Carroll was telling him that he ought to ask Joy to marry. And they both knew a man could marry and still be a misogynist. Carroll was telling him that he had to be open to asking even a deeper question. Slade was sure that question must be obvious to Carroll and that it should be clear to him. He could sense that it was right there before him, yet he couldn't see it.

Then Slade remembered. He had another fortune cookie in his pocket for Carroll. He reached in his pocket, pulled it out and slid it across the table.

"Oh, I need a good fortune," said Carroll, and he pulled off the cellophane paper, put the cookie aside and unfolded the small strip of paper: *"What you must have, you will lose; what you think you must have but you surrender, you will have in abundance."*

"Damn," said Carroll, "you don't need me as your barroom philosopher, you already got the goods in these little bitty cookies." He handed Slade the fortune to read himself, giving them both time for it to sink in.

"You know the problem, Slade. It is easy to get one-liners on what the truth is; the hard part is figuring out how to live into that truth. What I am telling you is not necessarily what I do. The answer to your question is not here." he said, thumping his forehead.

The next round of single malt scotch had arrived. With his right hand, Carroll raised his glass. With his left, he tapped his heart. Slade raised his glass and clinked Carroll's and slowly nodded.

CHAPTER 37

Blaine saw it happen on the immigration official's face as soon as he swiped Melissa's passport. She was so glad that Rat was right there with her and could see and hear what was happening to her. The immigration official left his booth and disappeared while she waited. He was not gone long. When he returned to the booth he simply stamped her passport, and she proceeded to the exit.

She exited the International Arrivals terminal at JFK with her carry-on bag, and because she had no checked luggage, she headed over to the adjacent terminal to get her domestic flight to Milwaukee. On the way over, she felt her cell phone vibrate. She flipped it open. There was a text message from Rat. "Start walking again, then turn around slowly. Then walk straight ahead, and then turn around slowly once again."

Blaine did as she was told. She knew that Rat was simply trying to identify who was watching her. After she got to the gate, she mumbled under her breath to Rat, "Who's watching?" then she waited for her cell phone to vibrate. It did not take long. Rat's text message said, "There are two, a man and a woman. Ninety degrees to your left. Do you see the man leaning against the pillar in the blue sweatshirt?"

Blaine responded yes under her breath.

"Then turn another ninety degrees left. See the smartly dressed woman standing at the newsstand, appearing to be looking at the newspapers? I think she is a tail also."

Blaine pulled a Swedish newspaper out of her carry-on and held it up before her face. "Thank you, Rat." She realized how anxious she felt knowing she was being watched, but not knowing who the watchers were. She felt her anxiety drop just in knowing who was watching her. "I suppose they would've stopped me at Immigration if they were going to try detain me in New York, so I guess these guys are along for the trip to Racine. Thank you, for looking after me. You are a real sweetie. How is Melissa doing?"

At the last minute they had decided not only to wire Blaine, but also to wire Melissa. Not only was Rat looking at exactly what was happening to Blaine on one monitor, he was also following each footstep Melissa was making on another.

Blaine felt her cell phone vibrate again. There was a new text from Rat. "Peachy," was Rat's concise report. A moment later the cell phone vibrated for the fourth time. Blaine looked down and read, "*!+@!", the prearranged signal meant that Rat was aware that someone was trying to tap their cell phone communications and he was signing off. Although Blaine knew that he would still be watching everything around her and listening to her, she began to feel apprehensive knowing she would only be able to communicate with Rat now by going to the pre-arranged Internet chat room on something besides her cellphone.

Just then, the gate agent called for boarding to commence for her flight to Milwaukee. Upon landing she would be met by the SOS sisters for the drive to Racine. She got up and headed for the queue that was forming in front of the gate. Soon she was standing beside her aisle seat in Row 15. Before sitting down, she turned around twice slowly. She knew now that it was important to give Rat a full view of what was going on around her. Just doing this gave her a feeling of security. As far as she could tell, neither of the two people who had been watching her earlier followed her onto the plane.

CHAPTER 38

Will Dawson was on his connecting flight from Denver to Milwaukee. From there he planned to rent a car and drive to Racine. He wished there had been time to drive so that Man and Ooljee could have come. Not only did he value their companionship, their being along assured that he was more grounded and, he sensed, able to make better decisions. He was not sure what he would do when he got to Racine. He just barely got Rat's message in time to catch the last flight to Milwaukee that would allow him to arrive in Racine before Mrs. Dowling's funeral. He would check the chat room when he got to Racine and see what instructions Rat had for him.

As the plane began to rumble down the taxiway, Dawson thought about some of the hair-raising operations he had been in as an officer. None of them could compare in emotional impact to the feeling of unease he had now. Feelings and thoughts whirled in his body and mind. What would he say to Melissa if he had the chance to talk to her? What would he say to Blaine? How was he going to be of any assistance to either of these two women who were trying to avoid being picked up by the CIA?

Dawson had only limited communication with Rat about what his role might be. Rat seemed to have the idea that at some point

Dawson might need to intervene and create a diversion to allow Melissa and Blaine to escape. How that might work, Dawson had no idea. The last thing he wanted to happen was to get himself detained by the Company. He was traveling under his Godfrey Adams identity; however, it would only take a quick scan of his fingerprints for the Company to know who he really was. He would at least have to remember his Australian accent. He had been stationed in Australia for a while as a liaison with the Australian intelligence agency, so the accent itself should not be a problem, if he could just remember to use it.

His greatest worry was that he had not had a chance to talk with Father O'Donnell before he left. He was not even sure that Father O'Donnell would approve of his coming to Racine. Dawson was good at following orders, and when the Rat had told him to go to Racine to be ready to help Melissa and Blaine, he had scrambled as fast as he could to figure out a way to get there. Father O'Donnell was still up in his hermitage and there had been no time to visit with him. Dawson realized that not only was there no time to get Father O'Donnell's advice, there was little time for Dawson to use the practices of discernment he was learning to figure out for himself whether this really was the right action. Okay, he admitted to himself, maybe he could have made time to figure out what was the next right thing in the mystery of contemplative silence, but it was much easier for him to jump into action than try to practice spiritual discernment.

CHAPTER 39

When Blaine's flight touched down in Milwaukee she exited the gate quickly. As she did she turned around twice, slowly, giving Rat the opportunity to see who was following her. She was not sure who they were, but she could feel their presence and she felt confident that Rat had identified them immediately. From an energetic standpoint she sensed that there were three individuals following her in rotation.

From there, events unfolded faster than Blaine could have imagined. She was met by two sisters from the SOS convent. Both of the sisters were dressed informally and greeted her like she was an old high school buddy. Blaine and the two sisters got into the sisters' car and drove straight to the funeral home in Racine.

Blaine followed the sisters' instructions and went into the room where Mrs. Dowling's body lay in her casket. This room, like the rest of the funeral home, had a hushed, sullen quietness, not at all like the sparkling silence she had experienced at the convent in Sweden. It was creepy to be mourning for someone else's dead mother.

Blaine kept checking her watch. As soon as ten minutes passed

Blaine returned to the lobby of the funeral home and with the two sisters headed across town. She would be staying with a woman, who was a friend of the two sisters and who evidently agreed to take all three of them in overnight until the funeral the next day. Blaine was not sure if the generous hostess taking them in was actually a friend of Melissa's or simply someone doing the sisters a favor.

When they got to the house where they would be staying, one of the sisters took Blaine into a bathroom with no windows in the center of the house. Blaine gave this sister the passport she had been traveling on, which was Melissa's passport. The sister returned Blaine's passport, which Melissa had used to travel to the United States.

The wordless passport exchange meant that so far the plan was going as anticipated and that Melissa was back in the United States and already in the area. Rat would also understand that when he saw the passports exchanged.

The only thing for Blaine to do now was to try to get some sleep—not an easy task. The critical part of the plan would unfold tonight, when Melissa would be taken to the funeral parlor after hours to visit her mother's body. Blaine did not know how the sisters were working out this part of the plan, and she guessed it was probably just as well that she did not.

At one of the sister's suggestion Blaine lay down in the spare bedroom. Sleep eluded her. Two hours later there was a knock on the bedroom door. One of the sisters came in to tell her that they would have to move later that night, at the same time that

Melissa would actually be visiting the funeral home. If they could keep the CIA officers busy watching Blaine, the possibility that they might discover Melissa's visit to the funeral home would be minimized.

Blaine told the young sister that at some point she wanted to go to a shopping center to visit a clothing store. She would be making her way back to Berlin immediately, if the plan worked successfully, and she wanted to pick up a couple items that were hard to find in Germany. It was colder than she expected and she needed something really warm to wear under the clothes of Melissa's that had been packed for her to wear to the funeral. Blaine also learned from the sisters escorting her that it was possible that her route out would be on foot through the convent grounds in northern Minnesota into Canada. She would need a good pair of hiking shoes. To her relief, the outfit provided fit her perfect and was all black. It was a comfort to be cloaked in her familiar all black camouflage.

CHAPTER 40

It was difficult for him to admit to himself, but Rat was having a hard time keeping up with everything on the array of computer screens in front of him. Usually the more there was going on, the more focused Rat became and the more precise he was able to be in responding. However, there is a human limit to the amount of stimulation that a person can process and that limit had been reached—even for Rat.

Maybe his attention was overly-focused on Blaine and how to keep her safe. Whatever the reason, he and Wiz had missed the millisecond timing needed to take over the Conficter botnet before it could begin to wreak havoc. Maybe it had only been possible to take it over in theory anyway, and there was no realistic way Rat and Wiz could have done that before some damage was caused. Rat and Wiz were simply a fraction of a second too late and the result was that the Conficter botnet attacked the military's computers in both North and South Korea and Iran and Israel. Conficter worked brilliantly and the attacks were successful against two of the four countries attacked, taking over the computers of the military services in South Korea and in Iran.

The intelligence services in the United States, Russia and China almost simultaneously became aware of the attacks on the military computer systems of North Korea, South Korea, Iran and Israel. All three great power countries immediately deployed nuclear attack submarines off the coast of the Korean Peninsula, in the Gulf of Oman along the Iranian coast and along Israel's Mediterranean coastline.

Even though its military computer system was not penetrated, the response of North Korea to the cyber attack was predictably paranoid. Orders immediately went out mobilizing the entire North Korean army, and satellite images showed a glow of activity around their nuclear weapons facilities.

Iran promptly accused the United States of the cyber attack and demanded a special United Nations investigation. Like North Korea, Iran was also in the process of mobilizing most of its armed forces. Unlike North Korea, there was no land target immediately adjacent to Iran where it could take out its eye-for-an-eye frustration. Israel had also gone on full-scale alert both in response to the unsuccessful cyber attack on its military computer system and the Iranian mobilization.

No one would ever know how successful Rat and Wiz were in minimizing the impact of the Conficter attack. Clearly their anti-worm worm was successful in significantly weakening its magnitude and degrading the scope of the attack. Additionally, they were successful in taking over about eighty percent of the botnet after the attack was mobilized. Nonetheless, the Ukrainian mafia got exactly what it wanted. The world stock markets immediately dropped between twenty and twenty-five percent, as soon as word of the mobilizations in North Korea and Iran hit the news. No doubt the computer gangsters made billions of dollars in a matter of a few minutes.

Of course, the entire time that Rat and Wiz had been trying to orchestrate their takeover of the Conficter botnet, Rat had been diligently following the journeys of Melissa and Blaine so that he could anticipate and thwart whatever moves the CIA would make to apprehend either woman.

CHAPTER 41

The funeral was still a few hours away, and Rat was hunkered over a computer screen showing a Google map of Calvary Catholic Cemetery in Racine, Wisconsin. The migration from Europe in the mid-1800s resulted in two groups of immigrants settling in this part of Wisconsin. One, largely from Germany, and part of the German-speaking Catholic tradition, had established a cemetery at St. Mary's. The other, consisting of Irish and English speaking immigrants, had established a Catholic cemetery at Calvary. It was appropriate that Mrs. Dowling with her Irish ancestry would be buried in the old Catholic Irish cemetery. Mrs. Dowling would be interred next to her husband. Her family had been from Donegal, his from Roscoman County.

Rat could see from the Google map that the Calvary Catholic Cemetery was just across Kinzie Avenue from the city-owned Mound Cemetery. Rat sent a text message to Will Dawson asking Dawson to check out the cemetery on the ground. Rat cautioned Dawson that the CIA would be scoping it out at the same time. The warning wasn't necessary. Dawson already assumed they were on the trail.

*   *   *

Dawson had followed Rat's instructions and driven his rental car from the Milwaukee airport to Calvary Cemetery in Racine. It was apparent to Dawson that driving back and forth on the grid of streets going north and south in Calvary Cemetery between West Boulevard and Belmont Avenue would make him an immediate object of interest to anybody watching the cemetery. So Dawson pulled his car off into the Mound Cemetery, parked and walked over to Calvary. It was still too early for many people to be out, and he would be much less noticeable walking around the cemetery than driving through it.

It was the kind of day he always associated with funerals. The sky was heavy and gray with clouds and there was a bitter coldness in the air. A number of maple trees and other medium-size deciduous trees in the cemetery obstructed clear views, and there was no obvious central vantage point. A funeral tent was set up at the Dowling gravesite. Three rows of folding chairs had been arranged under a tent.

A large obelisk monument in the cemetery with a cross etched on its side was the most prominent landmark. While the location of the obelisk did not offer particular advantage in observing people coming and going, it was the central point in the cemetery. Dawson decided this would be where the Company officer in charge of the operation would be standing during the funeral.

Dawson told himself to be patient. Those who were impatient were always the first to be discovered. He didn't have long to wait for his patience to pay off. Two men, who looked for all the world like wet-behind-the-ears officers, strode up to the obelisk and stopped. They had an animated discussion, with one occasionally pointing in different directions. Dawson watched closely.

An hour later Dawson felt confident he knew where the officers would be located. He surmised there would be three groups, with two officers in each group. It was a little more manpower than would normally be employed to detain one female suspect, but Melissa was no ordinary suspect.

Dawson texted Rat, and then the two chatted in the chat room. Looking at the Google map of the Calvary Cemetery, Rat was able to pinpoint exactly where Dawson believed each of the three groups of officers would be located during the funeral.

Since Blaine, posing as Melissa, had not been detained at the airport, Rat and Dawson were convinced that she would not be picked up until after the funeral and interment. However, neither believed the officers would let her get out of the cemetery.

Dawson decided to take another walking tour of the circumference of the cemetery. He was only about half way around when he got another text from Rat. He went to the chat room on his iPhone. Rat laid out the plan. Blaine, posing as Melissa still, would be driven by two of the sisters in full habit to a parking location that was as close to the gravesite as possible yet as far away as they could get from the CIA officers' vantage points. Melissa herself would not be at the graveside. There was no way she could safely be there and have a chance to get away. Rat had devised a method to download the video and audio that were streaming from Blaine's jewelry microphone and camera so that Melissa could watch the interment on a small portable screen as she sat in a car a quarter-mile away from the gravesite.

This arrangement was fine with Melissa since the clandestine trip to the funeral parlor the night before went off without a hitch and she was able to spend all the time she wanted with her mother, to give her mother's soul the energy transmission that Melissa knew was needed for her to make it to the other side. Melissa was not grieving the loss of her mother now but experiencing a sense of elation that she was not detained prior to getting to Racine and was able to help her mother's passage.

Dawson was thinking the plan looked okay and he was beginning to relax a bit, when Rat posted a chat message. After the burial service was over the two sisters would walk with Blaine back to their parked car. Another sister would remain in the car as the driver and keep the engine running. Once they were all back in the car they would take off immediately. As soon as they left, Dawson would pull in behind them in such a way that his car would be between their vehicle and any following vehicles. Once the block was effected, Dawson was to abandon his rental car and take off on foot. At a location nearby, another car driven by another sister would be waiting to pick him up.

Okay, thought Dawson. He had done things like this when he was a young officer—leaving the scene of a break-in on foot as fast as he could. However, he was a middle-aged man who had spent his last five years behind a desk at Langley and the chances of him outrunning a young officer were slim indeed. The only way for him to have a reasonable chance of escaping was to know the route ahead of time and hope there would be some back alleys where he could lose any pursuers.

He chatted back an acknowledgment of Rat's instructions and then headed over to walk the streets off of West Blvd. where his escape route would be.

CHAPTER 42

Even though picking up someone like Melissa ought to be a routine matter, Charles Redmon had at the first been closely watching his officers in the field plan the snatch. Now it'd been hours since he had thought about Melissa and operation 1776. His boss was on the phone with him every thirty minutes trying to see what further intelligence the Company had about the cyber attacks on the military computer systems of North and South Korea, Iran and Israel. Redmon knew that his boss was badgering him because the President's national security adviser was making the same repeated calls to the director of the CIA seeking information for the President. Nobody liked to tell the President of the United States that they did not know what was going on. In such circumstances it was always the tendency of the bureaucrats to make up more than they knew. Yet for the moment no one even knew what to conjecture.

What soon became clear to Redmon was that the cyber attack was causing a bigger problem. The problem was not so much that some group had tried to hack into the military intelligence systems of South Korea, North Korea, Iran and Israel, but the responses of China, Russia and the United States. They were all responding to the military escalation by the four countries that had been cyber attacked, but with no coordination among them.

The biggest threat was that one of the new, recently built Chinese nuclear submarines with a green commander might literally run into a U.S. nuclear attack submarine, and that this would lead to some kind of confrontation between China and the United States.

Redmon's boss was not concerned about a submarine pile-up. What he wanted to know was who the hackers were and how they had been able to launch such an effective cyber attack. The U.S. diplomatic strategy was to supply sufficient accurate intelligence to China and Russia so the U.S. would be allowed to take the lead in coordinating the defensive reactions of China and Russia with what the U.S. was doing. The United States always tried to have superior intelligence to use as a bargaining chip in foreign diplomacy. Plus, if the United States' intelligence looked better than China's and Russia's, it was a huge deterrent to those countries trying to out maneuver the U.S. later.

One good crisis could often achieve what years of peacetime diplomacy were unable to garner. But, for that to work, for greater coordination either between the U. S.'s allies or with the U. S.'s potential enemies to come about, there had to be superior U. S. intelligence. In the diplomatic game, knowledge was the only source of power.

The CIA was putting all of its resources to work on solving the mystery of what the cyber-attackers were up to. Consequently, Redmon had reduced the size of the Racine operation that was charged with picking up Melissa. Two officers should be more than enough for that task, and that way other officers could be back at their desks in Milwaukee on their computers helping the agency sift through the long list of rabbit trails that had to be run.

Despite the fact that the Internet and computer networks gave the agency the opportunity to immediately put most of its manpower to work on a specific case, so far they had not come up with an answer to the mystery of the cyber attack.

Redmon looked at the small TV on the bookcase across from his desk that was tuned to CNN. Geez, he thought, the stock market sure is taking a hit. He had been getting ready to move his retirement account out of equities into a conservative bond fund in anticipation of his retirement. Redmon mentally kicked himself for not having made that move sooner. If the drop in the market was reflected in his retirement account, which it probably was, he just lost close to twenty-five percent of his retirement savings.

Redmon was not a CIA section chief for nothing. His paranoia and keen imagination served him well in his career. He was feeling just paranoid enough to have the thought that perhaps twenty-five percent of his retirement account was going somewhere to finance terrorism. He picked up the phone and had his assistant place a call to a friend who worked as an investigator for the Securities Exchange Commission. Those guys should be able to do some screening and see who profited from the market collapse. The old adage, *Follow the money*, never seemed to become outdated.

His phone rang on an inside line. He knew before he answered it that his boss was calling wanting another update on where the cyber attack investigation stood. He had absolutely nothing new to tell him. He shrugged his shoulders and picked up the phone.

CHAPTER 43

Dawson could feel the cold and worry seeping into his bones. As the time approached for the interment he had only been able to pick up two officers standing next to the obelisk. No one showed up at the other two locations that he identified as being the most likely spots for two other surveillance teams. He let out a long slow sigh. He would just have to keep watching.

The burial was soon underway. The hearse pulled up as close to the gravesite as it could and the casket was being taken by the pallbearers to the grave. Family members and relatives of Mrs. Dowling were getting out of the funeral home limos and taking their places under the graveside tent. The priest had arrived and was pacing up and down beside the grave.

Just then, the car with Blaine, still posing as Melissa, pulled up on the far street about a hundred yards from the burial site. Dawson slipped the binoculars from his pocket and focused them on the car. One of the convent sisters got out of the back seat followed by Blaine and then another sister. Dawson swallowed hard. Blaine was dressed in black, as she had been when he first met her in Italy. How could he have not followed this intriguing woman to Berlin?

The group of three women made their way toward the gravesite. As soon as Blaine and the two sisters arrived and were seated, the priest began. An interment service is never long. Particularly, when it is cold and the sky is wearing a gray scowl.

The casket was lowered into its vault in the ground. Dawson noticed that the two officers stationed near the obelisk were beginning to move forward. As Dawson and Rat had planned, the car waiting to take Blaine and the two sisters away was on the opposite side of the grave site from the two officers.

Dawson could not help himself. He turned his binoculars in the direction of the car where Melissa was. He could see the vehicle and knew that she must be inside. As far as he knew, this was the closest he had been to her since their time together almost twenty years ago in Afghanistan. He could hardly take his binoculars off the car. The tinted windows were impenetrable to his gaze. It was only because the interment service was starting to break up, that Dawson focused back on the activity near the grave. Blaine and the two nuns accompanying her were starting at a good pace towards their car.

Some level of funeral etiquette prevailed so that the officers did not start running toward Blaine, and she and the sisters managed to reach the car before the officers could catch up with them. As soon as they were in the car, it accelerated down the street. Dawson could see the two officers were surprised that the car left so abruptly. They immediately turned and ran back toward the obelisk where their own vehicle was located. Dawson knew from his earlier inspection of the cemetery that they only had one way out—in the direction that Blaine's vehicle had gone.

Dawson jumped into his rental car and quickly brought it to the nearest intersecting blocking street. Luckily, the street was relatively narrow with vehicles parked on each side. He jerked the steering wheel hard in one direction and hit the accelerator and the brake. The vehicle swung in an arc into the center of the street. Dawson jumped out and surveyed the scene. Yes, his car would block all traffic on the street. He ran down the street in the direction of his pick-up point. Before getting out of sight, he stopped. Just then, the car with the two officers came around the corner barreling down the street. The officers' car came to a screeching stop just short of his vehicle. Both officers jumped out at the ready. They came up to Dawson's rental car and tried to move it one way or the other. He had left it locked with the parking brake on and their efforts were to no avail.

They were immediately on their cellphones seeking help, but as far as Dawson could see his blocking move had been effective. Knowing how the Company disdained the use of local law enforcement personnel, Dawson doubted that any reinforcements were close at hand. He opened the chat room window on his iPhone and sent a quick message to Rat to let him know that the block was in place and working. Then Dawson turned and headed down the street walking as fast as he could.

Three blocks and one alleyway later, he saw the coffee shop in sight that was his pick-up point. A car with Minnesota license plates pulled up in front of the coffee shop. Dawson headed across the street toward it. The driver side window came down and much to his surprise, there was a familiar face. It was Sister Theresa. Later he would wonder if she had asked for the assignment to pick him up. For the moment, he was just glad that

THE END OF DEMOCRACY

the car was there and that he knew it was for him. He opened the passenger-side door and slid into the front seat. Sister Theresa lost no time in maneuvering the car through several busy intersections onto Washington Avenue west and from there onto Interstate 94 heading north. From Milwaukee, they would head over to Madison, up to St. Paul and then north to the SOS convent.

As a precaution, Dawson slid way down in his seat, but after they got on Interstate 94 North he had gradually begun to sit back up. He realized that his real reason for sitting up was not to be in a more comfortable posture but to get a better view of Sister Theresa. She was not wearing her habit, but blue jeans, sweatshirt and a down vest. It was not because of her clothing that he wanted to see her better. Rather, it was his fascination with the glow of her energy and her stunning beauty.

"Good job," said Sister Theresa, looking over at Dawson as he pulled himself upright in his seat.

"Thanks," said Dawson, "it looks like everything is going off without a hitch. I can't believe the Company didn't have more resources out in the cemetery. But I guess you would say just be thankful for small blessings, huh?"

"Or big ones," said Sister Theresa, "this whole deal, if we can pull it off, is going to be one awesome blessing. And thank you, Mr. Dawson, for coming back north to help us out."

"Please, just call me Will," said Dawson. "How have you been, Sister Theresa?"

"I have been very well," said Sister Theresa. "Tell me about your journey. How have your practices been going with Father O'Donnell?"

Dawson paused, then he slowly let out his breath. This was the difficulty with these women that Dawson was attracted to. There was no such thing as trivial conversation. They got right to the point about the important things in life. Well, mused Dawson to himself, I guess I just don't like talking about the important things.

"I guess things have been going okay," said Dawson evasively. Not that he was intentionally evading Sister Theresa's question. He simply did not know himself. "I should say I have not gotten into a good routine. It was a long trip back to New Mexico, and then before Father O'Donnell came down from his hermitage and we had a chance to do work together, I got called by Rat to come up and help you guys out."

"Rat?" said Sister Theresa looking perplexed. "Who is this Rat?"

"Oh, you don't know about Rat? Rat is a friend of Blaine's. He is the one who got her the software job in Berlin. And he is the one who contacted your Mother Superior about coordinating the efforts to get Melissa back to Racine for her mother's funeral and to have Blaine act as a decoy. I met him in Turin, Italy at the International Enneagram Conference. He is a bit geeky, but all the girls love him, including Blaine, and he is a real phenomenon when it comes to doing stuff on the Internet."

"We all need talented friends, don't we?" said Sister Theresa.

"How are Man and Ooljee?"

Dawson began to relax just thinking about his two friends, a Native American boy and a Plott hound. "You know, they are probably the best friends I have right now. I had not realized that until you asked me how they were. The long miles together in the van coming up to the convent when I first met you, somehow we bonded."

"True friends are hard to come by. One of the advantages of convent life is you develop true and deep friendships whether you intend to or not. Was it the long ride together that caused you and Man to bond or something else?" asked Sister Theresa.

"Maybe it is because both Man and I are lonely. And as you sisters would probably say, a bit lost. The only one who is on solid footing in the whole group is Ooljee. Of course, he's got four of them. What I mean is—somehow that dog knows who he is. Maybe it is the Plott breeding, but he has no doubt that his job is to look after Man, and maybe now me too.

"You know the expression: 'Be yourself, the others are taken.' Ooljee doesn't even have to sniff at the others. He just knows what his life is all about and he could not be more pleased. Me, on the other hand, even though I am old enough to be retired from one career, I don't have a clue what my life is supposed to be about." Dawson had opened up more than he ever usually did with anyone and he wasn't sure how Sister Theresa would take his disclosures, but he knew it was because of her that he had opened up so.

Sister Theresa did not reply immediately. She sensed that Dawson's words needed to settle in his own mind. The rhythm of the tires counted the passage of time on the pavement. They were now past Milwaukee on the interstate headed for St. Paul.

"Will, what I have learned as a sister is that the journey is more important than getting there, and being deeply lost in the mystery of life is much more creative than knowing what you're doing. The challenge is not to be overcome by our own anxiety when we are in the mystery. That is what faith is and the contemplative practices of our Order—which allow us to experience the reality of faith—are all about."

"I think you are sounding like Father O'Donnell, telling me that what I really need to do is spend less time trying to figure out what my life is all about and more time engaging in practices which are going to allow me to be more fully present in the experience of my life."

"Very well put," said Sister Theresa, "you are a quick learner. That also means that you have the mind problem." She started laughing a deep belly laugh. Dawson felt he might have to grab the steering wheel so she wouldn't drive off the road.

"Don't worry, I've got the car," said Sister Theresa, "I have just wrestled with the same issue so often myself. It is such a paradox that the more easily the mind understands the problem, the more the mind is the barrier to solving the problem."

"Well, it is funnier for you, than it is for me," said Dawson. "But you are right. I seem to understand my issues pretty well, yet the

THE END OF DEMOCRACY

more I understand the more I seem to be stuck. So what am I supposed to do about that?"

Sister Teresa was still guffawing. "I keep being amazed that they didn't teach you about this in the CIA." She began to shake all over from another wave of deep laughter.

Dawson was a little irked by how funny she seemed to think this all was. "No, they didn't teach us these things. So what would you suggest?"

"I am sure that Father O'Donnell has already given you the practices that are going to bring you more out of your head and into the moment. Don't you have the traditional monastic routines of work and prayer and silence?"

"Yes, they keep getting interrupted by emergencies, but we do," said Dawson.

"Our Order probably engages in a greater variety of contemplative practices than you. Your Order puts such a great premium on silence. We value silence greatly, but we also engage in a number of active contemplative practices such as chanting and sacred dancing. The more physical the contemplative practices, the more helpful they have been to me in my getting out of my head. Mind you, there is nothing wrong with the deep spirituality of mental clarity. However, that is something entirely different from much of the chatter in our heads.

"After we get back to the convent, I am sure if you wanted to learn more about our practices, Mother Mary would let you visit for a while," said Sister Theresa gazing sideways at Dawson. "What do you say?"

Dawson was tongue-tied. He was trying to figure out whether Sister Theresa was giving this invitation because of an interest in him, or was she simply being inordinately decent like most of the sisters were. Dawson knew he was interested in being with Sister Theresa. Much more interested in her than whatever contemplative practices the nuns were doing at her convent.

This was always the challenge for Dawson. He would become enchanted by a woman like Melissa or Blaine, or now Sister Theresa. But when it came time for him to take the next natural step, or to become more vulnerable, he turned away and headed in the direction of whatever he could rationalize as being a higher calling. Suddenly he realized that because Sister Theresa was a nun, he had an easy way out of any commitment. Interestingly, the Sacred Order of the Sisters of Mary of Magdala did not practice celibacy, but he did not know exactly what that meant. He began to yawn from nervousness because he knew he needed to respond to Sister Theresa's question.

"Thank you for the invitation," said Dawson hesitantly, "let's see what Mother Mary has to say. I really do not know what I should be doing. After the Turin conference I came out to see Father O'Donnell in order to get his advice on trying to find Melissa, because Mrs. Dowling had given me a letter from Melissa asking me to try to find her. Now Mrs. Dowling is gone. Melissa is found, I guess you could say. I am not sure what Melissa wants me to do now or really what I want to do. As I was saying, I

THE END OF DEMOCRACY

guess I am a bit lost."

"That is great," said Sister Theresa, turning her warm, smiling countenance on him.

Dawson turned to look at her and for the first time felt a glimmer that everything might be all right.

*   *   *

Dawson and Sister Theresa arrived at the convent by late afternoon. They immediately went to talk with Mother Mary who let them know that Blaine had already arrived a couple hours earlier and was on her way overland to Canada.

Dawson was beginning to have that feeling of letdown that he used to have at the Company when an operation was completed. This time that feeling was mixed with his anxiety which had returned full force about the uncertainty of what he should do next.

"Mr. Dawson," said Mother Mary, "you look troubled. I do have one other message for you. Father O'Donnell and I have been in communication. He is aware that it would be impossible for you to fly back to the Southwest using the Godfrey Adams identity with which you traveled here. So he has suggested you stay here a while, and that when the weather gets better he will send Man and Ooljee in the van to come pick you up."

Dawson's face brightened. Maybe he had worked at the Company too long. He felt a sense of relief at being told what he should do, rather than having to figure that out for himself. Of course, being told that he needed to stay where he would be around Sister Theresa made him feel like Br'er Rabbit being thrown in the briar patch.

Dawson smiled, "that sounds good to me. Just let me know what you want me to do around here and I'll try to be useful."

"There are probably some things that you can do around here to help us," said Mother Mary, "but in my conversation with Father O'Donnell he made it clear that your time here was to be spent as much as possible in getting the same instruction that we give to our novitiates. If you can fall in love with Sister Theresa, then there is also the possibility that you can fall in love with God. While you are here you will see me for spiritual direction. Sister Theresa will be your mentor for learning and deepening the practices that we all engage in here at the convent. Do you have any questions?"

Dawson was astonished. She had read his feelings about Sister Theresa like he was an open book. He looked at Mother Mary. It was all he could do to nod his head yes.

CHAPTER 44

Norris and Walker were finally rescued, and Norris was in the infirmary at the Palmer Station recovering from frostbite. The station manager had done an incredible job of getting across the ice to retrieve the two men, after Norris had gotten lost in a snowstorm.

When the storm came through Norris had been out on the ice by himself. After the storm blew over Walker did everything he could to find Norris. Without success. When Walker realized he had no alternative, he radioed the Palmer Station and alerted them to the situation. It took two days to find Norris, but it appeared he would make it. The more immediate question was whether he might lose some toes or fingers from frostbite. No medical doctor was currently stationed at Palmer, but there were trained medics and a setup existed to get medical consultations about any problem over the Internet by satellite phone.

Terry Shaw, the bright energetic woman who was the manager of the Palmer Station, took Norris on as her personal project. She seemed to consider the well-being of everybody at the station as her personal responsibility, and she was not about to let Norris' injuries go unhealed if there was any way she could help him. It was, Walker thought, as if anything short of a full recovery by

Norris would be a blemish on her stewardship of the Palmer Station.

Whatever the reason for Shaw's motivation, she was constantly in Norris' room in the infirmary looking after him and joking with him about life in their frozen world. Norris was not sure that he would want to give up his toes in exchange for such careful attention from Terry Shaw, but the thought crossed his mind.

"How are you doing, Norris? Any toes fall off the great scientist today?" asked Terry, as she wheeled around the corner into his room for probably the tenth time that morning.

"Well, the last time I counted them there were at least nine," said Norris, happy as always to have Terry back in his room. "Of course, given the other fun activities you have for us to do at Palmer, counting your toes is pretty far up on the list of what is most fun, right up next to good scholarly research for my next journal article." Terry had been teasing Norris repeatedly about his scientific credentials, and he expected that she was on to his cover.

"As manager of the station, I have full authority, like the captain of the ship, to look after my personnel. That includes medical authority. Obviously, I need to order an enema for you so you can get a full appreciation of all the fun activities here at Palmer." She smiled at Norris, sat on his bedside, and with her right hand pushed his hair off his forehead.

Easy kidding and gallows humor were the perfect design for how she and Norris connected. Trying to entertain Norris with humor was as intimate as Terry would allow herself to get. The one exception was that, because Norris was the patient, she could allow herself to caress his forehead in an offhand way.

To Norris, her touch was electric and for a moment he would forget the witty repartee and gaze into her light gray eyes.

"You know, Terry, you were probably joking about the enema, but I think if you put a couple of shots of Scotch in one, I am more than ready." He said with an impish smile.

"Sure, we can do that. But it would have to be cheap Scotch. With the rest of what is in that enema, it's going to go through you so fast I would hate to waste good single malt."

"Next thing I know, you will be threatening me with a seal blubber dinner," said Norris. "Whatever happened to patient's rights?"

"Great idea," said Terry. "That is exactly what those little toes need, a little blubber to get the wiggle back in them."

Just then, Terry's pager went off. She unhooked it from her belt, looked at it and frowned.

"Don't die on me, Norris," she said with a quick smile. She turned and quickly left the room.

CHAPTER 45

"Jesus, am I glad to see you, Father," said Godfrey Adams, as he emerged from the holding cell and almost ran across the prisoner release room to be embraced by Father Hay.

"I am glad to see you, too," said Father Hay, as he looked into Godfrey's bloodshot eyes. "Looks like you need a little sleep."

"You're not kidding," said Godfrey. "But first I've got to talk to somebody about this. I don't understand what happened."

"I have my car right outside," said Father Hay "You can talk to me in the car and I will have you home shortly."

Once they were settled in the car and on the road, all of Godfrey's pent up emotions came spilling out in words.

"It was like in the old days, being pulled over and arrested for driving while gay," said Godfrey as he put on his seatbelt. "These guys who looked like local police just came by and took me away. I asked them if they were arresting me and for what, and I never got a clear answer. They took me in the back of this van so I couldn't see where we were going. They put a hood over my head. The next thing I remember was being in this interrogation room. I never again saw the local police who picked me up. There were just these two guys who kept me up all night asking me questions. They never told me who they were and they never let me call you, or a lawyer, or Jeff or anyone else. I thought we lived in America, 'the land of the free and the home of the brave.' Was I mistaken! I might as well have been in some Soviet gulag."

"I am just glad your ordeal is over," said Father Hay. "Right now you need some rest and food and I think we can take care of both of those."

"Yes," said Godfrey with a huge sigh. "You know, after the long interrogation and then being alone in a dark room for I don't know how many hours, I kept having this question in my mind: Why is this happening to me? I mean I think we have made progress together Father in our spiritual work, but all of a sudden I felt very empty when I was alone, isolated and imprisoned. Do you know what I mean?"

Father Hay did not expect to be having a spiritual direction session with Godfrey on the way home from the police station. However, he knew that one never gets to choose the timing of the right opportunity to follow the energy of big questions. "Tell me, Godfrey," asked Father Hay, "was there any time during this isolation and imprisonment that you were able to be connected to God?"

Godfrey paused. He realized he had been going on and on as if it was all emotional chaos, but as he reflected he realized this was not a totally accurate picture. "There were some times at night—I think it was night, I don't really know—when I was able to practice centering prayer. Not only did I feel connected with something larger than myself at one point I felt this inner fullness. In a strange way, I was almost happy."

"Excellent," said Father Hay, "I would say that all the spiritual work you have been doing has borne fruit. This is a bizarre and traumatic experience which you have had that came totally out of the blue. The fact that during that time you could practice being centered and connected is truly wonderful.

"I have tried to stress to you," said Father Hay, "that theological views are really not that important to spiritual progress. What is important is the continuity of your practices. What your experience does highlight is what I believe to be the central mission of Jesus—that he came as a teacher of transformation of consciousness."

Father Hay paused, took a deep breath and then went on. "The path Jesus defined to get to the Kingdom of Heaven is interesting in that it's almost completely counterintuitive. For the vast majority of the world's spiritual seekers, the way to God is up. To go up requires energy and most spiritual disciplines work on some variation of the principle of conservation of energy— practices that help build up the containment of energy in order to ascend the spiritual ladder. Through the disciplines of prayer, meditation and fasting, and by avoiding physical and emotional lust and ego gratification, one seeks to concentrate energy in order to reach the divine.

"Jesus' path of transformation built on these spiritual traditions.

He saw the necessity of the disciplines of prayer, of retreats in the desert, but his path did not stop there. Instead of concentrating his life force, Jesus' path was to teach surrender, to let go, to give it all away. Unitive consciousness is reached not through the ego's accumulation of effort—though effort and discipline are necessary—but ultimately only through self-surrender. This is the revolutionary path that Jesus introduced to the world. How does one make this shift in consciousness? How do we repent, or move into the larger mind of the heart? Sometimes it is in ordeals like you have had that such a breakthrough becomes possible."

As tired as he was, Godfrey was suddenly deeply attentive to what Father Hay was saying. He had the feeling that Father Hay was offering him a way to understand how his experience, bad though it was, might diminish his theological frustrations with Christianity. "I am all ears, Father. Tell me more."

"The route that Jesus suggested was different from anything that had ever been taught up to that point. It is still radical. You see the message throughout the Sermon on the Mount: 'You win, by losing.' We let go of our will and fall into a larger will in the unified field. This radical transformation of consciousness is only accessed through an attitude of inner receptivity which longs to experience this greater field of consciousness. We must be willing to experience the death of our own limited ego consciousness and enter the flow, and desire to live from our heart center which is a part of the larger field."

Godfrey interrupted. "This is a little abstract for me. Can you ground what you are saying in one of Jesus' teaching stories?"

"Okay. Let me see. An example would be how this path is outlined in what I call the difficult parables. Take the one of the five wise and five foolish bridesmaids in Matthew 25. A great wedding feast is about to take place and they are waiting on the bridegroom (Christ). They all fall asleep (the ego trance). Suddenly the bridegroom is coming. Five have remembered to bring oil for their lamps (they have been practicing centering prayer) and they light them and head into the banquet hall. Five haven't remembered to bring spare oil and their lamps are now out of fuel (they have neglected their spiritual practices). The five without ask their fellow bridesmaids if they can borrow oil so they can go to the wedding feast (into the unified field of consciousness which is love). The five with oil refuse.

"If this parable is viewed from a dualistic standpoint, it's about sharing and doesn't make any sense, because it would be teaching us not to share. But, if the parable is about transformation, then the reason the five bridesmaids who have oil can't give it to the five who don't, is that the oil symbolizes something that has to be created within you. If the oil stands for the ripeness of connection to the flow of love from God, nobody can give it to you and nobody can take it away. You don't get to the wedding feast unless you are tapped into a flow of love energy from being grounded in your essence that connects you to the unified field of God.

"The fact that you were able to make a connection to God, Godfrey, while subjected to this absurd random imprisonment is a tribute to the work you have done and God's Grace."

Godfrey shook his head. "I hear your words, Father; and maybe with time I will come to that appreciation, but right now it all seems too raw."

"Of course. It is difficult. So let's look at another difficult teaching. A prospective follower asked Jesus, 'First may I go home and bury my father?' Jesus' response is 'Let the dead bury their own dead.' Again if this teaching is about love, it makes no sense in a dualistic way. Jesus seems from that perspective to be giving unloving advice. However, if the teaching is about how to access a greater field of consciousness, it makes complete sense in a unitive way.

"Jesus is saying that if we are attached to our identity in this world, if that's our level of consciousness, then we will not be able to experience unity of consciousness. In other words, we will not be able to follow him.

"These examples show that Jesus' teachings were not simply 'be nice, share and trust.' No, the heart of his teachings were transform your consciousness and come with me into the unified field of consciousness, which he so beautifully called the Kingdom of Heaven, where we will be able to flow in God's abundant love.

"Father Hay," said Godfrey, "I did know some serenity during this ordeal, but it would be a stretch to say I was in any kind of flow of greater consciousness. I mostly felt anger at the injustice of what was happening to me."

"Did this injustice get bigger than you?" asked Father Hay.

"What do you mean?" asked Godfrey.

"What I am talking about," said Father Hay, "is the difference between anger for others or grief for the suffering of others, and personal anger or grief. Jesus' anger at the money changers was anger for others, not personal anger coming from an irritable self, but anger on behalf of the larger Self to which we are all connected. We call this kind of anger love."

"I can assure you that I did not feel any love toward those guys who were abusing me. They seemed absolutely certain that I knew something about some woman named Melissa. I do not have a clue who she is. But once I got over my initial fear, something did change. I am not sure what allowed me to get over my fear. Maybe it was just that it was all so absurd. There was no rational basis that allowed my fear to grow, so it began to recede. Whatever the reason, toward the end I did begin to feel some kindness toward my interrogators. I think one of them might have been a gay guy still in the closet. I had not thought about it at the time, but as soon as I began to feel some kindness toward them, the interrogation stopped."

"Here we are, Godfrey," said Father Hay as he stopped the car in front of Godfrey's condo. "I'm going to let you off here. I know Jeff is anxious to see you."

"Thank you again, so much," said Godfrey, and he paused as he began to open the car door. "You know, Father Hay, you might be right. Something must have happened that was bigger than the little me that felt so unjustly treated." With a huge smile, Godfrey reached over and shook Father Hay's hand and then pulled himself out of the car.

CHAPTER 46

The opportunity for Dawson to spend time with Sister Theresa at the convent evaporated quickly. It soon became apparent to Rat that the plan for Melissa's and Blaine's trip was woefully shortsighted. All of Rat's efforts had focused on getting Melissa to the United States, and he hadn't focused on getting Melissa and Blaine back to Europe again. Because Melissa and Blaine looked so similar, Blaine had been successful in allowing Melissa to return to the U. S. undetected using Blaine's passport, but now Rat realized there was absolutely no way that Blaine and Melissa could travel back to Europe using their real identities without being apprehended.

Once Rat realized that his brilliant plan had not provided an exit strategy, he was in touch with Mother Mary and Dawson. Dawson was then dispatched from the convent in Minnesota to obtain new passports for the two women. Dawson, of course, could no longer travel as Godfrey Adams, the identity he had used earlier.

So Dawson was back to 1950s travel mode, which did not require identification. That meant taking a bus back to Georgetown with passport pictures of both Melissa and Blaine, in the hopes of getting new travel documents for them from his friend Sergei Karsiloff. Despite Rat's insistence that Dawson go directly to Georgetown, Dawson decided to first return to the monastery to talk with Father O'Donnell. Dawson was beginning to recognize the importance of an authentic connection with himself before making a critical decision. He had grown enough along his spiritual path not to take off across the country at the behest of somebody else, without first becoming aware of his own feelings. Dawson also thought that his trip east would be better undertaken if Man and Ooljee traveled with him.

As the Trailways bus rolled across the center of America toward Denver, Dawson could not help but reflect that now, when Melissa and Blaine needed his help most, he realized he had to give first priority to deepening his own spiritual life. For the first time in his life, he was acutely aware of how spiritually inadequate he was and that ultimately he could be of little help to anyone until that changed. This meant that Melissa and Blaine might have to lay low in one of the convent's hermitages out in the Canadian wilderness for awhile.

It was new for Dawson to stop organizing his life around the priorities and emergencies of somebody else. This old habit was deeply ingrained in him after twenty years at the Company, and he had felt lost and depressed after he retired. As the miles unwound, he began to see that finding himself was the only path he could take.

*   *   *

It took three days for Sister Lisa to lead Melissa and Blaine to the hermitage. Most of the trip had been in the all-terrain vehicle which Sister Lisa had driven. They had gone for miles and miles deep into the wilderness and at some point Sister Lisa announced they had crossed into Canada. The last part of the trip was on foot—the virgin timber was simply so thick that there was no room to maneuver the all-terrain vehicle through it. After they got off of the ATV there was scant evidence of a trail, but Sister Lisa was confident of where she was going.

Sister Lisa's confidence was well-placed. At the end of the third day they emerged out of dense forest into a clearing. In the center of the clearing was a small hut apparently made from logs, cut from the trees when the clearing was made.

Melissa and Blaine had been told by Mother Mary that the hermitage was designed for silent, dark retreats. Neither Melissa nor Blaine knew what a dark retreat was. Only after they got to the hermitage, and Sister Lisa began to show them around, did this become clear.

The hermitage consisted of a round building inside of which were two windowless round rooms connected by a hallway. Sister Lisa explained to Melissa and Blaine that the purpose of the hermitage was to accommodate more advanced spiritual students. It provided a place for a silent retreat in total darkness. One room was for the retreatant and the other for the attender. One could not undertake a dark retreat on one's own, it was simply too dangerous. The possibility of a mental breakdown was too real. In fact, the hermitage had not been used since last year, when a sister on a dark retreat had suffered a severe psychic episode. It had taken the attender a week to get her back to the convent and then to a hospital.

Blaine was apprehensive about the idea of a dark retreat. On the other hand, Melissa seemed to think it was a great idea, and that maybe it was the reason that they were there after all. Particularly, when they were told by Sister Lisa that it might be a long time before Dawson was able to get them new passports to travel on.

Sister Lisa left them with simple, but ample provisions. They had a large bag of rice and a variety of dried beans as well as numerous packets of detox tea. For the first two days after Sister Lisa was gone Melissa and Blaine spent time exploring their immediate area. The hermitage was located by a wonderfully sweet spring only about 150 feet from the hermitage. On the opposite side of the hermitage a primitive privy had been constructed.

"Blaine, we ought to make the best use of our time here and use this place for the purpose it was intended. Why don't we both do a dark retreat?" said Melissa.

Blaine felt uncertain. "I am not sure this is the best time for me," said Blaine. "Maybe there is never a good time to take the next step into the unknown. As you know, Aasia and I recently finished an intensive time at the convent in Sweden. Do you really believe the timing is right for a dark retreat for me? And if we do this, doesn't somebody need to be at an attender?

"That is a most important question," said Melissa. "There is a risk if we both do a dark retreat at the same time. I know the

Mother Superior would be upset with me if we tried to do it together. Maybe that is not our only choice. We could take turns."

Blaine brightened. "Well, of course, that's a good idea."

"And you ought to go first, Blaine," said Melissa, "you would need to have the experience of what a dark retreat is like before you can know how to be an attender. Does that make sense?"

Blaine nodded her head. It did make sense, but it also made her more apprehensive. She preferred for Melissa to go first. That way, she thought, she could always decide not to do it if it appeared too hazardous.

"Blaine, I realize I'm pretty enthusiastic about this," said Melissa, "but it is absolutely up to you to decide if this is the right time for you to do a dark retreat. Don't let my enthusiasm for it sway you one way or the other. We have plenty of time for you to discern if it is the right thing for you at this time."

"Thanks," said Blaine, "it does make me feel a bit better to have the pressure off. Maybe I'll know in a day or two what I believe is right for me. That will also give me more time to read and study some of the material here in the hermitage about a dark retreat." She realized she had no idea how long dark retreats were supposed to last. And since she had no way to know how long it would take Dawson to get new passports, she had no idea how long they might be secluded away at the hermitage. She picked up a booklet entitled *Living in the Light—Making a Dark Retreat* and began to read.

CHAPTER 47

Slade could not believe what he was reading in *The New York Times*. Peter Wagner had not let go. He couldn't wait to tell Joe Carroll about this. Naturally, he would want to tell Dawson if he ever showed up again. Slade could hardly believe it himself.

The paper went into detail describing how a corporation, which Wagner set up some time back, was running for President. The article also went to great lengths to quote from legal scholars about whether this was proper and noting that lawsuits challenging it had already been filed, but the bottom line seemed to be that it was happening.

Slade put the paper down. He picked up the phone and called Joy to tell her.

"Joy, you will not believe what's happening. Do you remember the strange guy up in Maine who I had the job with that took me to Italy?"

"Hey, Sweetheart," said Joy, not nearly as concerned about what Slade had to say as she was glad that he had called.

"Yes, Beautiful," said Slade, immediately backtracking to first connect with his fiancée. "I was just reading the paper and was amazed to find out that this guy Wagner that I worked for at one time has a corporation that is running for President. Isn't that bizarre?"

"President of what?" asked Joy in a deadpan voice.

"The good old U.S. of A," replied Slade.

"Gosh, that is weird," said Joy, "you do hang around with some strange people. I'm just glad to know that there's somebody out there weirder than me."

Slade laughed. "You know, the really bizarre thing is that I even take this seriously. I guess it's because I once had a long conversation with Wagner, which told me how serious he was. What I am afraid of is that other people will take it seriously. The article says that other corporations are already making campaign contributions to the corporation seeking to be elected. Wagner kept talking about how individual democracy was dead. I guess he's about to prove it. The corporation is a news organization. One pollster, which of course is owned by the corporation running, has already come out with poll numbers indicating it has a good chance to win."

"You have won me," said Joy. "Am I going to see you tonight? I have to leave work a little earlier today because I have about two hours of work to do on fortune cookies. I was hoping you would be coming over later."

"Absolutely," said Slade, "you know it is my good fortune to have the chance to be with you, and I don't want to miss any opportunity. That's the way the cookie crumbles."

"Good grief, now I'm a prisoner of fortune cookie love," said Joy. She smiled at Slade, "and I couldn't be happier. See you about eight. Oh, and what is the name of the new candidate?"

"That makes it all the funnier, in an ironic sort of way, it is Good Opportunity for our Democracy, Inc.. Or, and here is the sick part, GOD, Inc..

"Hmm," said Joy, "maybe I can use this in the fortune cookies."

Slade smiled. Democracy was going, maybe already had gone, to hell in a hand-basket, but being in love with Joy made all the difference to him. He wondered if that could possibly make any difference to the world. He laughed out loud. He would need to talk to Joe Carroll about that.

CHAPTER 48

Father Hay could tell that Godfrey was upset even before Father Hay opened his mouth to greet him.

"Hey, Godfrey," said Father Hay, "it's good to see you."

"I just cannot believe it," said Godfrey, "a broadcasting corporation is running for president. What is the world coming to? I have never heard anything more absurd. And it's called GOD!"

Father Hay laughed. Their session today was starting even before they got to Father Hay's office. "Tell me why you are so upset by this news?" said Father Hay.

"That should be obvious," said Godfrey, "but I don't have a clue what the answer is. Somehow this really has got me upset."

Father Hay led Godfrey down the hallway to his office. Father Hay sat in the torn brown leather chair next to his desk and Godfrey sloughed into a brightly upholstered chair opposite.

"Focus on your body," said Father Hay, "what are you feeling?"

"As I am sensing my bodily sensations right now, I feel an overwhelming sadness. Maybe I have been out of touch with the way things really are, but somehow it seems to me there is this sense of huge loss, a loss of the way I thought the world was and should be."

"That makes a lot of sense, Godfrey," said Father Hay, "you have experienced much loss in your life. As a gay man you have spent a lot of time trying to understand how you fit into a culture that at times has been very antagonistic to you. Now there is more loss. I confess to you that for some time I have also felt this grief about the loss of constructive politics in our country. It was only in sharing about it with my spiritual director that I began to have some inkling of hope about it all. Would you like for me to share with you what he had to say?"

"Sure," said Godfrey. His curiosity having been aroused, he settled into a somewhat calmer disposition.

"My spiritual director believes that democracy, as it is idealized in this country, has long been worn out. He believes that maybe this is for the better. He thinks that democracy is the political expression of the majority of people choosing to live in a dualistic reality, choosing to live in our small ego selfs. In other words, democracy fits perfectly for those who have not yet attained unitive consciousness. Democracy is all about losers and winners. Democracy promotes abstract political philosophies by Republicans and Democrats, which they in turn apply to whatever problem is presented.

"Democracy as it plays out in this country never creates win-win solutions. It might be better named dualistic democracy. It is about power and control. It is about creating fear. Fear that the other party will win, fear that their philosophy will control, fear that their policies will hurt me, and on it goes. Democracy as we practice it has led to an alienated culture. It has left us with a second-rate education system, because people are so busy debating their abstract political philosophy that they can't come together in order to find practical solutions.

"Every now and then, a new candidate will come along who has the intention of overcoming our dualistic political approach. He or she won't last long. Either this person will not be re-elected or they will soon be overwhelmed by the dualistic approach of party politics. They will eventually be co-opted and nothing will change."

"I see what you're saying," said Godfrey, "but what is the alternative? Everybody knows that democracy is an inefficient system of government. It is just that there are no better alternatives."

"If you look at it in a dualistic way," said Father Hay, "it appears that you are right, that there are no better alternatives. However, if humankind's level of consciousness were raised to a unitive level all that would change. At that level, there would not be this huge drive for power and control. People would understand the transformative message of Christ—that 'the last shall be first.'

"I believe democracy is finished. The fact is that rather than creating good government, it tends to create fear, to alienate people and set groups apart from each other. These results show

how little vitality it has left. We are attached to the idealism of a democracy that the founders of our country had.

The reality is we live in a system of dualistic thinking, which our democracy promotes. It produces poorly educated people, lots of fear and mediocre results on the issues it tackles."

"I was feeling bad when I came in," said Godfrey squirming in his chair, "and it sounds like I should be feeling even worse."

"The situation we are in currently commonly arises when any old structure becomes worn out and is ready to be discarded. Yet, at this point, no one can see what will replace it. We will either go forward or regress badly. We cannot yet imagine how a unitive conscious democracy would work, but we can imagine the outcomes that would be available in a system based on unitive consciousness where the goal was always to create win-win solutions. Where, if you thought A was the answer and I felt B was the answer, we would always have a way to get to C. Can you imagine how much progress could be made in addressing the problems that face humankind if this were what motivated the political process?"

"Just thinking about it scares me," said Godfrey. "I see your vision of where you would like us to get to, but I don't see any way it can be done."

"It is scary," said Father Hay, "but the system we have created based on power and money—where a corporation can run for President—you have to admit it's bankrupt. Maybe back in the Middle Ages when a person did not have a sense of identity apart from tribe or kingdom, it was just as scary to contemplate not being subservient to a chief or a king. At that time, the thought of something different, of what eventually turned out to be democracy, was way beyond anybody's comprehension. One thing we know is that nothing stays the same. We are in a hard place—our democracy has changed from a system allowing diverse people to live in community to a system of people being controlled through power and money. Sometimes the hardest thing to give up is an ideal in our heads.

"This loss does not mean that our broken system cannot be replaced with something better. Do we think we would keep the same form of government for a hundred years or five hundred? Of course not. You get the point. Something better always comes down the pike. At this point it is just not clear what it might look like. But, we will change, and we will seek to adapt a better way to govern ourselves.

"Our American emphasis on individualism, which is a fear response to the complexity of modernity, has caused us to spend a good bit of time in the subjective experience of our own separated selves. We would not have all this political partisanship if we realized we were not really separate after all. We wouldn't worry about trying to control or dominate others if we experienced that all those someone elses were also part of us."

"What do you mean fear response to modernity? That is a bit sketchy for me," said Godfrey.

"Do you remember when the United States invaded Iraq and tried to establish a democracy there? The opportunity for the ideal of democracy soon slipped away. Why? Because democracy simply provided a format for warring factions to fight about power. It was not about bringing people together and moving the country forward, but dividing people into groups and fighting each other for control.

"Contrast this with what happened in Egypt in February of 2011. A dictatorship of many years was overturned by the united consciousness of the country. This peaceful revolution was accomplished not because of angry, warring factions, the usual products of democracy, but because the consciousness of the people was united together for something larger. People wanted something greater than just their various limited interests. The rallying cry of their victory became, 'Lift your head high, you are an Egyptian.' What won out was not the result of our old-fashioned paradigm of conservative versus liberal, or Islamist versus secularist, but unity of the desire for human dignity.

"Outwardly, the culturally correct West interpreted the united consciousness of Egypt as a desire for old-fashioned conventional democracy. However, structure and content are not the same thing. Yes, the people of Egypt wanted to move beyond the old authoritarian power structure, but not to a new divisive power structure. What the united consciousness of the people of Egypt desired was a structure that provided human dignity for all. Such a structure is one that requires a higher level of human consciousness than what is encouraged by the manipulative media and divisive political institutions that are the products of dualistic democracy. The desire of what the united consciousness of the Egyptian people wanted was, unfortunately, way ahead of the forms available to achieve their goal."

Godfrey took a deep gasping breath, unaware that he had not been breathing.

Father Hay nodded his understanding of the impact of what he was saying on Godfrey and kept on going. "What is certain is we will not get to something better if my idea and your idea are in competition. We will need a process that takes us beyond a dualistic approach. We will go backwards, or we will go forward because enough people's consciousnesses have evolved and unitive democracy becomes possible. The best hope I know for that process is to get on about the business of what brought you here to start with—continuing to walk deeper down the path of your own spiritual journey. So tell me, Godfrey, where is a divine reality most present today in your life?"

Godfrey was still reeling from the shock of what Father Hay had told him. He started to speak and stopped. He simply did not know what to say.

CHAPTER 49

Charles Redmon tossed the latest Project 1776 report back down on his desk. For the first time in his long career he understood why a CIA officer would break his oath and go to the press. Using an extraordinarily effective e-mail logarithm, one of his case officers had been able to intercept Melissa's e-mail. For the first time, Redmon had a grasp of what was at stake.

He had the feeling that everyone was preparing for an OK Corral showdown. Redmon was still not sure where Melissa was. He just knew that she was not in the United States and for long periods of time did not use e-mail. He was quite sure she was trying to raise her level of consciousness the last few increments in order to intervene in the conscious thoughts of people around the world.

The CIA had made some progress. Although Walker and Norris at first weren't getting anywhere, there were encouraging signs. After Norris nearly froze to death and got frostbitten, things began to turn around, at least for Norris, and he was making real progress in becoming aware of his energy field. Walker, on the other hand, had made no progress at all. Now Norris had requested that he continue his assignment at the Palmer Station in Antarctica, and Walker, his buddy, was asking to return stateside.

While Norris was making progress, Redmon had heard through the grapevine that he was totally infatuated with the station director, Terry Shaw. Good Company officers did not get infatuated or fall in love on the job—that was not part of the job description.

Redmon took out Norris' file. Norris was not helping the fight if he was spending his time at the Palmer Station falling in love. He would re-assign Norris to become a student at the University of Arizona's Center for Consciousness Studies. The University of Arizona's Center for Consciousness Studies had picked up where the Department of Defense's old remote viewing program left off. Remote viewing is seeing something in a location that is hidden, or distant, from the viewer. The Department of Defense sponsored research into remote viewing at Stanford University back in the Cold War when there was concern that the Russians were making progress doing similar work. This research was led by Hal Puthoff and Russel Targ. Uri Geller was their Exhibit A.

Redmon chuckled. He once went to a CIA demonstration where Uri Geller entertained the audience by bending spoons. As far as Redmon knew, Uri never gave the CIA much beyond some cheap entertainment and stalking horse research that encouraged the Russians to do research on something that would go nowhere.

Redmon suddenly realized what was bothering him about the 1776 report. The rationale it gave for Melissa's actions made sense. Furthermore, the articulation of the view that democracy had become an outmoded structure for governance was presented with unerring logic. Democracy has always been paired with capitalism. However, as the report sketched out, open-market

THE END OF DEMOCRACY

theory is also compatible with various structures of government. He was aware of the strong argument that government by an elite was much more effective and efficient than democracy. The Chinese version of a free-market economy has taken more people out of poverty and made them middle-class in the past twenty years than has ever occurred at any time in human history. Yet the Chinese still needed to go through the stage in which an individual's sense of self could evolve. Good old-fashioned democracy is the hothouse in which that transformation occurs.

In the United States the situation was totally different. Lines were being drawn in the sand between those who are attached to their ego's need to dominate and control on both the left and right. Out of sight are those people working with Melissa, whoever they are. This group is dedicated to raising their consciousness sufficiently so that they can overcome their ego's needs and at this higher level of consciousness affect the thought patterns of everyone else. They believe that at this higher level of consciousness they are not separate from everyone, therefore their thoughts are everyone's thoughts. These people think that democracy as it is being practiced in the United States is outmoded, that it encourages dualistic thinking that keeps people in fear, anxiety and anger. These emotions drive a need for security found in loyalty to an ideological group and the demonizing of everybody else. For those in this dualism there is no overriding principle that brings people, who are different, together.

The report concluded that apparently Melissa and her cohorts were not breaking any laws, unless you could call long retreats and contemplative practices terrorism. That would be a stretch for any judge, but that was not Redmon's problem. The CIA was not about bringing people to justice. Its job was to eliminate anyone who was a threat to the United States. But, mused Redmon, what if the real threat was the form of what the United States had become? He surely loved its people. But was the form of American democracy now, like the Wizard of Oz, something entirely different behind the curtain, than what everyone thought?

Redmon let loose a huge sigh. The politics of the United States was becoming more and more brittle and fragmented. His job was not to worry about what was behind the curtain. His job was to fight for what was supposed to be there, even if nothing was.

Yes, Redmon thought, maybe he should retire.

CHAPTER 50

Dawson was relieved to be reunited with Father O'Donnell. Simply being in Father O'Donnell's presence calmed Dawson down. And Father O'Donnell had the uncanny ability to reassure Dawson while at the same time making him aware of the challenges the priest saw occurring in Dawson's life. Father O'Donnell explained to Dawson that his compulsive need to go from one project to the next was a way for Dawson to prevent himself from feeling anxiety and fear—that impatience was actually a form of activity greed.

Dawson knew patience was not his strong suit, which was putting it mildly. Father O'Donnell suggested to Dawson that taking on a spiritual practice of patience would be helpful. Dawson, on the other hand, was feeling he would just as soon have his teeth pulled, but he knew he was back visiting Father O'Donnell so that he could be told what he needed to hear.

The reality was that in being forced into using old-fashioned transportation in order to avoid detection by the Company, Dawson was having to practice patience whether he wanted to or not. After traveling from Minnesota back to the Southwest to talk with Father O'Donnell, Dawson took a Trailways bus east to rendezvous with Sergei Karsiloff in Georgetown. It took Sergei several weeks to get new identity documents made for Melissa and Blaine. Dawson already had an extra identity for himself, but he had Sergei make a spare for him also, just in case. While checking in with Sergei in Georgetown, Dawson lay low, living in cheap D.C. motels and hanging out in public libraries.

Once Dawson had the new passports, he took another Trailways bus back to Denver. There he met up with Man and Ooljee. Father O'Donnell had agreed that Man could drive the monastery van up to Denver to meet Dawson. The three of them then headed back up to Minnesota.

After traveling almost non-stop for twelve hours in the van they arrived at the Sacred Order of the Sisters of Mary of Magdala convent in northern Minnesota. As soon as the van stopped Dawson, Man and Ooljee unfolded from the vehicle and stepped out to stretch, yawn and, in Ooljee's case, find a bush to pee on. Though it was late at night, a light was on in the convent office. Perhaps someone was still up. Dawson and Man walked stiffly toward the convent office.

When he opened the door to the convent office, Mother Mary looked up from behind a desk on the other side of the counter.

"It is good to see you back, Brother Issac," she said. "You know I am not complaining, but it sure took you awhile." Mother Mary looked tired and stressed.

"Yes," said Dawson, "it was a frustratingly long trip. And I'm glad to be here. I hope I can still be helpful."

THE END OF DEMOCRACY

"I hope you can too," said Mother Mary, "but things have gotten much more complicated since you left. We have been able to discern a change in the energy field here, which tells us we have come under more intense surveillance. This level of energy intrusion made it very difficult for our younger sisters who were just learning how to control their energy fields to make progress. For that reason, most of them have left and gone to Sweden. Unfortunately, this makes your task of delivering the passports to Melissa and Blaine difficult. No one is left here who knows the way to the dark retreat house."

Suddenly her mood seemed to shift. "Let's talk more about this in the morning. I know you need some sleep." She looked past him at Man. "I expect you both are hungry. Standing and looking over the counter where she could see Ooljee, she said, "I should say all three of you are probably hungry. Come with me back to the kitchen, I am sure we can find you something there."

Mother Mary started down the hallway then turned and looked back at Dawson. "Brother Issac, I am afraid Sister Theresa has gone back to Sweden. You are stuck with the likes of me, but then I don't expect you will have much time to hang around here either." With that, she turned and headed down the hallway toward the kitchen. Dawson, Man and Ooljee followed.

CHAPTER 51

Dawson struggled to pull himself up out of bed. Off in the distance he could hear the bell ringing, calling the sisters to the morning chapel service. He looked across the room at the cot on the other side. Man was already up. The space below Man's cot, where Ooljee had slept, was also empty. Those two must have gotten more nap time in the van than I realized, thought Dawson. He had a vague, fleeting thought that Mother Mary would expect him to be at chapel, but it passed even before his body collapsed back to sleep.

Two hours later, Dawson pulled himself out of bed and stepped into the shower. He pulled on jeans and a T-shirt, slipped on sneakers and made his way to the kitchen. Mother Mary was there waiting for him.

"Breakfast is over," she said, eyeing Dawson a bit critically as she pulled a chair up to the kitchen table. "However, I made you a couple of fried egg sandwiches." She pushed a plate with two white bread sandwiches on it toward him.

"Thanks," said Dawson. It was not what he would have picked to eat, but the eggs were still warm in the middle and the sandwiches tasted good.

"I know you're going to need to rest up a bit," said Mother Mary, "but I hope you can leave as soon as possible to try to find Blaine and Melissa. After most of the young sisters left to go back to Sweden there was no one here who knew the way to the hermitage. Because of the surveillance, it has not been safe for one of us to try and find them, so no one has checked on them or even taken them food. They have been out there now for over five weeks. In fact, I am not sure how you will be able to find their hermitage. All I know is you will simply have to find them," she said with an anxious frown.

Just then the back door of the kitchen swung open hard and in came Man followed closely by Ooljee and two young sisters whom Dawson did not recognize.

"Glad to see you guys are making yourselves at home," said Dawson. He was delighted to see the smile on Man's face. Dawson had forgotten how quickly Man and Ooljee became the center of attention the last time they had visited the convent. Turning toward Mother Mary he said, "and luckily for us, Mother Mary, we happen to have one of the best tracking hounds in the country right here." Dawson let Ooljee come up and lick traces of yellow off his fingers. Then he rubbed the dog behind the ears. "You are ready to go, aren't you, Ooljee?" He looked up at Mother Mary. "When do you want us to leave?"

"The sooner, the better," said Mother Mary.

"Okay," said Dawson, "We're going to need some help. Do you have aluminum foil?"

"We have plenty in the pantry," said Mother Mary, "what do you need us to do with it?"

"The Company will probably try to find us with heat sensing equipment either aboard satellites or surveillance aircraft. If you will have the sisters sew strips of aluminum foil on everyone's outer jackets and caps, I think there is a good chance we could break up the heat pattern that would reflect on their screens so it looks like small animals not humans. And, I want to get rid of the monastery van. Its out-of-state tags are sure to be spotted quickly if you're under the intense surveillance that it looks like you are. Soon as we get it stashed somewhere out of the way, get some supplies packed, and our outerwear foiled, we'll be ready to start."

"Don't worry about the van," said Mother Mary, "I already had one of the sisters arrange to drive it into Minneapolis and leave it at a large church, where it can be used. Let's see about getting your supplies packed, your clothes foiled and maybe you can leave after lunch. I am afraid that Melissa may push things too far given all the time she has at the hermitage. A dark retreat is risky and I know Melissa is impatient to deepen her already astonishing energy abilities as quickly as she can."

Dawson raised his eyebrows questioningly. He was not sure what Mother Mary meant about the retreat being risky, but he knew Melissa was fearless. "We'll find them, and we will leave right away." He looked at Man. Though young, Man was already a serious spiritual warrior. Man nodded his agreement, although he did seem a bit disappointed at the thought of having to leave the young sisters so quickly.

As Dawson had experienced before at the convent, everything needed had a way of appearing. By lunchtime, two well-used but reliable looking backpacks were being filled in the kitchen with food. In addition, both Dawson and Man were given sleeping bags and inflatable mats that could be attached to the bottom of their backpacks. Their jackets and caps were streaked with foil strips.

When lunch was over Dawson, Man and Ooljee left the convent kitchen under tree cover and headed north. Because of Dawson's concern that the convent might also be under audio surveillance they did not take the ATV. It would add a day, maybe two, of walking, but the last thing Dawson and Mother Mary wanted to do was have Dawson's rescue efforts alert the Company to where Melissa and Blaine might be.

Dawson knew that initially, because they were following the first leg of the journey that Melissa and Blaine had taken in the ATV, that it would be difficult for Ooljee to scent their trail. However, Dawson was anxious to get Ooljee on the job sooner rather than later. He pulled the Altoids box from out of his jeans pocket, opened it and took out the locket which he had given Blaine in Italy. He called Man over and gave the locket to him. Man let the dog sniff the locket and said a view words to Ooljee in Navajo.

Then—"Find her, good dog. Find her. Find her."

Ooljee was off, rapidly moving from side to side on the trail ahead of Dawson and Man. Dawson turned to Man, "I have no idea if Ooljee has picked up Blaine's scent, but he acts like he understands what we want."

"If any dog can do it, even though the scent trail is weeks old, Ooljee can," said Man. "Besides, I think Ooljee has the ability to time travel if we need for him to. He could pick the trail up by simply going back in time to get it."

"I don't know about that time traveling part," muttered Dawson, "but he sure looks like he knows what he's doing. He is one smart dog."

After all the time spent in the van, Man could feel himself relax just watching his dog work. He looked at Dawson and smiled.

CHAPTER 52

For the next week Dawson, Man and Ooljee hiked long stretches each day and slept hard each night. Each morning before they started off Dawson would pull out the locket from the Altoids box and Man would let Ooljee smell it good. They had no way to know for sure whether Ooljee was on the right trail. Occasionally, Dawson would check his compass and it provided some assurance, as it always showed that they were generally heading north.

By the tenth day, Dawson was fairly certain that they were at least a couple dozen miles into Canada. They were now hiking in virgin timber, mostly giant spruce. The trees were so large that there was not enough sunlight penetrating below the canopy to support the kind of bramble thickets they encountered earlier, which made their initial going extremely difficult. Now their passage was much easier.

Dawson knew they needed to find the two women soon, as they were already making a huge dent in the foodstuffs that they had brought along. He and Man and Ooljee were each eating lots of carbs each day and Dawson could feel his body strengthening from the daily exertion, even though he was dead tired at night. Despite their exhaustion, the past two nights they both were awakened by Ooljee growling, and on full alert, looking at two pairs of glowing eyes off in the distance. Their remoteness was palpable.

On the twelfth day out, they were on the trail early. They had only been walking for a couple hours when Man raised his hand, turned to Dawson and pointed at his nose. Then Dawson also got a whiff of the smell of wood smoke. He hoped it was from a fire made by Melissa and Blaine. If so, they were close. If not, it would be somebody else's fire and that would be trouble. No one else should be out in this remote area, unless Dawson and Man were being followed. Dawson nodded to Man to proceed cautiously.

An hour later they came to a clearing and saw a strangely designed round log hut. A gray plume of smoke came from a flue in the center of the hut. Dawson was trying to figure out what was the most careful way for them to make their approach, but Ooljee made that unnecessary. The dog immediately went to the door of the hut and began scratching on the door with his paw.

The door opened. There stood Blaine. She looked gaunt and worried, but Dawson immediately saw her as he had at the Trevi fountain where he first kissed her. He caught his breath.

Blaine looked out and saw Dawson and then Man beside him. "Oh my Gosh, Will, I am so glad to see you! I didn't know what I was going to do. I think something bad might have happened to Melissa, or maybe it's good, I just don't know."

Blaine looked as if she might faint and Dawson stepped quickly to her side. Man went to her other side and together they helped her sit down on a log bench just outside the door of the hut.

"How long has it been since you had anything to eat, Blaine?" asked Dawson.

"Just a few days."

"I was afraid of that. Man, can you get some of that rice and bean stew going? And we may need to find some protein we can add in."

Man nodded. He was already getting cooking gear out of his backpack. Dawson pulled his canteen off his belt unscrewed the top and offered some water to Blaine. She drank and this seemed to calm her.

While the fire was getting underway and the water for the rice coming to a boil, Man and Ooljee headed into the woods. They were back in no time with something that Man had already skinned. Maybe it was a rabbit, or perhaps a squirrel. Whatever it was did not really matter. It would provide much-needed protein for Blaine. Only after Blaine had eaten her fill of Man's stew did Dawson ask her what had happened to her and Melissa.

Blaine started at the beginning. She told Dawson and Man how she and Melissa got out to the dark hermitage site with the help of Sister Lisa. She explained that the purpose of this particular hermitage was to give the retreatant the opportunity for a silent retreat conducted in total darkness. A sensory deprivation retreat increased one's ability to go deep within. Melissa wanted both of them to have the opportunity to undergo such a retreat. Melissa was sure that it would provide a giant step forward in their spiritual paths. Blaine, however, reminded Melissa that she and Aasia were just back recently from doing much emotional cleansing work at the convent in Sweden.

"I told Melissa that I didn't think I was ready to do a dark retreat," said Blaine. "I think she was disappointed, but she understood. She then seemed to like the idea that if I did not do a dark retreat this would give her the opportunity to have a longer and deeper dark retreat. We spent some time talking about how I could be of greatest assistance to her as her attender. And then one day she began.

"While Melissa was on her dark retreat we had no conversation. I would bring a bowl of hot food to her in the mornings and evenings and leave it by her door. If she needed anything else, she would simply leave me a note, which she could shove under my door. Or, if her need was immediate she could break silence. I understood that it would be up to her to break silence though, not me."

Dawson and Man were aware how vivid Blaine's recollection was. Her face conveyed the emotions of the moments she was describing. She was speaking as if she were reporting from the scene itself.

"Melissa wanted to get the most out of this opportunity, so she set no time limit on her retreat. From what I had read in the booklet about dark retreats, that is unusual. Ordinarily, a time is agreed on and the attender keeps track of the number of days that go by. I imagine a retreatant loses track of time quickly and soon has no idea of whether it is day or night. I was instructed by Melissa to let her remain in dark silence until someone arrived here to help us return to the convent or to go on farther into Canada.

"After a couple of weeks, there came a time when it appeared she was not eating anything. After a couple of days I got worried and knocked on her door. There was no answer. So I opened her door. And, you won't believe this. Maybe you will. She wasn't there. The place where she had been sitting on her meditation cushion was still warm. I have been around these sisters enough to know that they do indeed have strange powers. I was stunned. And, I was alarmed. I didn't know what to do. Finally, I decided to meditate in the room where Melissa had been and see if I was led to know what to do. In some way, I was able to experience her presence. The message I got from this experience was that she was all right, and that she had decided to leave."

Blaine frowned. "No, it was more powerful than her just deciding. Somehow she had been told to leave, and to do so quickly."

"I don't know if she meant leave this life, or simply leave being out here in the middle of the wilderness, or what she meant," said Blaine, wiping her eyes with her shirt sleeve. "I just knew that I could not try to go anywhere alone. I have no idea how to get out of here. Quite frankly, I was afraid that if I tried to go back, no one at the convent would understand what happened. I mean you would think they would, but who knows, this is pretty strange."

Dawson was gradually taking it all in. He realized, with some embarrassment, that his first thought had been how his efforts to find Melissa had once again been thwarted. His second thought was how happy he was to see Blaine.

"Blaine, that is an incredible story. So much that is happening here is extraordinary. You know the locket with the icon in it that you gave back to me? Well, that is how we got here. Ooljee followed your scent from the locket. He is one incredible dog."

Ooljee, as if acknowledging the praise, got up from his position by the fire and walked over to Blaine so she could pat him. Blaine thought, well it is a cinch this dog knows how to enter the thought fields of others. Ooljee seems to know what everyone is going to say to him before they say it.

It was obvious to Dawson that Blaine was exhausted. Once she had eaten all she could, he took her into one of the rooms in the hut and laid her on the bed. Ooljee assumed it was his duty to watch over Blaine and situated himself right at the side of her bed.

The next morning they awoke to the sound of heavy rain. Dawson had been anxious to get back on the trail, but realized that the rain was giving them the opportunity for Blaine to gain nourishment and rest without the worry and anxiety of whether or not she would be rescued. The rain continued a second day. A greater reality seemed to be calling the shots. On the third day following Dawson's and Man's arrival at the dark retreat hermitage, they awoke to a chorus of bird songs and a bright blue sky. It was time to leave.

Dawson was not sure how long it would take for them to get to the Canadian safe house. He had a compass heading that Mother Mary had given him from the dark hermitage and he was a decent land navigator.

Fortunately, the next three days on the trail were without rain, and even though it was early November, Dawson and Man were able to make Blaine reasonably comfortable each night in Dawson's sleeping bag laid on a bed of spruce clippings. Each night Ooljee slept right beside Blaine.

On the fourth morning, the foursome walked out of virgin timber into the edge of a pasture. A farmhouse with smoke curling up from the chimney was in the distance. Dawson decided it was best for Blaine, Man and Ooljee to wait while he made sure that this was the safe house. Dawson had received a code word from Mother Mary that he was to use in casual conversation to confirm that he had the right house.

Dawson headed out across the pasture along a fence line. Blaine and Man sat down next to a small spring beneath a huge spruce tree. Ooljee, after getting a drink, settled at their feet.

"How are you feeling, Blaine?" asked Man. He knew that the past three days of hiking had been hard on her. The sedentary weeks attending to Melissa's dark retreat and the lack of food after Melissa left had taken a toll on her.

"I am not doing too badly," said Blaine looking directly at Man. She found that while most men made her uneasy—even Dawson because she could not trust her heart to him—she felt totally relaxed and herself with Man. "I'm glad you have been with me. I mean, I have to tell you, I think it would have been difficult for me to be rescued just by Will. Your being here has given me great comfort." She smiled and looked down at Ooljee. "And Ooljee has only added to that."

She paused. She liked the way Man paced his conversations with pauses. He had told her that in the Navajo way the pauses were important so that the mind did not run too far ahead of the heart. She continued, "I met Father O'Donnell in Italy. Will you be going back to the monastery where he is, after you and Dawson..." She paused again, her eyes sparkled. "...finish rescuing me?" She smiled at Man.

"I don't know if that is for me to decide," said Man, "but Ooljee and I would be glad to stay longer with you if that would be helpful."

Blaine stood up. She could see Dawson returning across the pasture. Man followed her gaze and stood up beside her. Even though he was only seventeen, he was a good ten inches taller than Blaine. She reached up and put her hand on his shoulder where his long black hair fell. "Thank you for coming to find me and wanting to continue to help me. I hope there will be a way that you can."

Man looked shyly into the piercing blaze of her dark eyes. "I hope so too. Before I left to meet Dawson in Denver, Father O'Donnell made me get a passport. He was not sure how we might get back into the U.S. after we smuggled you into Canada and said I better have one. He also told me that if you needed

THE END OF DEMOCRACY

someone to travel with, to make your escape easier, Ooljee and I should go with you. He said it would be too dangerous for you to travel with Dawson. I told Dawson that when I picked him up in Denver, but he just shrugged his shoulders and said that he didn't think that would be necessary."

"Oh, that would be wonderful, Man, if you and Ooljee could travel with me." Blaine took a deep breath. She realized she would feel so much better to have them traveling with her. "I would love that. Man, I am so glad you told me."

Man nodded and looked at the ground. She could see a twinkle of light glinting in his somber brown eyes.

CHAPTER 53

Dawson had a big smile on his face as he walked up to Blaine and Man. "This is the right place," he said. "The home of two middle-aged dairy farmers. Evidently they were once in the SOS, but left the order several years ago to heed the call to become farmers. We are in great luck that this is our safe house. I expect we're going to be treated to a true farmer's dinner with homemade cheese on the side. Let's get on over to the house."

Just a few hours later, true to Dawson's prediction—after the second milking was done—they were all settled around a large kitchen table before an enormous spread of food. It was the kind of late afternoon meal people have who work hard physically all day and live close to the earth—with plenty of fresh vegetables, farm-raised meat and, of course, in the case of dairy farmers, lots of fresh milk, cheese and butter. Sister Josephine presided at one end of the table. She was a large woman with broad shoulders, long brown hair with gray streaks and light blue eyes that seemed to bring everything within their gaze into sharp focus.

At the other end of the table was Sister Darcy. She was barely five feet tall. She seemed to have all the countervailing traits of Sister Josephine, but the same compelling presence. Not only was Sister Darcy tiny, her short hair was dark, almost black, without a trace of gray and her eyes were pools of liquid night that, like Sister Josephine's, captured and held you.

Sister Darcy bowed her head. "Shall we say grace?" It was a rhetorical question if there ever was one, and before anybody could think of responding, she continued.

"Beloved energy of Love that brings life into the world, from the rising to the setting of the sun, and radiates to all of us in perfect beauty, thank you for bringing these pilgrims safely to our table, thank you for the bounty we are all about to share, and keep us all in the mystery and awe of your Presence, Amen."

"That was a beautiful blessing," said Dawson.

"That blessing comes from Psalm 50," said Sister Darcy, "and pretty much sums up the theological thinking of our sisterhood. As you may know, Brother Isaac, our Order is long on presence and action and, for the most part, short on theology."

Dawson was taken aback. How did Sister Darcy know what his Order name was? He guessed he should be getting used to people like Father O'Donnell and the sisters in this Order knowing a great deal more about him than he told them. For the moment, Dawson was more interested in finding out more about the sisters.

"I may be a little confused," said Dawson, "but I was under the impression that you were former members of the Order, yet it sounds like you are still in it. You live on a farm, not at the convent. I am a little confused. Can you clear this up for me?"

Sister Josephine let out a guffaw and broke into another round of hearty laughter. "Tell them how it is, Dars. I was thinking the food was a lot more interesting, but some of these folks have anxious minds. As much as we feed our minds, they are always hungry. That's not the table where I want to eat." She continued to chuckle and picked up a huge plate of biscuits and placed a couple on her plate. Sister Josephine passed the platter of biscuits to Man who already had his plate piled high with fresh squash and beans and a huge slab of meatloaf covered with gravy. "Although I can see that some of us don't exactly suffer from that mental malady," she said, smiling at Man.

Man returned the smile and, following Sister Josephine's example, picked three saucer-size biscuits off the platter. He put two on his plate and deftly slipped one below his lap into the waiting mouth of Ooljee who lay next to his feet.

Sister Darcy raised her fork, put a bite in her mouth, swallowed and then responded to Dawson. "A lot of people don't understand our Order, and the truth is we don't go out of our way to try to explain things to people publicly because it is difficult for many people to understand. Our Order does not believe in celibacy. However, it does believe in Jesus' example of the necessity of time in the wilderness.

"We believe the monastic impulse to go into the wilderness was misunderstood by the Church after Christianity became the state religion under Constantine. After that, this idea of celibacy got a lot of traction as the role of women in the Church began to be repressed. You get a gay guy like Paul on a rant and, despite some of his wonderful presentations of Jesus' teachings about transformation, he apparently had no love of women and left the early misogynistic papacy with way too much ammunition to diminish the important role of the feminine.

"Our Order believes that in life everyone needs to spend time in the wilderness in order to grow emotionally and spiritually. Time for spiritual growth is best supported by a group of peers. Going into a religious order is the equivalent of going into a wilderness. It is going into the wilderness of your personal psychic landscape. It is a necessary journey. Then again, Jesus did not spend all of his time in the wilderness. Most of his time was spent with other men and women whom he loved, like John and Mary Magdalene.

"So being called into the wilderness, or into an order if you will, is a natural part of everyone's spiritual journey. It does not foreclose or replace the other natural part of everyone's spiritual journey, which is to develop and nurture an intimate relationship with another human being. So Sister Jo and I are still in SOS, but we are in that phase of our spiritual journey where we are learning the spiritual challenges and joys of intimacy. We believe that Jesus and Mary Magdalene both taught that the greatest reflection of God's love occurs in intimate relations between two people who are attracted to and love each other regardless of gender."

Dawson noticed that both Blaine and Man were paying close attention, as he was, to what Sister Darcy was saying. He couldn't resist the question. "I am not sure that I should ask, but tell me how does sex figure into all this?"

Sister Darcy gave an impish smile and Sister Josephine commenced laughing again. "That's a great question," said Sister

Darcy. "Sexuality is the most basic part of our incarnational expression of love. In other words, we believe that we make God happy by making love. This is why celibacy is so out of line with the Gospels' message of love. Our Order is not promiscuous. We do not promote a person having more than one intimate partner, because we believe in the example of Jesus and Mary Magdalene that the greatest love is found and expressed in a relationship between two people. There is a trinity, or, that is, a third in our relationships, but that is God. If there was a human third person sexually involved, God would be eliminated; there would be no reconciling of the natural energies of the universe expressed through the two partners."

Blaine had been thinking about Aasia's interest in becoming a member of the SOS. What Sister Darcy was saying would be very interesting to discuss with Aasia. She decided to ask a question. "Are the intimate relations that your Order fosters just between those of the same gender?"

Sister Josephine began laughing again. "Don't let a couple old gay gals like us give you the wrong idea. The SOS promotes intimate relations, once a person's wilderness work has been done, whether a person's attraction is to someone of the same gender or the opposite gender. The gender preference does not matter. What is important is that the attraction be authentic and have the same sense of calling that a call to join the Order has."

Sister Josephine's explanation gave Blaine a sense of relief. Blaine imagined that people like her and Aasia, who had histories of serious trauma wounding, needed to feel completely free and authentic to be able to develop relations with anyone on a physical level, since it was on the physical level that they had been grievously wounded.

Dawson jumped in. "So you mean there are a bunch of you SOS sisters living out there in the world like ordinary folks?"

"Yes," said Sister Darcy, "that's right. There are a lot of us out there, wherever 'out there' is. Our Order wants us to be in midst of life out in the world, not only experiencing deep love and intimacy with a partner, but also caring for and helping to heal the world. Some of us are able to do that by looking after and caring for a fine herd of Jersey cows. Jo and I are both city girls, so being led to this farmstead was something we never imagined, but what unimaginable joy it has brought us. And because we are on the end of the underground railroad from the convent in Minnesota we also get a number of interesting guests like you."

"So what kinds of other guests do you get?" asked Dawson.

"You guys really are not that special," said Sister Josephine with another laugh. "Well, you are special in one way. Most of the time, the folks who come here from the convent come by a more direct route. Only rarely do we get people coming from way off in the western wilderness where the dark retreat hut is. Yes, we get a number of people, many of them social activists who have sought political asylum in the United States and been denied. Their lives would be at risk if they were deported back to their home countries. So we help them get into Canada where they can more easily seek political asylum."

"Which reminds me," interrupted Sister Darcy, "I know you have been completely cut off from any news for weeks, but there is some political news from the United States that you may be interested in. This is totally bizarre to us since we have been living here long enough to become Canadians, but it seems like your country has elected a corporation as its President."

"We thought corporations had presidents, we didn't know they could become President," said Sister Josephine with another round of her jolly laughter.

Blaine and Dawson looked at each other in shock. The news did not seem to register in any particular way with Man. He simply reached down toward the floor and rubbed Ooljee behind his ears.

CHAPTER 54

Sister Darcy and Sister Josephine may have been way out in the backwoods, but they had a great satellite Internet connection. Blaine was immediately in communication with Rat, who was delighted to hear from Blaine and to know that she was safe. Rat was waiting all the while, for her to be in touch having received news of her journey from Father O'Donnell.

It appeared that, with the Americans electing a corporation President, the CIA was on hyper-alert. Rat had been able to discover that the CIA had determined that Will Dawson had used a Godfrey Adams identity and their hunt for Dawson had intensified. Both Rat and Father O'Donnell agreed that Dawson should not travel with Blaine, even in Canada. Dawson was at the top of the CIA's international pickup list and he would attract too much attention. As Man had confided to Blaine, their recommendation was that he accompany Blaine back to Berlin and that Dawson hike back into the United States, and then make his way from the convent overland to the monastery in New Mexico.

Blaine explained all of this to Dawson after her chat room conversation with Rat. She was delighted with the idea of having Man travel with her back to Berlin. Dawson, on the other hand, was very apprehensive about leaving her. And after the long trek he and Man made to rescue Blaine, he was not particularly excited about heading back into the forest alone. Nevertheless, after the matter was discussed with Sister Josephine and Sister Darcy, it was very clear to Dawson that he was expected to do exactly as instructed. After all, the most basic rule of life in an order was that you did not follow your own ego's needs or wishes, but what was best for the good of the order and who the order was trying to serve. Dawson was glum.

Sister Josephine and Sister Darcy ran their safe house by the book. That meant getting folks on to the next destination as soon as possible. The longer underground railroad passengers stayed in one stop, the greater the risk that the stop would be discovered and the whole method of safe passage imperiled. That was the last thing the sisters wanted to happen. By the end of the evening plans were made. Dawson, with a well provisioned pack, would set off into the woods right after breakfast. The sisters would then take Blaine and Man to the airport at Winnipeg.

The next morning as they gathered in the farmhouse kitchen for breakfast, Man stopped them. He told them that before they left he wished to perform a Navajo ceremony in order to assure everyone's safe journey. Sister Darcy and Sister Josephine were excited about this, exclaiming that they should have thought of it also. They led everyone to the small chapel that was built off the east side of the house. It had a simple stained glass window that faced directly east to catch the first rays of the morning sun.

Man asked everyone to be seated and he pulled out of his pack a bag of corn, a rattlesnake skin and the skull of an armadillo. He explained that the rattlesnake represents the primordial energy out of which everything arises, corn is the symbol of fertility and new life, and the armadillo represents the protection that the community must provide so that transformation is possible. At his request, Sister Josephine brought sage and cedar into the chapel. Man started the ceremony by putting the sage and cedar in the armadillo skull. Then he placed a hot coal from the morning fire into the skull. Soon the small room was filled with the pungent aroma of smoldering sage and cedar. Smell connects directly to emotions and the fragrance provided a path unimpeded by thought to take each participant to a place of openness to the other world.

Man then passed the snake skin to Blaine. She felt its feathery lightness. She passed it to Sister Darcy who experienced how beautifully it was designed. Sister Darcy passed it to Sister Josephine who sensed how strong it was and how powerful the snake was who had worn the skin. Man then took the skin in his hands and prayed in the language of the *Diné* to the Creator, to the source of all power, for the life force to be expressed powerfully in the lives of each one present so that they would travel safely and in Beauty.

Man then poured corn meal into each person's hands. They rubbed the meal on their hands and face. Each felt the scent of pollen and the elemental power of creativity. Again Man prayed in Navajo for creativity to flow into and from each person. This time he waited after his prayer for each person to add their creative prayer petition. Sister Josephine prayed for her favorite cow who was about to have a calf. Sister Darcy prayed for the role of the Order in bringing transformation to the world.

Blaine was unsure what to pray for, so when her turn came she glanced tentatively at Man. He smiled at her and touched his heart. She focused on her heart center and words came from her mouth asking that her heart protectiveness would break open and a germ of new love would sprout in her life for the benefit of others. If it had not been for the ritual process, where each person had one foot on the Canadian farmstead and the other foot in the transpersonal world, she would have been embarrassed; as it was, her petition seemed totally natural and appropriate. Dawson was the last to pray. He stumbled at first and then out flowed a paraphrased Thomas Merton prayer that Father O'Donnell often prayed, which reminded everyone that often we have no idea what is God's will for us, but our efforts to please God are what counts.

Man finished the prayers with a rather long chanted prayer in Navajo. Blaine would have to ask him later what it was all about. When he concluded, they all silently returned to the farmhouse kitchen.

As the beauty of the Navajo ceremony subsided, the anxiety of departure grew. Sister Josephine was not one to let unresolved emotional sentiment build up and bog down plans that needed to move forward briskly. She pushed her empty breakfast plate away from her. "Brother Isaac, it has been good to meet you. We will pray for your safe journey."

"Thank you, I think I'm all ready to leave, but I would like to have a few words alone with Blaine before I depart." said Dawson as he gave Blaine a pleading look.

Sister Josephine seemed to take in the emotional nuances of the

THE END OF DEMOCRACY

pair in one deep breath. "Certainly you should have time to say goodbye to Blaine. However, this is not the time to distract yourself or her with unfinished emotional issues that have not been worked through. You are a good man, Brother Isaac, and I believe you will do important work in your life. Your attraction to Blaine is understandable—she is a lovely woman. Frankly, you have not yet had the chance to be long enough in your personal wilderness to know how to love another. For now, your journey is back to Father O'Donnell who will help you find your way along this path."

Dawson had risen to his feet and was starting to speak, but Sister Josephine waved him away with her hand. "I'm sorry to be so blunt, but time is of the essence. Blaine, tell this good man good-bye, and get him on the trail. Blessings to you, Brother Isaac."

Dawson went out the farmhouse's backdoor and Blaine followed a short distance behind. When Blaine got just outside the door she stopped. Dawson was already at the edge of the porch. Blaine took a deep breath and centered herself, "For the time being, Will, you still have an invitation to come to Berlin to see me, but that invitation will not be there forever. Travel safe. I am sure Rat will find a way to be in touch with you as soon as I get back to Berlin. Goodbye."

Dawson, once again at a critical relationship moment in his life, was speechless. He simply did not know how to put into words the feelings that he had or, for that matter, any certainty about what his feelings truly were. He took the one step down from the porch to the ground. He nodded. "Okay, Blaine, I guess I don't know what to say. Travel well and don't keep Man in Europe too long. I guess I better go." And with that, he turned and set out across the pasture, shifting the heavy backpack as he went until it settled against the base of his spine.

It would be a long drive to deliver Blaine and Man to the airport at Winnipeg. Rat had arranged their itinerary, which would take them first on a non-stop flight to Reykjavik, Iceland. From Reykjavik they would catch a connecting flight to Copenhagen. From Copenhagen they would get the train to Berlin. Rat believed this was a much safer route than going through London. He made the reservations for Blaine with her new identity. Ooljee might get quarantined a while in Copenhagen, but Man would not have to leave him there long.

After Dawson left, Blaine and Man gathered their few belongings and walked outside. One by one each began to embrace the other. Blaine melted into the unrestrained earthy embrace of Sister Josephine and the calm serenity of Sister Darcy's hug. She was tentative as Man put his arms around her, they were traveling together so a good-bye hug was not really called for, but she was in awe of the ceremony that he had led and she let herself open to the energy and protective power of his strong masculine embrace. She could feel heat rising up her spine and a sense of something in her chest, like an old rag being torn apart.

Man too felt the unrestrained love from being embraced by Sister Josephine and Sister Darcy. He didn't know what it would mean to embrace Blaine, but he followed the tide of the ritual without stopping to let his mind analyze his feelings. He held her tightly and he could feel the electricity coming off her skin and heat rising from the crown of her head just below his chin. He had the same feeling which he had on the rez as a boy when a traveling circus had come to town—when he rode the Ferris wheel, and it got to the top the first time and then began to drop through the cool night air. He breathed in this feeling of mystery, awe and exhilaration as long as he could until he noticed that Ooljee, who was standing at their feet, was beginning to whine. Blaine pulled apart and reached down and patted Ooljee. Oh my, she thought, I think Ooljee is jealous of me.

"It is time to get you guys on the road if you are going to get to Winnipeg in time to catch your flight," said Sister Josephine. "Plus, we have to go by the vet on the way to get shots and paperwork for Ooljee, so we better hurry."

CHAPTER 55

Man had not been able to sleep at all on the first leg of their journey to Reykjavik. Blaine had insisted that he pack the long-bladed knife that he kept in his boot in his checked luggage. He did not like being in this strange environment without any way to defend himself. Plus, the tedious hours of waiting to board the plane and making sure that Ooljee would be traveling comfortably added to his anxiety.

On the second leg of the journey to Copenhagen he had finally fallen asleep exhausted. He awoke suddenly with a start. Blaine who was sitting in the window seat, was asleep and her head had fallen over against his shoulder. He was surprised he had not disturbed her. He turned slowly in order to avoid awakening Blaine as he sat upright.

Before it slipped away, he knew that he needed to try to understand the dream that he had been having. It was a violent dream. He had been in a strange room full of boxes and shelves. Four men dressed in long overcoats had appeared in the room. This was when he awoke. He sensed that the message of the dream was that he would need to be prepared to fight for his survival.

He also had the feeling from the dream that whatever was happening would not be a threat to Blaine. He was glad for that. He looked down at her head on his shoulder. He shut his eyes almost all the way so that he was squinting out of them and he could see sparks of light coming off of her head. He was reminded of the pictures of the Virgin Mary in medieval paintings he had seen in one of the books the nuns had brought to his elementary school. Except, not only did Blaine have the sparks of golden light coming from her head, he could also see clouds of dark brown and gray energy. She must be doing some fierce dreaming herself, he thought.

With his eyes almost shut he scanned the rest of her body and saw crossed hatched lines going everywhere. He also had the sense that she was painted like a warrior. That's bizarre, he thought, but he had learned not to question what came to him from reading another person's energy. Maybe he would have to ask Blaine about this. Just then, she stirred and looked up at him sleepily.

"How are you?" he whispered.

"Not too bad, I guess," said Blaine stretching as she pulled herself back over into her seat. "Thanks for letting me fall sleep on your shoulder."

"Not at all." He paused. "Blaine, I was reading your energy just now, and it was very curious."

"What do you mean you were reading my energy?" Blaine was surprised. He seemed to be talking like one of the nuns.

"It's nothing really," said Man, "all the young Indian boys in my clan learn about reading energy in order to track game. And, you need to learn to read energy in order to avoid evil energy. In my tradition, we have lots of names for the different kinds of evil energy, or evil spirits, that might cause problems.

"What I want to ask you about is very curious," said Man. "I had been dreaming when I awoke just now, so I was partially in that dream state where the barriers between the worlds are down and it is possible to see more. I looked at you and saw your energy patterns and all these marks like scratches across your body and these paintings like you were painted as a warrior, like you had been a very brave warrior and fought in many battles."

Blaine was dumbstruck. How in the world was Man able to see that she had cuts and tattoos all over her body? What struck her most deeply was the realization that Man did not see her cuts and tattoos as terrible—just the opposite. They seem to engender his respect and maybe even admiration. How different his perspective was from the feeling of embarrassment and shame she once felt about the cutting she had done to her body.

"So, what if you're right?" said Blaine defensively. "I'm not saying you are. Only what if you're right, that there are cuts and paintings, what would that mean to you?"

Man paused so that his response would not be off the cuff, but what he really felt in his heart. Finally he said, "It would mean that I would be willing to go into battle with you. I would respect you as a warrior who has fought some battle internally, or externally, and survived. The cuts and paintings would honor you. I would have great respect for you."

Blaine sat a moment with what Man just told her. This certainly was a new perspective for her. She wanted to know just a little more. "Would you like to sleep with a woman who had cuts and paintings on her body, or would that repulse you? Don't worry, Man, I'm not suggesting anything about you and me, but I'm asking in the abstract. Hypothetically, would you?"

"In the native tradition, generally marks and paintings on the body that are there because of real-life experiences are seen as much more beautiful than ornaments that you wear and take off. We have a particular love for turquoise and silver, but even these are not valued above the lines of wisdom on an old man's or woman's face."

"Thank you for telling me that," said Blaine, and she put her head back against his shoulder.

Then she looked up again quickly. "Now, you couldn't see anything else could you?"

Man was too dark skinned to appear visibly to be blushing but she could sense the heat rising up his neck and face.

"Of course you couldn't," she said before he could reply, "that would not be polite would it?" Before he could say anything, she snuggled her head back down into his chest.

CHAPTER 56

After landing in Copenhagen, Blaine, Man and Ooljee took the train to Berlin as planned. Ooljee's recent updated shots had allowed him to avoid quarantine. Rat was there at the Berlin Hauptbahnhof, the central Berlin station, to meet them. They decided that Rat and Man would take Blaine to her apartment. Aasia was staying there while Blaine was away, and Aasia was anxious to see Blaine again.

Man and Ooljee then went with Rat over to the storage room where Rat lived to spend the night there until they could make further plans. When they got to the storage room, Man immediately experienced a feeling of apprehension. Man looked at Ooljee. He could see that Ooljee, who seemed to have relaxed after they arrived in Berlin out of an instinctive familiarity that he was back in the homeland of his ancestors, was suddenly also on hyper-alert. It was hard for Man to determine whether the tense sensations came from being in Rat's strange environment or whether there was something seriously wrong in the offing.

Man settled into a chair right below the exposed fuse box and Ooljee was at his feet. Rat got something cold for them to drink out of the refrigerator across the room. They were relaxing enough to begin to think about going to bed, when the door to the storage room came crashing open.

Four men in long overcoats rushed into the room. They were speaking quickly in a strange language. Man remembered his dream, which he was now re-experiencing in slow motion. When the four men started to swing something up from beneath their overcoats, Man reached behind his head and pulled the switch on the fuse box sending the room into total darkness.

"Get down!" he cried to Rat, and he rolled across the floor toward the refrigerator. Immediately a hail of bullets went over his head as the four men fired their automatic weapons. When the burst of firing stopped Man peered out from behind the refrigerator. Even though it was totally dark, he could see the energy shapes of the four men. He reached into his boot and pulled out his long-bladed knife.

At the sound of the knife clicking open, memories of his knife practice as a young boy flashed through his head. He and the other young boys would practice on watermelons and squash. The idea was to learn how to use your knife and make a cut on the watermelon that sliced into the white rind, but not into the red meat. The goal was to make a meaningful superficial wound, one that upheld honor but did not cause serious injury. If the wound was serious and somebody died, then the likelihood was that the matter would be taken out of the tribal courts and into the federal courts. No one wanted an altercation over honor to end up in a trial for murder in the white man's court.

Once he had been called out to fight another teenage boy after an athletic event at the local high school. He had dodged the other youth's knife and managed to make a long twelve-inch cut across the other boy's chest. The skin had been cut apart but the wound was not so serious that the other boy needed immediate medical care.

All these thoughts went through Man's head in an instant. His cuts would need to be a little deeper than the one he had made on the boy in the school yard, but not too deep. He moved silently through the room with his arm outstretched so that the force of his body turning slashed the knife across the chest of each of the four men in turn. Ooljee was right behind him, sinking his teeth in the leg of first one man and then the next. When Man's knife slashed the chest of the last of the four men, he realized that the man's automatic weapon fell to the floor. Man turned and picked up the weapon and, at the same time, reached above the chair where he had been sitting and flipped the power switch back on.

He leveled the automatic weapon at the four men and motioned for them to lie on the floor. He spoke to Ooljee in Navajo, telling him to release the last man and to step back a few paces from the men to give them room to lay down. Man turned and looked toward the back of the room. He saw Rat getting up off the floor. Without taking his gaze from the four intruders, Man backed over toward Rat.

"Are you okay?" Man asked Rat. Rat was shaking, but he nodded his head that he was okay. "We have to get out of here as quickly as we can. You better get anything that you don't want to leave behind, that you would not like to have end up in somebody else's hands."

Rat nodded again and he began to survey his bullet-riddled computers. Most had oddly twisted metal and plastic on some surface. His quick check revealed that all of them were damaged in some way except for his slim new MacBook. Quickly he removed the hard drives from each of his computers. At the same time, Man was tying the hands behind their backs of each of the four intruders lying on the floor. Suddenly an idea occurred to him and he walked over to where he could talk quietly to Rat.

"We need to make sure these guys don't go anywhere, until we have a chance to get out of the country." said Man.

"Sure let's make them watch really bad video games until they die," said Rat almost in tears as he worked over his damaged computers.

Man's brow furrowed. "I'm thinking we make up some kind of fake bomb or something that keeps them from leaving."

"No problemo," said Rat, who was becoming more composed as he began to automatically do what needed to be done in order to take all of his computer hard drives with him. He felt the composure of a father getting his children quickly out of harm's way. "You figure out a way to make them think there is something that'll blow up, and I'll wire it to one of these prepaid cell phones."

Man went to his knapsack and pulled out the bag of cornmeal that he had brought with him. He poured the cornmeal into a plastic bag and placed it on the floor a few feet above the men's heads. Rat then wired the cornmeal to a cell phone.

"Can you check and see how soon we can catch a train to Stockholm?" asked Man. Rat pulled out his MacBook and went to work. There was a train leaving from the central station in Berlin for Stockholm in three hours. Rat also sent an e-mail to Blaine telling her that the Conficter guys had paid a visit, that he and Man were both all right but that they needed to leave immediately and thought it was best that they go to Sweden to hide out for a while with the nuns in the convent there. Blaine and Aasia should meet them at the Berlin Hauptbahnhof in time to catch the next train to Stockholm. They would need Blaine's help in getting to the convent from Stockholm.

Man moved close to Rat and motioned toward the guys on the floor, "Tell them that if they move even one inch, or do anything before three hours has gone by that the bomb will go off. After three hours we will call the phone. After they hear it ring then they will know that it is safe to move about and leave. Otherwise, any movement they make before the phone rings will trigger the bomb."

Rat spoke to the four men in German, and Man collected all their automatic weapons and put them in a duffel bag. They could drop them in the ship canal they had walked by on the way from the train station. Rat threw all his hard drives and the MacBook into a knapsack. Man hoisted his own pack on to his back. They headed out the door and down the stairs. When they emerged into the arcade, they realized it was so noisy that it was possible no one heard the shots overhead. Even if someone had and went to investigate, Rat and Man were already disappearing into the crowd.

CHAPTER 57

Will hiked for almost three weeks through virgin timber wilderness before he got back to the convent. Except for the short visit at the safe house in Canada, Will had been hiking rugged terrain for almost five weeks. He was in the best physical shape he had been in twenty plus years. He felt much more centered in his life than he had when he started on his rescue mission and he was calmer than he had ever been in his life.

He slipped back into the convent after dark one evening. Mother Mary was delighted to see him. She knew that his mission was accomplished and that Blaine reached the safe house in Canada and from there was taken to the airport to catch a flight to Reykjavík. However, Mother Mary was concerned that the level of surveillance of the convent had intensified. She didn't have specific proof of this, but all the sisters were picking up on an intrusive foreign energy. She felt Dawson should leave the convent as quickly and surreptitiously as possible.

The next morning Dawson was in the back of a laundry truck bound for Minneapolis. From there he caught the bus to New Mexico. As the bus rumbled across the great America prairie, Dawson began to feel a shift in his perspective. Maybe his mission now was not to pursue Melissa or to follow Blaine to

Germany. Even though it was a complete mystery to him what had become of Melissa, both she and Blaine seemed to have been well taken care of by the Sacred Order of the Sisters of Mary of Magdala and Rat. In his travels the knowledge that he needed to focus on his own journey had settled more deeply into his emotional outlook on his life. He would talk to Father O'Donnell about this as soon as he got back to the monastery.

Two days later he was there. Brother Will wrote a note telling him that he just missed Father O'Donnell who had gone back up the mountain to his hermitage. Brother Will surmised that Father O'Donnell must be worried about something since he was increasing the amount of time he spent at his hermitage. After a night's rest, Dawson decided that he could not wait for Father O'Donnell to return. He needed to tell him everything that had happened with Melissa and Blaine and learn what he should do next.

The hike up the side of the mountain, which had been such a struggle for him before, was now a cakewalk. The air was clear and crisp, and walking almost straight up the side of a mountain for two hours was exhilarating.

When he got to the ledge where Father O'Donnell's hermitage was, Dawson knew immediately that Father O'Donnell had seen him coming—the kettle was already on the propane burner.

Father O'Donnell embraced Dawson with a big hug. "It is sure good to see you, Brother Isaac," said Father O'Donnell. "I know you had some adventures. Sit down and let me fix a cup of tea for you. I want to hear everything. I only got up here two days ago so I have not really settled into a routine of deep silence. I am glad you came. Your timing is good."

Two hours later, Dawson had finished telling Father O'Donnell about his adventures over the past two months. When he got to the part about getting to the dark retreat hut and finding that Melissa had simply disappeared, he asked Father O'Donnell what could have happened to her. Father O'Donnell simply smiled and shrugged his shoulders in his wise way of accepting the unknown.

"Brother Isaac, I am glad you have decided to focus on your own spiritual journey," said Father O'Donnell. "Ultimately we never get where we're going by following others' adventures. Finding ourselves is our most elusive and wary quarry. If you are willing, I think I know a way that we can up the stakes for you on your journey."

"Whatever you say, I am willing," said Dawson. Although as the words came out of his mouth, he realized that he was not quite as willing as he sounded. However, he was very willing to hear what Father O'Donnell would recommend for him.

Father O'Donnell smiled at Dawson and paused, as if he were aware of the threads of ambivalence within Dawson.

"I want you to continue to spend as much time at the monastery as you can, engaging in the spiritual practices which all the monks do. In addition, I think you should attend the University of Arizona's Center for Consciousness Studies. The commute won't be too bad, and the Center is on the cutting edge of research into the plasticity of the brain and the neurobiology of consciousness. I do not want the contemplative movement in the United States, which has gained such momentum in the past ten years, to miss out on any of the new understandings that quantum biology is teaching. It would be a shame for the contemplative movement, simply out of ignorance, to have a Galileo-moment like the Church had a few hundred years ago." Father O'Donnell stopped talking and looked at Dawson to see how his words were being received.

Dawson was surprised. He had not known what Father O'Donnell would recommend for him to do, but this was certainly not something he expected. His first thought was that he was a little old to be going back to school as a university student. His second thought was that maybe the timing was right. He seemed to be at a starting over place in his life, and he always liked learning and discovering new knowledge.

"Obviously, this is not something I had thought a thing about," said Dawson, "but I'm ready to follow your recommendations. Quite frankly, it appeals to me."

Father O'Donnell nodded and smiled. "Good. You can enroll online and the monastery will pay your fees. You will need to enroll under a different identity than your own. I would suggest you enroll as Brother Will. Check with him, I don't think he would mind. Brother Will did well as an undergraduate. Anyway, the name fits and that should make it comfortable. I'm sure you wouldn't have any difficulty being accepted in your own name. I expect you did reasonably well as an undergraduate. I don't imagine the CIA accepts officers except those who have outstanding academic records. I believe the next semester begins in just a couple of weeks."

Father O'Donnell and Dawson continued to talk. Their conversation was punctuated by long peaceful pauses. Finally Father O'Donnell looked out at the sun moving down in its arc across the western sky. "Brother Isaac, if you're going get down before dark, it's probably best for you to get started. Is there anything else that we should talk about before you leave?"

Dawson yawned and then sighed. "When I got back to the monastery there was a message that had been left for me in a secret chat room by my friend Gordon Slade. Slade recently got engaged, and his fiancée is a woman named Joy who is a librarian but who also works part-time for a fortune cookie factory. Slade's message was that he had asked Joy to give him a fortune cookie for me. She did, and when he opened the cookie, the message for me was: *In order for you to hear, you must first be silent.* So maybe this is not the right question for me to ask, but I am torn by it. I realize deeply that I need to be on my own spiritual journey, but I still can't get Melissa and what might have happened to her out of my mind. Is there anything more you can tell me?"

There was a long pause. "Brother Isaac, I am not sure whether this is helpful or not, but maybe the reason Melissa reappeared in your life after twenty years had nothing to do with you finding her, but was all about you finding you. From everything you've said, she really loved you, and sometimes an opportunity for self-discovery is the best gift we can give to someone we love. I know this doesn't literally answer your question, but maybe it is the best way to live into that question for now."

Dawson nodded. He stood up and embraced Father O'Donnell, pulled the supply backpack loaded with trash up onto his shoulders, turned into the rays of the distant sun and headed toward the path down the mountain. At the edge of the ledge he turned to look back at Father O'Donnell. Just as he did, a golden eagle passed overhead and let out a piercing cry. For the first time in his life, Dawson knew that there is nothing that needs to be said in the face of ultimate reality. He waved at Father O'Donnell and started down the mountain.

CHAPTER 58

As he walked toward the front door of CIA headquarters at Langley, Redmon realized that he was probably walking by the seal of the CIA, carved in stone on the floor, for the last time. He was filled with mixed emotions. He had given the best part of his life to the Company. However, he knew it was time to leave. Not only did he have the requisite number of years in for a good retirement check each month, he was not sure he could stay and be reasonably content inside himself. He had always followed the directives of his superiors—even when he was not sure if the approach being taken by his superiors was the best one. He always had confidence that there was integrity in the goal the Company was seeking to achieve.

Not anymore. As he headed toward the parking lot he once again pulled *The New York Times* from under his arm and glanced at the obituary. The obituary in the *Times* for Peter Wagner was more than enough of an excuse to retire. Evidently, Wagner had passed away in his sleep. The article mostly talked about his corporation, GOD, that had won the election and was about to be inaugurated President. The obituary stated that there would be no funeral or memorial service. Maybe, thought Redmon, that was because not even the Board of Directors of GOD, the unelected people who would be running the country, cared enough about

Wagner to come.

CHAPTER 59

The Olds spluttered to life. Slade pulled out of his parking place at his condo near Fenway Park and headed for Joy's house. Commuting to her place would be over soon—their wedding was just a few days off. He thought about delaying it to see if there was any chance that he would hear from Will Dawson. He would love for Dawson to be a part of the celebration, but Slade had heard nothing from Dawson.

Joy greeted him at the door with a big smile and a kiss. He would have never guessed when he first met her that this mousy little introverted librarian would turn out to be the exuberant love of his life. What wonderful, absurd miracle caused him to persist in getting to know Joy.

"Gordon, you just missed someone, a government guy looking for you. He said he needed your help finding someone. He told me he tried your office phone but missed you. I told him to try you tomorrow. I am thinking of carrying one calla lily when I walk down the aisle, what do you think of that?"

"Whoa, too much, too fast. Did you find out this guy's name or what government agency he was with?" asked Slade.

"No. What do you think about the calla lily idea?"

"I think, you are the lily of my heart and I can't wait to be married to you," said Slade, pulling Joy close to him.

"Come in," said Joy, "Mom and I have fixed you a special dinner, but first I want to give you a fortune cookie from the Contemplative series I have been working on."

Slade took the cookie and held it up to the light like it was a rare gem. Then he tore off the cellophane, broke the cookie in two and extracted the little scroll of paper.

Slade looked at Joy, "Will this tell us about our future?" he asked.

Joy thought a minute, then answered wistfully, "I don't think this is about us. I think it is about our country or maybe the world."

Dawson unfurled the tiny scroll. The message looked long. He frowned and read aloud: *"So then every seed that my Father in Heaven has not planted shall be uprooted. Those who were separated shall be united, and all who are empty shall be filled, so that everyone may enter into the Bridal Chamber where they will be born into the Light."*

Joy's eyes sparkled as if he had just read some profound truth. Maybe he had, but in that moment he did not know what it meant. Perhaps he would in a few days or a few months. There were so many new things he was discovering in life because of the woman who was standing right before him. For now, he was thinking of another bridal chamber. He smiled and kissed his bride. He had found Joy.

THE END OF DEMOCRACY

ABOUT THE AUTHOR

Don Carroll is a spiritual director and the author of *A Lawyer's Guide to Healing*, the *Connect* interactive journal and THE CONSCIOUSNESS TRILOGY. He completed his spiritual direction training at Sursum Corda. He is a member of the Wesleyan Contemplative Order and leads workshops using the Enneagram as a tool for spiritual transformation and as a tool for deepening spiritual transformation in 12 Step recovery.

Don received his undergraduate degree from Davidson College. He has a Masters of Philosophy from the University of Dundee in Scotland and he received his law degree with honors from the University of Virginia. He holds a MFA in writing from Vermont College. From 1994 to 2011 Don served as Director of the North Carolina Lawyer Assistance Program. He is a certified Professional Coach and a certified Strozzi Institute Somatic Coach.

In November 2011, Governor Bev Perdue conferred on him membership in the Order of the Long Leaf Pine for outstanding service to the citizens of North Carolina.

www.doncarroll.com

THE END OF DEMOCRACY

Coming Soon…

THE ARMAGEDDON CHOICE